Choose your Lane to love!
Readers love Romantic Suspense
by AMY LANE

Racing for the Sun

"This book opens with impact and never lets go. Not once. The characters were beautifully nuanced and intricately drawn by a very skilled writer."
—On Top Down Under

"…this was an interesting story filled with characters that needed to be loved."
—The Romance Reviews

Fish Out of Water

"*Fish Out of Water*… really captured my attention and kept it. This book is gritty and urban. It's suspenseful and I found myself gasping more than a few times."
—Diverse Reader

Red Fish, Dead Fish

"Packed full of action, suspense, and of course steamy goodness, *Red Fish, Dead Fish* is the sequel we have all been anxiously waiting for."
—Love Bytes

"The passion in her words of love and family somehow come through like no other author I know."
—Paranormal Romance Guild

By Amy Lane

Published by DREAMSPINNER PRESS
www.dreamspinnerpress.com

By AMY LANE (CONT.)

FISH OUT OF WATER
Fish Out of Water
Red Fish, Dead Fish
A Few Good Fish
Hiding the Moon

KEEPING PROMISE ROCK
Keeping Promise Rock
Making Promises
Living Promises
Forever Promised

JOHNNIES
Chase in Shadow • Dex in Blue
Ethan in Gold • Black John
Bobby Green
Super Sock Man

GRANBY KNITTING
The Winter Courtship Rituals of
Fur-Bearing Critters
How to Raise an Honest Rabbit
Knitter in His Natural Habitat
Blackbird Knitting in a Bunny's Lair
The Granby Knitting Menagerie
Anthology

TALKER
Talker • Talker's Redemption
Talker's Graduation
The Talker Collection Anthology

WINTER BALL
Winter Ball • Summer Lessons

Published by Harmony Ink Press
BITTER MOON SAGA
Triane's Son Rising
Triane's Son Learning
Triane's Son Fighting
Triane's Son Reigning

Published by DREAMSPINNER PRESS
www.dreamspinnerpress.com

Hiding
the
Moon

AMY LANE

Published by

DREAMSPINNER PRESS

5032 Capital Circle SW, Suite 2, PMB# 279, Tallahassee, FL 32305-7886 USA
www.dreamspinnerpress.com

Hiding the Moon
© 2018 Amy Lane.

Cover Art
© 2018 Reese Dante.
http://www.reesedante.com
Cover content is for illustrative purposes only and any person depicted on the cover is a model.

Trade Paperback ISBN: 978-1-64080-937-6
Digital ISBN: 978-1-64080-936-9
Library of Congress Control Number: 2018907630
Trade Paperback published October 2018
v. 1.0

Printed in the United States of America
∞
This paper meets the requirements of
ANSI/NISO Z39.48-1992 (Permanence of Paper).

Mate gets jealous because Mary is on every dedication, but he is too! When I acknowledge my family, he's front and center. Mary never gets jealous; she's always surprised, like her friendship is something that just grows on trees and isn't one of the most wondrous things to happen to me. The kids don't really care, but someday they will, so I can't forget them. The dogs don't read, so they don't even get mention. This book is dedicated, as they all are, to the people I love, who allow me to function, who tell me I don't suck, who give me a reason to get out of bed. Thanks, guys. It's no small thing.

Acknowledgments

THANKS, KAREN Rose, for all of the professional advice. The failures are mine, but the improvements are almost unilaterally yours.

Author's Note

THIS STORY is a sequel to *two* different novels. *Racing for the Sun* came out five years ago, and it featured a character named Lee Burton, a black ops military genius, the kind of guy who fades into the background but makes big things happen. I wanted to write his character's story right then—I even had Ernie planned as a psychic, because that seemed incredibly unlikely. Anyway, I moved on to other shiny things, and Burton got left as unfinished business. Then, when I was writing *A Few Good Fish*, I realized that Jackson and Ellery were in *way* over their heads. They needed help—and since Sonny wasn't much of a planner, who better to help than the superhero I'd already planted and the psychic I'd matched him with in my head, even if I hadn't actually *written* the book, right?

So I put them in *A Few Good Fish*. But I couldn't just *do* that. Burton had his own story—dammit, it had been floating around in my head for *years*. So to flesh out the characters, I began writing what I thought was a series of shorts on my blog, which turned into the first 18,000 words of this story here.

I've always liked the guys in the background. I've always loved the people who had great stories but kept them quiet. Burton and Ernie are two of my favorite kinds of characters—the watchers, the guardians, the quiet people with the giant agenda and positive impact.

I just didn't want you to think I pulled them out of my ass for *A Few Good Fish*, that was all.

Oh, also—

The military base in Barstow is completely made up. So is Burton's fictional and vague black ops division. So is Karl Lacey's little rogue military operation, and the assassin's group, Corduroy. I'm not sure why I feel compelled to point this out, but really, I just wanted to write shit-go-boom, then-there's-pecs-and-peen! This one's fantasy. Eat popcorn and enjoy.

You Got the Wrong Guy

BURTON DIDN'T like the meet.

He didn't like the timing, he didn't like the place, and he didn't like the way Jason Constance, his handler, was fidgeting with the manila envelope in his hands.

None of it spoke of good things to come.

"I hate fuckin' Denny's," Burton snapped, scowling. He had a degree in computer science and had graduated from Officer Candidate School fifth in a class of two hundred. But the only person he talked to that he liked and knew as a friend had been fighting in alleyways when he should have been taking his SATs, and Burton sounded more like Ace Atchison and his boyfriend, Sonny, every goddamned day.

"Well, they're disappearing for a reason," Constance muttered, toying with the envelope again. "Look—"

"What in the hell is wrong?" Burton didn't believe in fiddlefucking around.

Constance sighed and ran his hand through tightly curled hair that pulled back from a widow's peak. "I don't like this," he said. "I don't like this assignment. I don't like that they specifically asked for my division. I don't like the asshole this request came from. I'm putting it out there. I don't fucking like this. You have the right to say no here. And if you say yes, and this doesn't look kosher in any fucking way, you have the right to bug out and leave the target pristine, you understand?"

Burton blinked.

He was a military assassin.

He worked primarily on American soil, although he'd been overseas enough to get pulled for some gigs in the Middle East. Mostly he took care of people who couldn't be legally identified as terrorists—but who had the stacks of guns and the agenda and the covert acts of violence that actually made them terrorists.

A surprising number of his targets had blond hair and blue eyes and had done some heinous fucking shit.

Burton didn't see innocent a lot. And he certainly hadn't seen a target that had tempted him to neglect his duty.

Burton palmed the back of his shaved head with a hand the color of burnished dark oak and reached out for the folder.

"At least let me see the op," he muttered.

Constance handed him the envelope and darted his eyes back and forth like a fucking spy, when the first thing you learned in black ops training was how not to act like a fucking spy. Burton's curiosity—a thing he thought had been yanked out of his chest along with his conscience—surfaced unexpectedly.

What had Constance spooked?

He opened the folder and blinked.

"This kid?" he asked, staring at the photos.

The kid had an unshorn abundance of curly black hair. It hung around his ears, was being constantly pushed out of his eyes—a full three-quarters of the pictures showed the kid fucking with his hair. It didn't look like a fashion statement; it just looked like the kid forgot it was there.

The rest of his face was sort of pretty—narrow chin, narrow cheekbones, tiny blade of a nose. He had eyes a man could drown in.

Burton blinked and tried to slow-breathe that thought away. He hadn't had a feeling like that since he told his girlfriend back home he was breaking up with her.

The breakup had hurt—they'd been friends since grade school—but not as much as becoming the man he knew he'd become while he was bedding his pretty high school sweetheart and lying his ass off.

But this kid's eyes—big, brown, luminous in a pale face.... Burton had to swallow. He usually took care of those urges with a girl for a night, but he'd known they were in there for men as well.

He just kept those to himself.

"There is...." Constance made a frustrated sound and took a long swig of his dank coffee. "There is nothing in that kid's jacket that looks like he should be in that fucking jacket."

Burton scanned the details and had to agree.

He saw a lot of half-finished classes and trips to the dance floors. A lot of pretty bedmates, but no man in particular. And a lot of jobs he'd lost for being late or for forgetting something important or for general flakiness. *He's a nice kid*, one employer had stated, *but he's as reliable as a rabbit.*

Criminals who ended up on the wrong end of Burton's scope were often very reliable. "Oh, he killed people on a regular basis? But he punched the clock every day and ate lunch with my wife!" That was who Burton was assigned to.

X-blowing disco bunnies?

Not so much.

"Hinky," Burton muttered, looking Constance in the eyes.

"I'll say this one more time," Jason Constance told him, the lines around his mouth seeming particularly deep and bitter today. "If this kid doesn't smell right, walk away."

"Who asked you to off this kid?" Burton asked.

"Some fucking commander from a naval base in Las Vegas—"

"Las Vegas?"

"Man, that place is so far off the grid it makes us look like a billboard in Burbank. I'm not sure which favor he pulled to get access to our division, but—"

"This was the kid he pulled the favor for." Burton's chest turned icy.

"Yeah."

"I hate being used as a tool."

"So do I."

"I'll scope out the sitch. If this kid's bad—"

"Do what you have to."

"If not—" Burton didn't sign on to shoot the innocent.

"Walk away."

Burton studied the pictures again—this one a long-distance shot of the kid waking up in a pile of happy naked limbs, looking around him like he was surprised to be there.

"Ernie James Caulfield," Burton murmured, reading from the jacket. "Boy, who did you screw?"

One Month Later

GAH! ALBUQUERQUE sucked in July! The day's temperature had been 113 fucking degrees, and in the city all that heat just sat and baked into the juicy asphalt and the stoic brick and adobe. Yeah, sure, most places had air-conditioning on the inside, but Burton was on a rooftop, covered with a tarp and trying not to hallucinate about Fallujah.

Fallujah had been bad. He'd been with his first Marine unit then, and the guys were the best. Well trained, smart as hell, they goddamned had your back if they had their next breath. But bad intel was bad intel, and when you found yourself facing a preschool through the scope of your gun, that intel was as bad as it got.

One spooked kid, a new recruit, hadn't held his wad. They'd been told the place was full of chemical weapons, and everybody had their fucking phobias.

Burton would have taken any assignment after that—any goddamned one—to not have to look at another dead four-year-old and know he'd been part of the team responsible.

His CO knew that. So his next assignment had been the guy leaking them the bad intel.

It had been a shot much like this one—covert, from a building rooftop, down into a crowd. Burton hadn't hesitated. One kill shot, no collateral damage.

It had all felt so neat and simple then.

This was not neat and simple.

Tracking Ernie Caulfield hadn't been a cakewalk so much as it had been a walk through cake. The kid was working at a bakery at the moment, and he'd get home at ten in the morning, sleep through the hottest part of the day, get up at eight, eat sunbeams and rainbows for all Burton could see, and go dance at his favorite club—appropriately called the Flower Child.

He'd dance his heart out for hours. Fucking hours. Yeah, he'd take a tab of X—Burton could see that—but he wasn't an addict. Burton had camped out in opium dens. He knew what addicts looked like getting their fixes.

That was not the look on his face by a long shot.

Ernie took that tab—always handed to him by a sweet little girl who worked at the Flower Child wearing a tie-dyed dress—with the expression of someone who suffered from chronic headaches downing their first Motrin of the day. Like the X was soothing him, keeping the pain from making him crazy.

So Burton had sat watch from the building top for three days, sighting Ernie through a sniper's scope, trying to figure out what this kid's deal was.

He seemed to do okay at the baker's. Burton had gone in for a donut on the first day, and Ernie had been happily involved in the back, probably mixing up dough for all Burton could tell.

The bell had tinkled, and he'd called up, "Don't worry, Max—he's good."

"Thanks, Ernie. Gets tetchy at 4:00 a.m...."

"Yeah—don't worry about this one. And tell him the crullers are about ten minutes from done, so if he can have a cup of coffee, it'll be fine."

Burton had blinked, but Max—paunchy, grizzled, fiftyish—didn't even look up. "How many crullers would you like, sir?"

"Are they good?" he asked, because that had been a really specific guess and he was a little bit unnerved.

"Donuts fresh out of the fryer. How bad could they be?"

Well, yeah. "Three," he answered promptly. Sugar and water—it was all a growing boy needed in this temperature. "And cream for the coffee."

He hadn't seen Ernie that morning—the kid had stayed back and baked or whatever. But the crullers had been delicious, and the coffee beat Starbucks by a mile.

But Burton had scoped him out that night across from his apartment, when he'd gotten up, opened the window, and let in stray cats from all over the neighborhood and fed them. He'd shooed them out on his way out the front door as he headed for the club, and Burton had trailed him in the shadows. The kid didn't... move like other people moved.

He swayed; he wandered.

Burton had watched him disappear into alleyways and then pull himself back, looking surprised to find himself in that part of town. The walk was four blocks, and it took him half an hour. Burton was a breath away from grabbing the kid by the back of the neck and steering him toward the club.

And now Burton was up on the roof across from the club, watching as Ernie windmilled his arms harmlessly in a mash of bodies bopping to a song Burton had never heard before.

Just watching them made him feel old, but watching Ernie—that made Burton feel whole other things as well.

"Okay, little hamster boy," Burton murmured, watching the boy's gyrations. "Why do you do this every night? I am highly curious."

But Burton wasn't the only one.

From his vantage point, Burton saw two distinctly disturbing things.

One was God's gift to all gay and bi boys, who had latched on to Ernie's back and was dancing with him with way too much familiarity. Burton couldn't look at the guy without growling, because even if Ernie returned his interest, it was damned hard to tell when the boy was as wasted as he appeared to be.

No, Smarmy Dance Kid shoving his hand down the front of Ernie's pants was not even acknowledged, and Burton was a heartbeat away from

5

going down there, grabbing the kid by the ear, and hauling him away from the fucking club, just because somebody should, dammit!

The other thing was potentially much more dangerous than Smarmy Dance Kid.

"Who are those guys?" he asked himself. They were trained. That was the first thing he could tell. One had point, the other had follow-up, and the one in the middle was scoping out all the angles. They also moved their lips, indicating earpieces and military-esque technology. Burton could spot their weapons—the obvious ones—tucked into shoulder holsters and hidden by sport coats, and he got a lot of bitter satisfaction out of how easy they were to make and how much they must have been suffering in all that gear.

They ranged themselves throughout the club, moving from the bar to the corners and back again but generally forming a net around Burton's very own sweet-eyed stoner boy.

It made Burton twitchy.

A part of him very dryly noted that how dare they stalk the guy he was supposed to kill—but most of him had given it up from the moment he'd scoped out Max's Pastries and Coffee.

If this kid was a threat to national security, Lee Burton was President of the United States and a Russian traitor to boot.

"Seriously," he mumbled. "Who are those fuckin' guys?"

He studied them again, but when he went to check on their position relative to Ernie, he'd disappeared.

"Fuck!"

The logical thing to do was to remain up top. The club didn't have a back entrance, but it did have a side entrance that led to an alleyway and the outdoor-access restrooms. Logic—Burton's friend since his first A in math—dictated that he stay up top on that building and scope out the goings-on with the full weight of his very expensive government-issue personally modified sniper's rifle at his beck and call.

Ninety-nine percent of the time, Burton relied on that part of his brain. It functioned very well, thank you, and he credited it for keeping him alive in some very hairy shit.

But the one percent of his brain that stayed friends with guys who knew him in the military that nobody knew he knew—that part of his brain was the one running the show.

Burton charged down the fire escape of the old brick warehouse at full speed, the heat forgotten in his need to be on the ground, in that alleyway before Smarmy Dance Guy got Ernie into the dark and shadows where military ops guys could do worse things.

By the time Burton got down the stairs, the sounds coming from the shadows were both intimate and nonconsensual—and the three gorillas with guns were nowhere to be seen.

"Mm… no. No. Not you. You're not good—"

"C'mon, club boy—you put out for everybody. You're legendary—"

"Who're you? You're not good. Don't touch me. It feels like bugs when you touch me!"

The scream came from the pit of the boy's stomach, but the next sound made Burton sick to his.

A crunch, a scuffle, and a low moan of mortal pain, and Burton could not run fast enough. His heart started beating in two more breaths when Ernie's voice—a low, dreamy tenor—echoed out of the alleyway.

"Stop touching me with bugs!"

Jesus, kid, what did you take?

Burton crashed into the alleyway, pistol drawn and laser sight active, while his eyes adjusted quickly to the darkness.

Club Kid was down in a crumpled pile in the corner of the alley. His body was twitching, but Burton thought maybe that wouldn't last long. Ernie stood panting in the center of the three operatives, crouched, jeans sliding down his hips and his hands out in front of him in a classic martial arts pose. Burton would have found it laughable, like a little kid faking karate, but two of the assailants were bleeding and one was cradling his arm.

The kid had bought himself some time with the element of surprise, but there were two laser lights dotting him, one in center mass and one on his head.

Burton took out the headshot shooter first and the center-mass guy next, through the head, both of them, and had the gun aimed at the guy who couldn't draw before the bodies hit the floor.

"Corduroy Company," the man barked. "I'm going for my ID."

"So I'm not supposed to shoot you because you're a merc?" Burton asked, undeterred. "That club bunny with the mushed brain didn't get to pull his stupidity card. What are you doing here?"

"Man, you should know! We got hired by the US military—this here's a high-priority target!"

"When'd the contract come through?" Burton asked.

"Two days ago—apparently the guy assigned to the kid didn't follow through."

"The guy assigned to the target thought the job was hinky and wasn't taking a life without asking any goddamned questions," Burton snapped, feeling grumpy. Two kills defending this kid? Three if you counted the club bunny with his nose through his brain, but Burton had no way of knowing if that had been the Corduroy mercenaries or the kid himself. "And look what you made me do."

Mr. Corduroy Company rolled his eyes. "We take orders, soldier—I don't know how you get to have a conscience."

Burton felt his brain and his chest go cold. He was going to have to kill this guy method-like, without any more talk, because there was no reasoning with him.

"Wait," Ernie said, holding up his hand. He practically wafted to where the mercenary stood.

"You broke my fucking wrist," Merc snarled.

"You're a bad man," the boy told him, eyes wide. Gently he laid his hand on the merc's wrist through his jacket, then shuddered and dropped his hand. "Bad through and through," he told Burton with a shrug. His shoulders drooped dejectedly, and he moved to Burton's other side.

He was well out of the line of fire when Burton dropped the final Corduroy mercenary, his silencer loud in the late-night air.

"WHERE ARE we going, Cruller?" the boy asked five minutes later.

Burton wasn't taking the easy route—he'd left his sniper rifle bolted to the top of the building, prints and all. First things first, and the first thing was to force the kid up the fire escape in front of him in a minute and a half so Burton could disassemble the rifle and they could beat a hasty retreat through the inside of the building.

"What'd you call me? And move your ass before I kick you up there myself!"

"It's five stories," the kid said mildly. "Nobody heard. That's why the dance club is out here in the warehouse district."

Burton growled and glared balefully at the kid's back, wondering if sheer irritation would make him move any faster. "So noted. Now what did you call me?"

"Cruller. It's your donut. The kind with the glaze but not the flavor," he recited dutifully.

"You didn't even see me that day," Burton muttered, breathing a sigh of relief when they finally broke through to the roof.

8

"Yes, but you're very definitely good. It radiates. That is a big gun. What are you going to do with that big gun? Why didn't you just pick off the bug-touching guys with that? I was scared, you know. They were going to kill me."

"They disappeared," Burton muttered, getting on his knees and using the air drill to unbolt the base of the gun. "I couldn't see them to shoot. And they *were* going to kill you—you're lucky to still be alive."

"Mm." The kid nodded and then sat down bonelessly, like a cat flopping on a carpet, and closed his eyes while Burton worked.

"Did you take out Mr. Date-Raping Octopus Hands?" Burton asked into the silence, because the question was making him crazy.

"No," Ernie said sadly. "He would have left after I yelled. He was bad, but… there's bad that can be fixed and there's those guys you killed. He could have been fixed. Those other guys are just bugs."

Burton shuddered and clamped the case shut. "Fair enough. C'mon, Ernie, you and me need to get out of this bug-ridden town before those fuckers get you."

"Who's going to feed my cats?" Ernie asked—but he was following Burton without question, which was nice.

"How about half of Albuquerque?" Burton was taking the steps two at a time, and he wished fervently that Ernie could keep up with him. "That was every stray cat in the residential district!"

Ernie let out a laugh that should have been on a playground. "But I know all their names!" he said plaintively.

"I'll make arrangements," Burton told him, mind already going to the phone calls he'd have to make to take care of the matter.

"Really? Okay, Cruller—you are a good guy!"

"Burton." *Cruller* could haunt a guy through four branches of the military. Burton had seen it happen.

"Cruller," the boy said, the stubbornness a surprise when the tone was so amiable.

"Get a move on," Burton snapped. "I got transport three blocks down, but we don't know how many more Corduroys we've got on our tail."

"Mm…." Ernie seemed to shut down then, his eyes going to half-mast, his body doing what Burton asked, but not at triple time. Finally they were in Burton's white Tahoe, heading west.

"Ernie!" Burton snapped, and Ernie's eyes popped open.

"Yessir."

"Keep awake!"

"I was. You said you didn't know how many Corduroys were there. Two. There were two more in one of the apartments we passed. They were getting upset." He sighed sadly. "Do you think they'll miss their friends?"

"Yes," Burton said, thinking about the four bodies in the alleyway. "I think all of them are going to be missed, which is why we need to be in California in less than six hours."

"What's in California?" Ernie asked.

"Haven, I hope."

"Mm… that's nice. We need to stay in a hotel first, though."

Burton did a double take before gluing his eyes back on the road. "I'm sorry?"

"You need to call your boss, and then you need to call your friends, and you need to get to know me."

"Why in the world would I want to do that?" Burton snarled.

"I don't know—you're the one who's screaming with need."

"I'm screaming with frustration is what I'm doing—"

"Well, that too. It's okay, Cruller. A crappy hotel will be fine. But at ten o'clock I need to sleep, so maybe find something soon."

Burton could see the sun flirting with the horizon in his rearview mirror. "Damn—where did that time go? It's almost six in the morning!"

"It was five when the killing started," Ernie said sadly. "I don't want to think about it. Tell me when you find the hotel."

And then he closed his eyes and checked out. Just… checked out. No amount of calling his name made him open his eyes, and no attempts at conversation stirred him.

Burton screamed, long and satisfyingly, after five minutes of trying to get his attention, and still the kid didn't even interrupt his breathing.

"God," Burton muttered to himself. "My God. What am I going to tell my boss?"

And that got the kid's attention. "You're going to tell him you walked away, Cruller. Because if you didn't, the Corduroy people will be after you too."

Burton blinked and checked on him again.

He hadn't even opened his eyes.

Jesus.

Fucking Jesus.

Who was this kid?

Meet the Moon

BURTON YAWNED and looked at the clock on the dash. Seven o'clock.

It was true; he could drive straight through to Victoriana and be there in another three hours—but, maddeningly enough, Ernie was right.

Burton wanted to talk to his boss first, and it would be nice of him to offer a heads-up to the people in Victoriana. Yeah, Ace owed him a few, but Burton had been raised to be polite.

Besides, Ace would be fine with it, but Sonny always needed a little warning, and Burton didn't want to piss Sonny off. Idly he thought back to his interactions with the laconic Ace and the highly unstable Sonny Daye and wondered if Ernie would think they were "good" or "full of bugs."

"Good," Ernie mumbled, turning sideways in the seat and curling up like a little kid. The Tahoe came fully loaded, and Burton hit the passenger seat adjustments to tilt the thing back and make Ernie more comfortable. "Like you," he said happily. "I'm hungry. I usually eat at the bakery by now. Stop, get some food, find a room. Your friends will be there tomorrow morning."

Burton snorted. Yeah, sure, a hotel room was probably a good idea—there was a Motel 6 at the next turnoff and he had cash—but he wasn't planning to spend more than a few hours there.

The thought had no sooner crossed his mind than Ernie chuckled, like he knew something Burton didn't.

"Goddammit!" The fine hairs on the back of Burton's neck stood up. "Why are you laughing like that?"

He knew when the kid's eyes opened.

"I'm a pretty good lay," Ernie murmured. "You're going to want to take more time than that."

"So help me, I will wreck the car." The idea was preposterous. Burton had urges—he knew them for what they were. But he'd never taken a man to his bed, and he certainly wasn't going to do so now, in the middle of a failed op and the… the frickin' mystery that was Ernie Caulfield.

"That'd be a shame," Ernie said, sitting up and readjusting the seat. "I think I wouldn't mind you touching me."

Burton growled. "You're stoned. It's not happening."

11

Ernie gurgled happily. "Nope. Wore off before…." His voice dropped. "Before the Corduroy guys thing." He sighed. "I… I wish it lasted longer. That would… it would have been nice to be stoned when that happened."

"Why?" Burton wanted his wits as sharp as possible when shit was going down.

"Don't feel so much. The X or the pot takes over, and it… it muffles shit. All the bad shit—hell, even the good shit's bad when there's too much of it. I… I really wish it had all been muffled when the bad shit went." He whimpered. "The club guy grabbed my dick. That… that wasn't pleasant."

"Not the first time it happened," Burton wagered.

"It's better when I want it," Ernie said dispiritedly. "I mean, got lots I didn't want, but some of it I wanted. I didn't want that."

"Why do you take it when you don't want it?" he asked, curious. So many pictures of Ernie naked with other people. Always with the same dreamy expression, like he wasn't really there.

"'Cause you can ride it," Ernie said, eyes closed. "Like, ride their endorphins like you ride the drugs. Both ways suck, but one way you're not alone. Until I found the club. That was perfect."

A week ago Burton would have dismissed what Ernie was talking about out of hand. But Ernie had unnerved him, pretty much from the beginning, and he found himself flirting with the possibility, the outright probability of the impossible thing that Ernie was in his head.

"Maybe be somewhere without so many people?" Burton suggested. Hell, even if the kid was simply agoraphobic, the self-medication he was talking about wasn't good for him.

"They can find me in the empty." Ernie pulled his knees up and wrapped his arms around his shins, which spoke well of his flexibility, since he was using the seat belt. "But now they found me in the city, and I don't know what to do."

And then Lee Burton, once in Marine special ops, now in special division covert ops, soldier, assassin, all-around logical guy, found himself making the rashest of promises.

"I'm taking you someplace safe," he said. "Someplace not even my boss knows about. You tell me why people are after you, and I'll find a way to make it stop. I swear."

Ernie looked at him sideways from his big brown eyes. "Why would you do that? We haven't even rented the hotel room yet." He stared back out into the desert moodily. "Everybody wants sex first."

"Kid, I'm not in it for sex—"

Ernie snorted derisively.

"I was supposed to kill you, you understand? I am a finely trained killing machine—I'm great at it. But I don't kill club bunnies or witchy little bakers or kids who feed all the stray cats in downtown Albuquerque. I kill bad men—and somebody put you on my list, and on Corduroy's list, and for all I know on the CIA's list, and Jesus, you probably have a fucking SEAL team hunting down your scrawny ass, and I want to know why! My boss didn't like this op and I don't like it, and I'm going to find out who tried to make me a murderer."

"But aren't you—"

"Like you said, kid. It matters if I want it. I kill bad men who like to kill innocent people. I don't kill innocent people who are hunted by bad men."

Ernie *hmm*ed, appearing to be thinking very carefully. "You still want me," he breathed. "This is your exit. There's a donut shop down past the motel. Let's go there first."

Burton hesitated to ask, because like this kid would know, right?

"They have crullers," Ernie murmured, looking sublimely happy.

"How do you do that?" Burton asked bluntly. He'd been all ready to go for the donut question, but seriously, how did this kid keep reading his mind?

"I'm not usually so good at it," Ernie said, looking down at his tennis shoes on Burton's upholstery and picking at the stitching. "But your mind is very clear. I think it's because of that assassin thing. You need to be totally focused. So it's like reading something etched in stone. But most people aren't like that. I just get fuzzy sorts of auras. I… I wish I'd learned how to tamp down on it when I had the chance."

"You had the chance to learn how to use this… this thing in your head?" Burton wasn't sure how he was going to tell Jason Constance that their target was psychic, and that was probably why he was the target—but he was really interested in why that made someone want him dead.

"Yeah." Ernie sighed again, like this was the heaviest concept on the planet. "But they didn't want me to make it stop or quiet it down. They just wanted me to tell them who was good and who was bad."

This was interesting.

"What did they do then?"

Ernie's face fell. "They hurt the good people to see if it would make them bad. And sometimes it would."

Burton sucked in air. It sounded like something illegal. It sounded like behavior modification—of the most monstrous type.

It sounded like a reason to kill a dreamy kid who just wanted to get stoned enough to stay in his own head. "Donuts," he said grimly. "You and me need some sugar before I call my boss, and then we need to talk about what's next."

"Okay, Cruller." The kid closed his eyes happily. "You can ask me anything you want after donuts. But maybe make sure we get a king-sized bed for that other thing—"

"Ain't happening."

Ernie's laughter tinkled, low and charming, and Burton wondered exactly what sort of pictures he was painting in the kid's mind.

It would be nice if Burton knew himself, wouldn't it!

"IT'S NOT as good as yours," Burton blurted after his first cruller.

Ernie looked up from his cream-filled and grinned. "I'm good at the bakery," he admitted proudly, and then his shoulders slumped and he looked tired and dispirited. "Good to be good at something."

Don't ask, don't ask, don't ask.... "Your high school grades were so good," Burton said, because this had been bothering him. "But they dropped in the last semester, and you didn't even go to college. What happened?"

Ernie frowned at him. "That's all my file says? My grades were good and then they slipped?"

"Says your folks died in a car wreck, and you didn't do well in foster care," Burton told him cautiously and was unprepared for Ernie to stand up, face crumpling as he fought tears.

"Didn't do well?" he demanded. "Didn't do well? Jesus—that's all you know about me? There's so much truth missing, it's like you only know me as the lie." He turned toward the exit, entire posture screaming about storming out into the strange city of Cletus, and Burton couldn't let him.

He stood and put a quiet hand on his elbow. "Ernie," he said softly, "I didn't pull the trigger. I wanted more info. If my intel isn't good, you're the only source I've got for better."

14

Ernie slumped against the glass door of the donut shop. "Get a box," he said, voice breaking. "And some iced coffee. I'll stay here. I promise. I need to go to bed anyway."

"Sure."

Five minutes later they were headed for the Holiday Inn.

"Not the Motel 6?" Ernie asked, only a little curious.

"All fleeing hit men stop at the Motel 6," Burton answered semifacetiously. "It's just too damned obvious." The truth was he wanted something… better, for Ernie. The slump of his shoulders, the obvious pain of speaking of his family—Burton had disrupted the life, the peace he'd forged for himself already. He was going to have to do it some more. If there'd been a five-star place, Burton would have taken his disposable credit cards and gotten a room there, but the Holiday Inn would have to do.

Ernie's smile lightened up a fraction. "You're being kind. Thank you."

"So what happened to your folks?" Burton asked softly.

"I'll never have any proof," Ernie answered back, just as softly. "But I think they were forced off the road."

"By who?"

"Same military motherfuckers who hunted me down in foster care when they couldn't place me." Ernie sighed—and yawned. "No offense, Cruller—"

"Burton—"

"I might not remember that. But I need to sleep soon. I…." He let out an unhappy breath. "I know you probably think I'm just all moonbeams and sunshine and shit. But one of the reasons 'my grades fell,' as you so nicely put it, is that it's hard. It's hard for me to… to focus… when the world comes at me like it does. Knowing who's good and who's bad, if there's donuts around the corner, if someone's going to want me and listen to no, or trying to figure out how to say no if they won't—it's hard. I get lost. I forget what street I'm on or what day it is. So I need to sleep at the same time and wake up at the same time and do the same things every day. And there's none of that now. So I need my sleep." And again, he was perilously close to tears. "You understand?" he begged. "I need my sleep when I need it."

"Understood," Burton told him. "If you can hang on while I'm checking in, I can bend to your schedule a bit. Do we have a deal?"

"Yeah," Ernie said, sighing into his chest. "Thanks."

He didn't say much more as they got to the hotel, not even when Burton went inside and made the hotel arrangements—under the name of Smythe.

15

He parked the car and proceeded to lead Ernie up to their room, his sniper rifle over one shoulder, his packed duffel of clean clothes over the other. When he got to the room, he put both bags under the desk.

Then he watched in bemusement as Ernie stripped down to nakedness, dropping his clothes on the floor, before sliding under the covers and falling fast asleep.

Well, damn. Burton wouldn't mind some shut-eye himself, but not now.

Something about the way Ernie's face relaxed told him that Ernie was going to sleep for the full seven hours here just like he did at home.

Just as well.

Burton was going to have to place a whole lot of booby traps before he got so much as a catnap.

Burton set up security measures at the windows and the doorway, including mirrors in the high corners of the windows to see if anybody was approaching their front-facing hotel room who shouldn't, and setting up his laptop so he could tap into the lobby camera footage and see if anybody was crossing the front who looked suspicious. Then he checked access to the ventilation system through the ceiling vent in the bathroom and set tiny charges in a hole configuration in the closet—if the doors and the window were both blocked, Ernie could hide in the ventilation while Burton escaped through the closet.

Three exits and a contingency plan—Burton had been an A student in special ops, and he didn't let shit hang.

Finally he was done securing their locale and it was time to make a decision.

He dug through his duffel, pulled out his emergency phone, and set it up to charge, then sat for a second, staring from his company phone to the emergency phone. Both of them were smartphones, but one had been outfitted for him by his op commander and given to him by his handler, and he'd trusted both of them to have his back.

The other one he'd outfitted all on his lonesome, and it was set to bounce off a number of satellites and receiving stations with every call.

One of these was untraceable except by friends.

The other assumed he had no friends in the one place he was supposed to have brothers.

He looked at both phones and then looked at Ernie, asleep and as trusting as a child.

Ernie needed him to give up any illusions to safety and to trust a murderer and a thief with his well-being.

God, Burton hated ambiguity.

With a sigh he picked up the untraceable phone and called Jason's number.

"Who in the fuck has this numb—"

"Jason!" Burton hissed. "Stop talking and call me Snider." Their code name over the years. *Don't contact me unless Snider calls* was code for *I'm out unless there's a death in the family or a military coup of our nation.* If Burton wanted Jason to call him Snider, then shit had hit the fan.

"Snider," Jason said, voice cooling to glacial. "So good to hear your voice. We thought everything was proceeding normally."

"The target was... unviable," Burton told him, which was a little bit of a lie, but not too much if it kept Ernie off his radar. "I walked away. He was wearing uncomfortable pants, if you know what I mean."

C'mon, Jason... remember all the people their unit considered enemies.

"Not denim?" Jason asked carefully. "Something heavier?"

"Yup—but still making headlines, right?" A child's joke—corduroy pillows making headlines, but Burton was pretty sure Jason would get it.

"Fuck," Jason rasped. "Seriously? Those kinds of pants? Not, like, linen?"

"No, Jason, not linen pants. Jesus. Who gave you that fucking contract?"

Burton could hear Jason's caught breath. "A naval commander from Las Vegas, like I told you," he said softly. "But I've done some digging of my own, and I seriously think he's pulling a Bob's-in-the-bathroom here."

"I'm sorry?"

They'd joked about it. When a target had been too hard to find, when too many people had claimed to have seen somebody who eluded surveillance again and again, they'd told the story about the high school student who'd never gone to class and had all his friends tell people that Bob was in the bathroom. Ninety-eight percent of the time the target was just lucky. The other two percent he was already dead. Bob was never, ever in the bathroom—he was just damned hard to find.

"Seriously—he's stationed in San Diego—"

"You said Las Vegas!"

"Well, yeah. That's where we were getting our orders from—but I looked into the guy's billet, and sure enough it *says* San Diego, because that would make sense because *Navy*, right? But he's having all his calls routed to a number in Nevada. He used to be in charge of a unit called Behavior Modification—but there was some sort of… I don't know. Scandal. Nobody's talking, and everybody looks fucking uncomfortable when it's mentioned. And this guy is everywhere except in his office doing his fucking job."

Burton chuffed out a breath. "Well, he tried to use the Marines like a sledgehammer on a baby seal's head, and I want blood."

Jason grunted. "You…." He took another deep breath. "I can grant you leave," he said after a moment. "Six months' leave. In six months, come back looking rested and able or turn in your papers. And don't tell me about your trip to Tahiti, and there'd better not be any fucking pictures, understand?"

Burton understood completely. His job was to take care of domestic terrorists under the radar. If someone in the US military was working as a terrorist—or just as a cog in a mercenary assassin guild—the military didn't want to acknowledge a fucking thing.

But they wouldn't mind if Burton took care of the problem either.

Burton looked over to where Ernie was sleeping again, except Ernie was regarding him soberly with big brown eyes. He didn't say a word, just blinked slowly, like he was trusting Burton to take care of the scary things so he could focus on the tiny little rituals that Burton was starting to suspect kept him sane.

"I'll turn this phone on again in six months," Burton said coldly.

"Take care," Jason told him. "And out."

The line went dead, and Burton shut off both the phones. He made a mental note to buy a couple of burners, including a set that went from him to Ernie and Ace without stopping to pass Go.

"You chose me," Ernie said softly.

"Kid, you'd better have a good story to tell." Seriously—Burton hadn't even heard all of it.

Ernie closed his eyes and nodded. "When I wake up," he said distantly. Then, "No bad men, Cruller. Nobody but us. Can you hold me? I'm frightened."

Burton blinked in surprise. He was built like a tank, and he cultivated his silence. He didn't like to be messed with, so he worked to make sure nobody messed with him—worked hard at a preemptive shutdown of any friendly overtures—but Ernie didn't seem to notice that.

"It'll be okay," he said softly, but Ernie shook his head.

"Touch," he said simply. "Let me touch 'okay.'"

Burton stood from his crouch on the floor, by the outlet where he'd charged his phones, and stretched. "For a minute." He tried and failed to hold back a yawn.

"Take off your pants," Ernie said mutinously.

"I beg your—"

"They're full of metal and deadly things, and they have edges and buttons," Ernie told him, and Burton could not help but stare at him in surprise. He was armed—heavily—but not many people guessed that.

"But what about—"

"Ankle holsters, knives, and the gun in the small of your back." Ernie was scowling now, like Burton was being obtuse. "A knife under the pillow I can live with. I want you to hold me, dammit. You took me away from my city and my cats and my donuts and you owe me."

Burton wanted to argue that he'd already saved the kid's life, but he swallowed the retort with another yawn.

No bad guys.

Burton had done everything he could—and this could be the last good sleep he got in the next six months. With a sigh he stripped down, setting all his weapons on his desk and taking the hunting knife—as ordered—and shoving it under the pillow. He crawled in under the covers and pulled the scant sheet and blanket up over his shoulder, reaching out tentatively to put a hand on Ernie's arm.

Ernie scooted back until his bottom was nestled up against Burton's groin, and Burton's sleepiness disappeared as his eyes popped open.

"Uh, kid—"

"Not now." Ernie yawned. "Later. Hold me."

Unbidden, Burton remembered the last time he'd been in bed with Ariana, his childhood sweetheart. How her skin had been so soft and she'd smelled so sweet. Ernie smelled like sweat and like donuts, oddly enough, and like cats—not like Ariana at all. But still, his warmth was appealing, and the thought of holding a human being so close—male or female—that his heart felt warm soothed a cold spot he hated to admit he had.

But it was there.

And Ernie was warming it now, body flush with Burton's, and Burton sighed and relaxed against him, resisting the urge to run his lips over the back of Ernie's neck.

"This is good," Ernie murmured. "I can sleep now. You should too."

Burton's eyes closed of their own volition, but he double-checked his computer screen before he could doze off completely.

Well, he'd already thrown his career to the four winds—he was going to have to trust in Ernie for the next few hours. He found himself falling into the comfort of the young man's body and realized that wasn't going to be as hard as it should have been.

Learning New Things

BURTON WOKE up on a sudden inhale, panic flooding his body. The boy in his arms (there was a boy in his arms?) mumbled, "Go back to sleep. An SUV passed by. Bad guys, but not your bad guys. Sleep some more."

Burton thought *It is time to wake up*, and then his eyes closed and he slept for another two hours.

This time when he woke up, Ernie had rolled away and was facing him. His skin was pale—almost pasty, given the kid's hours—but his eyes, luminous brown under the fall of hair, held an appeal Burton couldn't explain.

"What?" Burton asked grumpily. He could feel the lateness of the afternoon in his bones, and he was still sluggish with sleep. A part of him knew he could leap up and commence giving orders at any time, but….

But the kid was just looking at him, almost in wonder.

"What?" Burton demanded again. "Was I snoring?"

"Yes, but who cares." Slowly the boy reached out to brush Burton's lips with his fingertips. "They're, like, cut from stone. You must press them together a lot."

Burton blinked and tried to remember if he did that a lot. "My job is sort of tense," he said, feeling silly.

"You think?" Ernie rolled his eyes and then pressed his hand to the side of Burton's neck. Burton didn't flinch from a man touching him—it was something he'd dreamed about enough that it felt… natural. "Warm. Just… body heat. Lots of it. You must be very fit." Ernie's mouth twisted wickedly, and he squeezed Burton's hard bicep with impish delight. "Very fit."

Burton licked his lips and hated himself a little for it. "I work out," he said with dignity.

Ernie nodded, a slight smile pulling at his full mouth. "You do. And nobody ever gets to appreciate it. I mean, there's girls sometimes. One-nights, because you gotta keep moving, but…." Ernie ran his hand appreciatively over the contours of Burton's arm—bicep, tricep, shoulder—coming to a stop with his hand splayed over Burton's collarbone, close to his neck. "No chance for someone to feel every hard inch."

21

Burton almost told the lie then—it was on his lips. *Son, you're barking up the wrong tree. Sorry, Ernie, but I'm not bi. Please stop touching me, it feels invasive.*

But Ernie arched a sardonic eyebrow, and Burton's heart rate sped up, all his blood rushing to the surface of his skin. Ernie's touch didn't feel invasive at all. It felt amazing.

"We shouldn't be doing this," Burton managed, and Ernie scooted a little closer.

"I need a shower," he whispered, and Burton could feel his breath dusting along Burton's throat. "And I need to brush my teeth."

Burton swallowed and nodded. "Me too."

"You go first," Ernie told him gravely. "Brush your teeth before you get in the shower."

Burton's brows snapped together, and he scowled. "Who does that? People brush their teeth while their nuts are drying—everybody knows that! Why are you giving me—"

Ernie brushed those lush, playboy lips against his, and Burton opened his mouth on a gasp. Ernie sucked his lower lip into his mouth and nibbled before letting it go.

"Yes, Lee Xavier Burton, I'm giving you orders. You can blow me off if you want, but you'll regret worrying about bad breath for the next few hours, so maybe just don't fight me here."

Oh Lord, Burton's blood was pounding in his ears. A kiss. A man's kiss. It trembled along the edge of his skin, and Burton could suddenly taste the acidic paste of morning breath.

"How'd you know my—"

Ernie's grin was a force to be reckoned with. "I can't always tell if the bad guys are after me," he said honestly. "If I'm stoned, I can't always read the scumbag who wants to feel me up. But I'm cold sober right now, and I know who's in my bed." His voice was low and mesmerizing, and Burton couldn't look away from his wide brown eyes.

"Who do you think I am?" he asked, curious. For all Ernie's dreamy oddness, Burton couldn't fault his accuracy.

"You kill the bugs," Ernie said, cupping his neck again. "You're good. Dangerous, but good. And you... you look at me like I'm nectar. I've never been nectar before. I really want you to drink me."

Burton shuddered, thinking about "drinking" him, and rolled out of bed jerkily, shocked and aroused by the mental picture. "You're right," he said, pretending that terrible suspended moment of intimacy had never happened. "I should shower first."

Ernie chuckled and propped his head up on his hand. "Sure." But he didn't sound put out, and he sounded like he knew something Burton didn't, which made Burton just a little bit nuts.

He stomped to his duffel bag, pulled out his shaving kit and a fresh pair of boxers and a tee, then stomped to the bathroom.

He was in the shower, letting the water pound his neck and chest, before he felt the cool of mint at the inhale and realized he'd done exactly what the kid had asked and brushed his teeth first. He groaned softly to himself and rested his head against the wall while the water pounded his back. The hotel wasn't bad—and the shower was amazing. A big space with enough water pressure to power-hose all his crevices. He was still there, leaning his head on his arms, when Ernie came into the bathroom and started going through his shaving kit.

"What're you doing?" Burton asked, staring through the clear glass of the cubicle.

"You got an extra brush," Ernie said happily, pulling it out and using the toothpaste. "That's nice." He started brushing his teeth, and Burton felt embarrassment crawl up his spine.

"The, uh, glass is clear," he muttered. He'd been in the military. He'd showered in the barracks with his entire unit. You didn't worry about some other guy seeing your pits, and he didn't worry about you scoping him out. That was the rule.

"I don't mind," Ernie said guilelessly, looking at him through the glass.

"I'm sure you don't," Burton muttered, grabbing the washcloth and squirting some soap on it. He'd managed his face, neck, and chest before Ernie spit and put his hand on the shower door handle. "Hey, what're you—"

The door slid open and Ernie stepped in, naked, pale body glowing like the moon.

Burton swallowed hard. Ernie was lean—almost skinny—but his chest and arms had some definition, probably from working at the bakery. His thighs and calves were wiry—he walked lots and danced all night, so of course they were—and his stomach was flat, almost concave.

His little pink nipples were fascinating, and for a moment Burton stared at them, the only bit of color in that lean body besides that thatch of dark pubic hair at the end of the happy trail below.

23

Ernie held out his hand for the washrag, and Burton passed it to him in a daze. Ernie took a step forward, then another one, close enough to catch the shower spray, close enough for their bodies to touch if either one of them took so much as a deep breath.

"Did you finish?" Ernie asked, the water spiking his dark lashes around his eyes like points in a star.

"No," Burton said, voice dry. "Uh… pits, crevices—"

"Mm… lift your arms."

Burton did. The washrag was wielded firmly—it didn't tickle under each arm, but it did scrub, and Ernie turned him so his back was to Ernie's front.

"I'm going to get real personal," Ernie said softly in his ear. He was taller than he seemed, only an inch or two shorter than Burton himself, who was over six feet. "You are built like a tank, but all you gotta do to stop me is tell me no."

No. I don't do this. I don't do this with strangers. I've never done this with a man before. You and me need to talk—

"I'll tell you everything when we're done," Ernie murmured, lips skimming Burton's shoulders. "But Lee, I think you need this now. I mean, it's practically the only skill I have."

The washrag moved low over Burton's stomach, and Burton took a breath to tell him that wasn't true.

Then it drifted to his cock, and Burton lost the wind to tell him anything at all.

"Spread your legs a little," Ernie whispered. "I'm going to get your… ah, yeah."

Personal wasn't even the word for it. The washrag moved between his legs, spending a lavish, soapy moment on each ball, and then… oh Lord, the crease of Burton's ass. Burton made a whimpering sound.

"You want me to stop?"

Yes, because I like this and I shouldn't and—

Burton put his hands flat against the wall and leaned forward, spreading his legs. It was like his brain was saying all the things it should be but his body was on a whole other mission.

Ernie reached over him and grabbed the showerhead, then hosed off all Burton's vulnerable bits. For a moment Burton watched as the soap went down the drain and wondered if his inhibitions went with it.

"Your turn," Ernie said, sounding happy. Well, of course. Ernie was just fine with sex, just fine with being gay. Ernie went to clubs and trusted that only the nice people would feel him up, put their hands on him, take him home to those tangles of bodies where the sex protected his fragile mind.

Burton felt a moment of hostility as he took the washrag, thinking it wasn't fair that Ernie should know all these things about showers and bodies and how what they were doing was going to end. But when he turned around, Ernie had assumed the same position Burton had, and his bitterness washed away too.

He was totally and completely vulnerable.

And Burton had just made himself that way for Ernie, and Ernie had done nothing but wash him, gently and firmly.

Burton took a deep breath and began to soap his back. Ernie let out a happy sigh and wiggled his shoulders, helping Burton out. Then Burton worked his way to Ernie's pits and took his cues from Ernie's own ministration, being firm so he didn't tickle. Flanks, hips, backside—but not too personal—and the back of the thighs followed, and then he paused.

"Chickening out?" Ernie taunted softly.

Burton moved closer so he could wrap his arms around the boy's (man's!) chest and soap that. His front to Ernie's back, his groin pressed against Ernie's bottom.

His cock swelled, and he pretended it wasn't happening.

Instead he kept his movements to the washrag, but he could tell by the way Ernie shivered that he liked the roughness over his nipples.

Just keep going... and then what? You're going to wash each other and this is going to end?

His hand stalled out below Ernie's navel, and for a moment he couldn't breathe. Then Ernie grabbed his wrist and guided him, slowly, over his groin, between his thighs. He let go of Burton's hand for a moment and propped his foot on the side of the shower and spoke into the sudden silence.

"Everything, Lee. You can do it."

Burton closed his eyes against the wave of arousal that swept him, and his cock, already thick and hard, swelled to the point of aching. More than anything, he wanted to wash this guy's crease, his asshole, the taint below his balls.

His hands shook and he tried not to be rough, but Ernie grunted, not sounding put off at all.

"My God, you want me," he moaned breathily. "Now rinse."

Burton didn't even ask why. Ernie leaned forward, legs spread, and Burton could see his hole, clean and pink, and fought the urge to lick absolutely everything he'd just dragged the washrag over.

Everything.

He used the showerhead to rinse away the suds and thought longingly of clean skin and not too much soap. He turned around and shut off the shower, almost disappointed when he realized Ernie had reached outside for a towel for each of them. Burton took the towel and wiped his face first, then started drying everything off, when Ernie stopped him.

"What?" Burton whispered, cock aching, body confused and aroused, heart crying out for a thing it had never defined.

"Now's when you're glad you brushed your teeth," Ernie whispered back, and after touching each other privately, intimately, his mouth on Burton's felt overdue, like they should have kissed the moment they met.

Burton groaned, pushed harder, devouring him....

Drinking him in like nectar.

Ernie pulled his hips forward until their bodies were grinding together, only the towels between them. Burton dropped his towel and cupped Ernie's lean behind, kneading and pulling, until Ernie broke away and moaned.

"Are you ready?" he asked.

"For what?" Obvious question. Obvious answer. But Burton had never felt less like the obvious was true.

"To taste all the parts of me," Ernie asked. "To know my body inside."

Weak. Burton's knees went weak as he imagined thrusting inside Ernie's pink and winking hole.

"All of it," he begged, no longer surprised when his mouth or his hands or his cock took over and ran the operation. "I want to know all of you."

Ernie bit his lip again, sucking it into his mouth.

"I've been waiting my whole life for you to ask."

BURTON GOT back to the room in time to see Ernie pull back the covers, revealing the slightly rumpled sheets, before he grabbed something from the back pocket of his jeans and lay down.

"What's that?" Burton asked, his suspicion hitting him hard. No drugs. No X. None of that crap in his bed—"Oh."

His entire body washed hot. A condom and lubricant.

"You just kept that in your pocket?" he asked. Ernie was stretching out luxuriously on the high-thread-count cotton sheets, his soft pink body almost too delicate to be real.

"Sex keeps my brain safe," Ernie said, a sad little smile on his face. "I don't often get to have it with somebody I actually like."

"You don't even know me," Burton mumbled, embarrassed. Like he was a reward or something. "And we're not having—"

"Sh." Ernie stood and placed two fingers over Burton's lips. "Don't lie," he whispered. "Not now. You promised."

Oh. It really had been a promise. Burton closed his eyes and licked Ernie's fingers. Ernie moaned and shivered, tilting his head back like Burton's mouth was a luxury, and Burton's skin cried out for more. He sucked those fingers into his mouth all the way, tongue hard on his palate. Ernie sagged against him, their bodies soft from the shower, bare, clean, and warm.

He opened his eyes when Ernie pulled his fingers out with a pop and darted a wicked glance up from under thick black lashes.

"See?" Ernie said, voice as wicked as his eyes. "That wasn't hard. Better things to do with your mouth than lie." He punctuated this with a kiss along Burton's shoulder, the glide of his lips down Burton's collarbone, and tiny fingertip pucker-kisses down Burton's other side. Burton slid his arms up Ernie's biceps, feeling the hard little muscles under that soft moon-pale skin. Ernie kept teasing him, his shoulders, his collarbones, his chest, until his lips accidentally on purpose brushed Burton's nipples.

All the air left his body, and he whimpered. Oh God, so close… his nipples were tingling, and he wanted… he wanted….

Ernie paused, breath brushing the sensitive nerve bundle, and stuck out a teasing tongue. Burton, naked and needy, blurted out his biggest fear.

"I don't know how to make love to a man."

Ernie's low, breathy chuckle sent ripples of reaction across his skin. "Touch my face," he whispered, lapping his nipple once.

Burton looked down at him and moved a tentative hand from his arm to his cheek. Ernie smiled shyly and stuck his tongue out again. He licked harder, and Burton slid his fingers into that glossy dark hair and tightened them.

Ernie clamped his lips over the nipple and sucked hard.

Burton let out a moan and tried to keep his knees from buckling.

"Mm…." More sucking, and then Ernie traced a line to the other nipple, his hand flattening on Burton's abdomen as he went. He suckled on the other side while the air teased the first nipple and Burton cupped his skull through his hair.

"But you're… ah… ah God…. You're… oh Jesus, Ernie… you're doing all the work!"

Ernie popped off the second nipple and grinned again. "You're letting me touch you."

He was so beautiful.

Burton cupped his cheek again as he stood up straight, then bent his head and touched Ernie's lips with his own.

Ernie's mouth fell open, and he melted into Burton's arms, that sinuous, boneless kind of melt that Burton had felt girls do. The kind that said Ernie trusted Burton to take care of him, to touch him kindly, to not hurt him. With a growl Burton took over the kiss, ravished his mouth, and backed him up to the bed, where he went willingly. He hit the mattress and scooted back, spreading his thighs wantonly, inviting Burton into the glow of him. Burton paused for a moment and took him in, and Ernie returned his stare.

"You're beautiful."

They both covered their mouths, and Burton stared at him with wide eyes. They'd both said it. Whispered holy words at the same time.

Like a prayer.

Burton had to touch him. Had to run his fingers over his neck, his ribs.

He clamped his mouth over a pink nipple and sucked, gratified when Ernie arched his back and gasped. "Good," Ernie urged. "So good."

The other one was just as delicious.

Ernie's body underneath his responded with abandon, undulating against him. His cock wobbled, a wild thing, streaking a damp trail against Burton's hip, his stomach, his inner thigh. As Burton plied his tongue, Ernie gave a little cry and ground up against Burton's groin. A hot spurt of precome spread between them.

"What do you want to do?" Ernie whispered, grinding again.

Burton collapsed against him, burying his face against Ernie's throat, and tried hard to pull himself together. With a girl this would be the part where they fucked—Mother Nature's lock and key—but this was a man, and the lock and key fit differently, and Burton needed the rules.

"Everything," he said, half laughing into the haven of Ernie's hair and his shoulder. "Kid, I want to eat you alive."

"Then let's start there." Ernie kissed his forehead, a benediction of desire. "Go ahead, Lee. Touch it. Taste it. Do what you want done. No teeth, that's all I ask."

He smelled so good! Burton sucked on his neck, then licked to his earlobe, sucked that into his mouth and nibbled.

"That's right," Ernie hissed. "Just, you know, lower."

Down. Every inch of skin a salty, smooth, sweet, and naughty temptation. Burton paused at his happy trail, running his fingers through the surprisingly silky hair, then following it down, down, down....

"Mm...."

It was all the encouragement he needed to wrap his fingers around it, surprised at the width, the length.

"Big," he murmured, watching a shiny bit of fluid gather in the slit.

It fascinated him.

"Not as big as yours," Ernie told him breathlessly, and Burton bucked against the bed, reminded that he needed release too.

"But I'm a bulkier guy." It was almost purple now as Burton stroked, and dripping, hot and... he stuck his tongue out and tasted.

Good. So good.

He shuddered and licked it some more.

"Nungh...."

In the back of his mind, Burton thought about teasing him, playing with his harp string, flirting his tongue along the edge of the bell. But not now. Not with Ernie bucking against his hand and his precome filling his senses with the bitter salt of desire.

Not when he wanted so bad to feel it in the back of his throat.

"Go ahead," Ernie begged. "God, Lee, please, I'm dying—ahhhhhh!"

It felt huge, filling his mouth, and he kept his lips over his teeth and let his mouth fill with spit, making himself a hot, wet cave for Ernie to thrust in.

Ernie bucked, crying out, and Burton kept sucking, squeezing his base with every stroke.

"My balls," Ernie begged. "Just... tug... a little harder.... God yes! I'm coming—God, you need to—"

Taste. Burton needed to taste him.

He sucked harder, tugged harder, flirted his tongue when he pulled back, and Ernie kicked his feet into the mattress and came.

Wet and thick, it filled Burton's throat, and he swallowed.

It wasn't oysters like the porn said, but it wasn't bitter, and he didn't gag.

He swallowed again, cock aching, as Ernie continued to spasm at the ministrations of his hand and his mouth.

Finally Ernie went limp, his hands searching for purchase in the stubble of Burton's head. Burton let himself be urged up to Ernie's shoulder, where he rested his cheek for a moment and arched his own hips, desperate for release.

"You shouldn't swallow unless you know my history," Ernie said weakly, sounding guilty.

"We take PrEP," Burton said without self-consciousness. "It's part of our hygiene protocol." He didn't add because there was often blood loss on both sides, but Ernie's little chuff of air told him he got it. "What is your history?" He propped himself up on his elbow and looked soberly at Ernie.

"My history," Ernie told him softly, skating his thumb over Burton's cheekbone, "is that I've sucked a lot of dicks and bent over for a lot of guys, but I've never looked into eyes like yours and thought I wanted more."

Burton closed his eyes, and Ernie invaded his mouth with his thumb. A brief suck, a pop, and Ernie rubbed his lower lip.

"You still hard?" Ernie asked.

"God, yes."

"Good. Because I... I would really like you to fuck me. Not fair, I know. You just spent all that time making me come and I just want more."

Burton smiled, eyes still closed. "I want all of you."

"Good."

Something about Ernie's voice, a break, a catch, something, made Burton open his eyes again. Ernie's eyes were red-rimmed, like he was close to tears.

"What?"

"I won't be able to go back to strangers," Ernie said, sounding helpless. "Not after this."

A surge of possessiveness shook Burton to his toes. He pushed himself up and took Ernie's mouth, hard, angry, needy. He pulled back and pinned Ernie with a glare.

"Good," he said, voice hoarse. It wasn't fair of him—he knew that. He had to leave this boy and go back into the surf of undercover, and claiming him wasn't kind. But Burton had held Ernie's cock in his mouth, had tasted his spend, and was going to bury himself in the heaven of his body, and Burton didn't want him to belong to strangers.

Burton wanted Ernie to belong to him.

"You're going," Ernie murmured.

"But not yet."

Burton kissed down his chin, down his neck, knowing where he was going this time. Here, in this bed, their bodies bare and speaking the same language, he knew exactly what to do.

The Problem
with Homeschooling

BURTON WAS still fascinated with his body—his cock, growing fat again as Burton kissed his inner thigh. His balls, furry and saggy and heavy and masculine, unmistakably so, when much of Ernie seemed delicate, almost ethereal.

The mystery of his taint, his cleft, the hidden little pucker there.

Ernie splayed his knees then, reached under his body, and grabbed his cheeks, spreading himself wide, giving Burton permission to touch, to explore while Ernie arched and moaned. Burton could have done that for hours—maybe—but as he played he found he was rippling his body, grinding up against the bed.

He needed.

"Lube," he demanded, and Ernie fumbled with his hand, shoving the lube ampoule and the condom into grasp. Burton took the condom and rolled it on in a hurry and then squeezed the lubricant on his fingers.

Gently, teasing, he thrust a finger inside, just to hear Ernie gasp. Oh, that was promising—that little choked cry. He thrust in again, and pulled out, and in and out, and then added another finger, fascinated by what he was doing.

"Proud of yourself," Ernie teased, still pulling his cheeks apart, ready and vulnerable and taking whatever Burton wanted to give.

"Your body is amazing," Burton said bluntly.

"Then come inside."

That quickly, Burton was almost there. He thrust his fingers in to the hilt and buried his face against Ernie's thigh, suddenly so damned close it wasn't fair.

"Now!" Ernie demanded, and that alone was enough to get Burton to wipe his hand on the sheets and shove up, dominating Ernie's thinner body with his shoulders alone. He positioned his cock right... oh God. Right there. He'd seen the mechanics, of course, but looking down, seeing his body disappearing into Ernie's... this felt magical.

He was becoming a part of another human being.

He'd done this before—but this was the first time he felt that magic. He looked into Ernie's wide brown eyes, surprised, and fell.

Tumbled.

Deep and deeper, only his physical sensation remained.

His body was exploding, atoms and quarks, and he pumped his hips desperately, needing to disappear completely into the warmth, needing that tight grip to make him come, spill, become part of his lover's body in a way he'd never felt before.

On the physical plane, Ernie whispered "Harder!" and Burton's muscles trembled with the force of driving inside him.

In his soul, in his mind, he was still tumbling through the sweet haven of Ernie's eyes, as safe as he'd ever been in his life. Ernie tilted his head back, eyes closed, and cried out, and the scald of his come on Burton's chest brought Burton back completely to his physical self.

His physical self was complete, immediate, tingling from taint to toes, on the verge of an orgasm that would turn him inside out, and for a moment he was afraid. Then Ernie clenched and spasmed around him, and he had no choice. He had to take that leap, had to give himself over, allow orgasm to swamp him, capsize him, drag him under, and expect Ernie to pull him back to himself and not let him drown.

He buried his face against Ernie's neck and screamed, and Ernie ran his fingertips in soothing circles over Burton's shoulders.

"Sh...," he whispered. "Sh... it's all right. Look what we did. We made love."

"It's not all right," he whispered, voice muffled. "I'm not all right."

"I got ya," Ernie told him, dotting his cheeks and forehead with tender kisses. "Don't doubt that I've still got ya."

For how long? How long can we cling to each other? Oh Jesus, kid, I miss you already.

"Kiss me," Ernie demanded, and Burton, lost and afraid and still buried in his ass, did exactly what he asked. Their mouths opened, and that curious merging sensation, that loss of himself and gain of the things Ernie loved the most—that resumed. They were sliding inside each other, their souls, their bodies. Burton had conjured sex magic with all his other lovers, but he'd been the magician.

He'd never been the magic.

For the first time, he was part of the wonder and not just the performer on stage.

With a moan he collapsed, pulling out of Ernie's body and falling into the wrap of his long arms.

"Forever," Ernie said, like he was answering a question.

"What?"

"You asked how long. As long as you want me. I'm going to want you forever."

Hokum. Bullshit. Burton should have doubted everything that came out of his mouth.

But instead he felt comforted. Relieved. His body tingled from release, and his soul throbbed from ripping away the veil of innocence he'd kept so fiercely wrapped around his desire.

But part of him was comforted. A wonderstruck, childlike part of his heart was convinced he and Ernie were going to be together forever, and in that moment, that vulnerable, fragile moment after sex, he believed it. Burton fell asleep for an hour, safer in Ernie's arms than he'd felt since he'd joined the Marines.

He awoke with a jerk, Ernie's head snuggled against his chest, and he had to smile when Ernie patted him like a kid.

"You're awake," Burton grumbled.

"I'm always awake at this time," Ernie said.

Burton shoved himself up on the bed, bare-chested, and Ernie rested his cheek against his midriff, fingers walking across his muscle groups just firmly enough not to tickle.

"Why is that?"

"World's too loud in the day," Ernie said. "Too many people, so close by." He shuddered. "Albuquerque isn't a big city either. But too big. About five thousand people is perfect. Just open stretches of desert feels weird—it's like being in a sensory deprivation tank. But that many—there's enough white noise to sleep."

Burton grunted. His family called it *witchiness*. His father held to this day this his great-aunt Gertie could read a person's palm like reading their job résumé and family history all rolled into one. He didn't necessarily have a problem believing in Ernie's gifts—or believing that Ernie needed to be gentle with himself to sustain them.

But he couldn't figure out how it had earned the kid a bevy of his own personal assassins either.

"You basically read people," Burton said, thinking. "Good intentions, bad intentions—whether they mean harm to you or others or not. Who knows about this?"

"The Navy," Ernie said guilelessly.

Burton knew his eyes grew really large.

"And that happened because...."

"My parents died," Ernie said, his voice dropping. "I was... I was seventeen. And... I mean, they did all the right stuff with a will and everything, but... I was so close, you know? They didn't figure on going out together, and they didn't appoint a guardian or whatever."

Burton started rubbing gentle circles on his back, just like he would if Ernie were a girl in distress. Ernie's entire body went slack against his, and their nakedness became important. They were skin to skin, and Burton had become the chief comforter.

This was... a big deal. This was how people became close.

"So, you went into the foster care system." That was logical, right?

"Yes. My first family wasn't...." Ernie shuddered. "I was so sad, and when the older brother tried to comfort me... it was easy at first, to let him touch me. And then... then there he was, hands everywhere, and my own... grief I guess, rolled away, and it was like being touched by a greasy octopus all over my body. So I started to scream, and the whole world showed up, and it was a big fucking mess."

"Oh, baby...."

"Mm." Ernie was so boneless. Like a light-boned cat or a really sleepy small dog. "But I went back into the system, and the next family... the social worker walked me to the front door, the mom answered, and I said, 'She's glad I'm here. She needs more money for her coke dealer.'"

Burton let out a chuff of air. "Well called."

"Yeah. Well. I was taken to a sort of holding place, an orphanage of sorts, and that was all kinds of bad. I'd stay awake all night, terrified, because I could feel all the bad—and so much of it wasn't the kids' fault, but it was there. And finally, the week before I turned eighteen, a guy in a uniform showed up and said, 'We have a special ROTC program just for kids who need scholarships.'"

Burton stared. "That's convenient. And unlikely. And—"

"And I slept in barracks for a year. I mean, I ate, had PT, got individual martial arts training, and didn't have to sleep near too many people. But… I was, you know. All alone."

"What did you do there?"

Ernie shuddered. "Do I have to talk about that? It…." His voice dropped. "I'm hungry. Can we eat? I don't want to talk about that anymore. We had donuts hours ago. Can we have dinner now?"

Burton took a deep breath. He was pretty good at interrogation—had done it a number of times on the job and overseas. But Ernie felt warm and sweet—they were naked together. They were close. Pushing him now felt like a violation.

And this kid had been violated plenty.

"Yeah, kid. Sure. Pick something out of the takeout menu. We'll order in."

Ernie's smile at him was transparent—he'd played Burton like a violin. But he also seemed grateful, maybe because Burton had allowed himself to be played.

"Can we hear stories about you now?" he asked, all but batting his eyes.

"Don't you know everything?" This was important, actually. How far did the gift extend?

"I know… I know good intentions or bad intentions. I get bursts of specifics, of speech, of pictures, but that's not consistent. When I think hard, I can scan the people around me for what they think about me or about the people I'm with. It's… difficult. If, say, a group of people were to walk into the hotel looking for us specifically, it would wake me up like a smack to the face."

Burton stared at him. "That's happened to you before?"

Ernie nodded. "Oh yeah. It's sort of how I left the military. But I'm hungry. Let me get food first. I swear I'll tell the rest."

Burton wasn't sure what made him cup Ernie's cheek. "My father's name is Roger. My mom is Anita. I have two little brothers. Eddie's a business major, and John can play the violin like a dream. I was engaged to my high school sweetheart all the way through two tours with the Marines, but I broke up with her when I joined black ops, because it didn't seem fair to be in a relationship with someone when I was going to be a ghost in her life. And I love Chinese food. Good Chinese food. If your gift can help me tell the good stuff from the weakshit tempura chicken in red sugar glaze, I'll be forever grateful."

Ernie's eyes grew big and limpid. "My parents were Glen and Sharon. They… they used to tuck me in every night, even when I was seventeen.

They were my… my scale for good. If someone had a heart like my mother or father, they were good. When… when I was suddenly in a world with people not like that….” He bit his lip.

“You were helpless,” Burton whispered.

Ernie nodded. “I… I had to work really hard to find… to find a life that wouldn’t make me insane.”

“I’m so sorry I ripped that away from you.”

And this next smile—shaky, hurt, and glorious. “I’m not. I might never have known what sex was for. It was beautiful. But I will miss my cats.”

Gently Burton placed a kiss on his forehead. “I’m sure there’s somewhere else, somewhere small, where you can feed every cat for miles.”

“You understand.”

“I’ll do what I can for you, Ernie.”

“Chinese food.” But Ernie didn’t move. He just stayed there, looking at Burton like he held the secret of peace in a painful world.

Burton leaned down and claimed his mouth and drank in his trust like wine. He’d make it happen. He’d save this boy. Maybe not for himself—who lived a life where that was possible? Where he worked as an assassin but had this much sweetness in his home, his bed?

But Burton would save him. It was his mission now. It was why he took the job in the first place.

Ernie’s taste flooded him and Burton groaned, falling into the kiss in earnest.

Of course it was.

BURTON CLEANED up the last of the Chinese food at around two in the morning. Ernie helped him—well, helped by licking some of it off his chest—and then they ended up in bed again, and this time when Burton fell back against the rumpled sheets, he felt well and truly done.

He couldn’t remember the last time he’d fucked himself out like that—but he obviously had been missing something in the meantime.

“What are you thinking?” Ernie asked, snuggling in against his chest. “I’m thinking I wish I’d charged my phone—I need to read something right now. It’s reading time, if I’m not out at the club, you know?”

“Mmm….” Burton’s phone had a reading app. “What do you like?”

Ernie’s chuckle was so wicked. “Action adventure and spy stuff.”

Burton pulled it up for him and paused, phone in midair.

"You want the rest of my story," Ernie said softly.

"Please. I need to know what I'm dealing with here."

Ernie chuffed out air. "Whatever I was supposed to be doing, I failed. I mean, you'd think a ranking officer would understand, right?"

"What didn't they get?"

"That good and bad are subjective!"

Burton blinked. "That's pretty fucking obvious, actually."

"Right? But they would ask me to talk to a guy and tell them if he was good or bad. I asked them what sort of criteria they wanted—because I'm not a moron! And they said, 'Just good or bad, son.' So, well, I'd tell them. Except… I guess I thought 'good' was someone who wouldn't kill without cause."

Burton took a quick breath. "That's my general definition too. Someone who's not cruel. Someone who's kind to all people, not just special friends." He didn't mention racism—he didn't have to, he figured, because Ernie patted his chest unhappily, like he was apologizing for something.

Hell, wasn't Ernie's fault.

And this other thing didn't seem to be either.

"That's what I thought," Ernie said, voice dropping. "But they wanted someone who would… you know. Follow rules. Regardless. So, like…."

Burton's heart turned cold and pumped ice through all his veins. "So, like, someone who would look at a picture of a clueless club kid who fed every stray cat in town and take him out without asking why."

Ernie shrugged. "And I could have told them that—but they kept saying they wanted someone who could be molded into the perfect soldier. Eventually, every man I shook hands with gave me a sweat-screaming, wet-the-bed nightmare. One day they just… just took me to Albuquerque. I have no idea even why that city, although it wasn't so bad, really."

"Maybe they thought the same thing you would," Burton said thoughtfully. "Maybe they thought it would be a place where not too many voices were in your head."

"Well they were fuckin' wrong," Ernie said unhappily. "They gave me money for my education—"

"Which you couldn't use." Burton remembered those grades—someone who wanted an education but who probably couldn't manage all the people.

"Yeah." He sounded so disheartened. "They added a year's worth of cash in the bank on top of my inheritance and an honorable discharge. I…

I have no idea what happened next, but… but I'm telling you, some of the men I had to assess…." He shuddered.

"Any names stick out?" Burton had seen a lot of good men in the military. But he'd seen the few bad apples too. The ones who came to the States from deployment and beat up their wives and made the news with a lot of blood on their hands. They weren't his job—weren't his business—but sometimes he really wished they were.

"This one guy…." Ernie sighed. "Had red hair and this ugly knife scar across his face—"

Burton sucked in his breath. "Galway," he muttered. Oh Lord—he knew what had happened to that guy, and it was bad news.

"Whatever. Anyway—he liked hurting people. And when I told my CO that, he promoted the guy. Another guy named Owens…. God, the inside of his head was like a dirty toilet. He… he was definitely going to kill. And a bunch more."

Oh hell.

"Ernie," Burton said, his voice dropping to a dangerous quiet.

"Yeah?"

"I'm going to call some friends in the morning. Some people who will take you in, and not ask questions, and be kind to you." It had been his plan from the first—but it seemed even more urgent now. "But I need you to do me a favor."

"Why can't I stay with you?"

Burton remembered Jason's warning that he was on his own. "Because I'm about to find out how to join this unit. You wouldn't happen to remember your CO's name, would you?"

"Commander Karl Lacey," Ernie said promptly. "But you're… what? What branch are you?"

"Multijurisdictional covert operations." Burton kept his voice bland, and Ernie rolled his eyes.

"Black ops. I'm not stupid."

"You are if you mention me to anybody but my friends in SoCal."

Ernie sighed. "You're going to… what? Infiltrate the enemy? Can you do that?"

Burton shrugged, feeling sleep pull at him. "It's my job," he said, yawning.

"Here. Give me your phone—"

"Only that app," Burton said, unworried. Yeah, his phone could be a scary place—if he hadn't locked everything down but the entertainment apps.

Ernie snorted. "I'm not stupid. I don't want you to have to kill me for real."

"For real?"

Ernie snuggled back into his arms. "Didn't you tell your handler I was dead?"

"I said I walked away—"

"But he assumed. No, that's fine. I can be dead. As long as I can read this book on your phone and maybe play Two Dots."

"All the scary stuff is locked," Burton said with a yawn.

"Yeah. I know. But I'm not going to tempt fate." Ernie smiled, so sweetly Burton's heart about broke. "I mean, we've had this night. How much better can my life get?"

He started reading then, and Lee Burton, who trusted nobody, yawned and fell asleep with Ernie on his chest.

He woke up a few hours later, and Ernie was right where Lee had left him, phone off and shoved under the pillow. His mouth was parted just a little, and he was snoring softly.

Burton paused and stroked his hair from his face. "Okay, my boy, I'm going to find a place for you to be safe for a while. If I'm any sort of person at all, I'll find you a home before this is over, just so you know."

"You're my home," Ernie mumbled. "Two more hours, Burton. Then we'll be on the run."

Burton didn't say anything, thinking about how this kid needed some peace and Burton was the last person to give him that. Thinking about how he was going to just leave the kid with strangers and run back into an operation where he might not talk to anybody for months. Thinking about how this kid deserved so much more than just a wonderful night and a promise that Burton might not be able to keep.

He figured he'd keep his promises to himself, then, and maybe wouldn't voice any of them until he knew for sure what he could make come true.

With a sigh he set his alarm for two more hours, but before he fell back asleep, he texted *Ace, I need a huge-assed favor. Hear me out before you say yes.*

When he woke up, he saw the message almost immediately.

Yes.

And that's why he'd trust Ace Atchison with Ernie, he thought, giving thanks for his few good deeds. Because Ace had so much faith in him that he'd die before he let Burton down.

Burton felt the same about Ace.

And now he felt the same about Ernie.

Burt and Ernie in the Desert

ERNIE LOOKED around the little nontown of Victoriana with a feeling of intense joy. The place was mostly a gas station with a fast food place on one side of the highway and a tiny garage with a house for the owners on the other. Desert surrounded it, and even in the encroaching fall, the landscape was flat and unexciting, with saguaro and creosote bushes for miles.

But for Ernie, this was the best place on earth.

"Really?" He turned toward Burton, body practically thrumming with excitement. "I'm staying here?"

Burton arched a suspicious eyebrow in his sculpted bronze-toned face and said nothing.

"It is, right? I mean, that house—it's got an add-on to it. Like, new. Even the siding is new. That's your place, right?"

Burton frowned. "How would you know that?"

Ernie grinned, unrepentant. "I heard you talking to Ace. He's nice. Your voice said so."

Burton's frown intensified. "You were supposed to be asleep."

Ernie bit his lip shyly. He had been, until he'd heard Burton talking next to him. He didn't need the gift to reckon Lee was uncomfortable with where their relationship had gone.

Well, not that Ernie wasn't slutty as hell on any given day, but the thing that had bloomed between him and Lee was based solely on the fact that when they looked at each other and touched, the world stopped spinning, and that included Ernie's ever-questing, witchy trouble-magnet of a brain.

Ernie didn't need to be slutty anymore. He'd found the safety he'd been looking for his entire life.

"Safety" just didn't know it yet.

"I was mostly asleep," Ernie soothed. "You like Ace."

Burton let out a sigh. "Yeah. Ace is good people. Not educated, mind you, so—"

"He's smart, though," Ernie said sunnily. Yeah, he'd read that much from the voice on the other end of the phone. That and the fact that Burton was scary smart, and he'd never be able to tolerate someone not scary smart like he was. But he was also—whether he knew it or not—intuitive, in the same way Ernie was intuitive, but not nearly as powerful.

Burton could see through what people were supposed to be and right into what they were. He'd watched Ernie for days when he should have just done his job and shot. Ernie was still walking around converting oxygen because Burton had seen there was more to Ernie than a brainless party boy who liked to make donuts.

"Yeah, he's smart." Burton let out a sigh. "Look, kid—"

"You know my name." Ernie knew all the tricks to making somebody not important. It was why he'd called Burton "Cruller" for the first two hours. It hadn't worked for Ernie; he wouldn't let it work for Burton.

"Ernie…." And it came out like a plea, just like it had in the hotel room they'd shared—in the bed they'd shared not hours ago.

"Yeah?" he said sweetly.

"I need to go away—you understand—"

"Undercover." Ernie wasn't stupid either. "The guy who put the hit out on me—he's bad news—"

"And he's legit. Like, a real guy in the real military, and he wanted you dead. I need to find a way to work for him so I know why. This isn't… the hit out on you should never have happened—"

"You're not just saving me," Ernie said. "You're saving anybody who carried out orders in good faith."

Burton started a grimace, but it came out a look of complete tenderness. "You're so… so very wise." Like he couldn't help himself, he reached out and cupped Ernie's cheek. "God… so pretty." For a moment his muscles tensed, like he was going to pull his hand back, but Ernie licked his lips on purpose, knowing it would make him look soft and vulnerable and wanting Burton to kiss him at least one more time before he fled.

Burton didn't disappoint him. He leaned forward, claiming Ernie's mouth with his own, and Ernie opened for him, as soft and as giving as he knew how to be.

He knew a lot. He was a sexual genius, mostly, and it took Burton a whole thirty seconds before he was groaning into Ernie's mouth and trying to haul him across the center island of the SUV they were sitting in.

Ernie would have gone. Ernie would have shucked his jeans and sat on Burton's cock dry if that's what it would take to get Burton to commit, but the damned SUV was too small, and Burton smacked his elbow on the steering wheel in mid-Ernie-maul-maneuver.

"Ouch!" He jerked back, letting Ernie go and looking damned embarrassed. "Dammit. Why can't I...? It's weird what you do to me, kid."

"Ernie," Ernie corrected throatily. "Don't go. Stay here. We can have all the sex you want until it doesn't seem so strange anymore that you want me. You can quit being an assassin-super-black-ops guy and be my guy. Nobody will even know our names."

He pulled in a quick breath, surprised at himself. That's not what he'd intended to come out of his mouth at all, even a little.

Burton was looking torn as a man could get. "Ernie... I... even if I come back, I might not be the guy for—"

Ernie pulled away and opened his door. "Let's go meet Ace and Sonny," he said, not wanting to hear it. At least when Burton was talking to his friend, Ernie wouldn't have to hear him lie—not to himself and not to Ernie. "Will you at least be able to come visit over holidays?" he asked after he'd slid out.

Burton stopped and grabbed the duffel of clothes they'd bought Ernie on their way from Albuquerque. They'd had to leave Santa Fe, not even stopping at Ernie's apartment with his cats and everything. They'd had to stop at Walmart and get clothes. Burton had called the super and made arrangements for the cats—even the strays that would just show up unbidden—and Ernie didn't even want to know what a colossal pain in the ass tying up that loose end had been.

But Burton had done it for him. It wasn't even part of his job, just like being Ernie's savior wasn't part of his job, and Ernie didn't want to think of the prices Lee Burton had paid for stepping out of himself in order to successfully not kill Ernie James Caulfield's scrawny psychic ass.

But he had. And he seemed to be willing to pay any price needed to keep Ernie as happy as possible considering he was a target or a dead man or worse.

Ernie was going to just keep on hoping the man would recognize that what they shared in the hotel room on the way here didn't happen every time two men met, fell into each other's eyes, and touched each other's bare skin.

"No," Burton said, sighing. "No, I won't see you for Thanksgiving. Do you have the phone I bought you?"

Ernie nodded. "Yeah." Clean, untraceable. It had been preloaded with Ace's number, Sonny's number, and Burton's number.

The end.

"I'll text you when I can."

Ernie brightened. "I'll text you when you can't."

Lee clapped his hands over his eyes. "Kid—"

"Ernie."

"Ernie—"

"Don't worry. Once you start thinking about me, I'll fill in the gaps in the conversation just fine." That wasn't really how the gift worked, except Ernie was pretty sure he'd be just as connected to Burton from however far away as he was now.

"That, uh, actually makes me a little itchy...," Burton said, slamming his door in a fit of what was probably pique.

Ernie smiled, so relieved he couldn't even let Burton piss on his parade. "It shouldn't. You just have to tell the truth. To yourself. Especially to yourself."

Burton's low moan reassured Ernie to no end. It meant the man believed him. Took him seriously. Would work hard to be as truthful as possible.

Ernie already knew what Burton felt for him. He could wait until Burton figured it out in his own head.

ACE WAS exactly what Ernie expected except way better-looking, but Sonny was not.

For one thing, Ernie had figured Sonny to be spelled with a *u* and Sonny to be a she, which just went to show you that sometimes the gift was a reliable way to get information and sometimes it was a big fat nuisance that overloaded Ernie's synapses and made him absolute garbage at dealing with the rest of the human race like a sane person.

Ace was a solid guy with a chest like a brick wall and arms built like pistons. He had hazel-brown eyes and a mouth that could be cruel, Ernie supposed, but when he shook Ace's hand, all he felt was decent guy trying to live a decent life.

There was a current of darkness, but everybody had that. This guy had just negotiated his current and decided how it flowed, was all.

Sonny was much smaller, muscular too, but in the whip-thin way of someone who was all activity and nerves and not so much effort. He had blond hair—almost pretty—and a fox-pointed but narrow face.

His darkness was like a box, and Sonny would rabbit into his box and bound out even as they were talking. The three-billionth time Sonny rabbited into the dark box in his soul, Ernie let out a rough sigh and grabbed his arm.

"I'm not here to take him away from you," Ernie said, exasperated. "As if anybody could. Now calm down. You're making Burton jumpy."

Sonny gave a long, slow blink with his enormous blue-gray eyes, and some of the rabbit jumped out of him. "Yeah. Sure." He retreated behind Ace then, touching him at the shoulder before he scooped up the tiny dog yapping at his feet. The dog shut up, and Ernie had a chance to look around their little house.

And it *was* little. The little kitchen opened up into a little dining room with a small table, which in turn opened up into a little living room. The living room was made smaller by the almost laughably large dog crate in the corner, complete with a little cushion, a blanket, and food and water on a plastic mat. It was the most palatial thing about the house.

Otherwise there were four doors—the laundry room, which was on the same side as the bathroom; Ace and Sonny's bedroom, which opened behind the couch; and a newly painted portal to what was obviously Burton's personal space.

Ernie interrupted the grand tour with a yawn. "Thank you, Ace and Sonny, for letting me stay here." It was getting time to sleep again. "I'll get up and you can show me how to earn my keep, okay? But I have to nap and say goodbye to Burton."

With that he grabbed Burton's hand and dragged him away from their surprised hosts and through the door to Burton's space.

Ernie looked around carefully once they were there, biting his lip.

"He made this for you," he said, awe apparent. "Like… like he loves you. Like a friend—'cause he's romantically attached to Sonny, which must be hard because Sonny's not easy, but look."

Burton looked around, saw what Ernie did. The simplicity of the room and the small, serviceable attached bathroom, the nice queen-sized bed with the good mattress and a plain high-quality quilt in a warm tan that matched the curtains, the wood paneling that matched the dresser. Ernie moved toward it and picked up a piece of driftwood sanded into a ball until it gleamed. There were a couple of other doodads there—a glass boat from San Diego, a snow globe from Tahoe, a small picture at the Chandelier Tree.

"Ace and Sonny," Burton said quietly. "They go on vacations now and then, and they bring back things. Something for Alba, their receptionist at the garage, something for Jai, their employee, something for Kat, a girl Ace sort of adopted who's living with Ace's parents, and something for me. Every time."

"It makes them really happy to bring stuff home for you guys," Ernie said easily. "It's… nice. You brought me to a nice place. This is your…." He looked around, feeling a sort of peace here.

"Haven," Burton said softly.

"Church," Ernie said, naming it for what it was. "When you go out and do the things you have to, you're thinking about Ace and Sonny, and protecting them."

Burton shrugged. "Somebody's got to."

Ernie nodded. "So now you're protecting me here too."

"Somebody's got to," Burton rasped, and Ernie heard the need.

He turned and rushed into Burton's arms, held him tight. "Be careful," he begged softly. "Come back. Become a part of this, of these people you love. They're here for you."

"I'm a—"

"A man." Ernie tilted his face up and took Burton's kiss like it was a given. Ernie knew it wasn't. But he'd lost himself already. Burton was going to do dangerous things to try to bring the people behind Ernie's contract to justice, but afterward, Ernie was going to hope for Burton by his side.

Burton ripped away from the kiss like he was gulping air.

"Kid—"

"Ernie."

"Ernie…." His voice ached with tenderness. "You and me, we're not over."

Ernie smiled. "At last, he sees."

Burton laughed gruffly. "Okay—I've got to—"

And then, dammit, the goddamned shining hit Ernie right in the gut. "You've got to protect them too," he said, his voice remote.

"Ace and Sonny?"

"They're far away, and they're tied into this and…." Ernie sighed. "Broken. One of them is broken. Tiny little pieces, a shattered fish in a bowl of refracted light. A shark who loves him. And they're coming. You'll know them. You'll protect them. They'll need you."

Burton blinked. "I, uh…."

45

Oh, goddammit. Ernie liked these people in his brain, the tough, battered one and the slick one in the suit. He couldn't see their faces, but he could feel their decency, even through the shining. He rose to his tiptoes and kissed Burton's cheek. "Come back to me," he said simply.

Because that's what you did when you loved a force of nature. You let him go be a force for good.

Burton left, and Ernie fell onto the bed dispiritedly. He was crying, because his heart was on his sleeve, would always be on his sleeve, had never not been on his sleeve.

He knew the door opened, and the small dog bounded on the bed and licked his face, but it wasn't until he felt the tentative hand in his hair that he realized he might have, for once, truly landed someplace that would feel like home.

"Don't mind Duke," Sonny Daye said, voice matter-of-fact. "He knows you're sad. I'm just gonna leave him here to keep you company while me and Ace go open the garage. You feel free to eat what you wanna—we'll go shopping for you later, and Ace says that's fine if you help with paperwork and stuff and—"

Ernie rolled over and grabbed Sonny's hand. "Sonny Daye?"

"Yessir?"

"We're friends already. Don't worry about making me happy. Burton wouldn't have brought me here if it wasn't a good place. I'm comfortable. I get up around six or seven. Want me to make dinner?"

Sonny smiled a little, and while Ernie caught the undercurrent of reluctance, he managed to say "That would be kind" in a way that was almost civil.

"Okay, then. Don't worry. I'll get along here just fine."

Sonny stood and left, and Ernie yawned and sank back down onto the bed. In his pocket his phone buzzed.

Was damned hard leaving you, kid. Be good until I get back.

Yeah. Until the fish and the shark got here, it was gonna be okay.

Waiting for Fish

OKAY FOR Ernie—but not so much for Sonny, not at first. He really was reluctant to turn the cooking over to a stranger.

Or, well, territorial as hell.

"What the fuck is this on the mac and cheese?" he'd asked the second day of Ernie's stay. "Breadcrumbs? Who in the hell puts breadcrumbs on their mac and—"

"It's real good," Ace had said, like he meant it. "Sonny, are you tired when you get off work? I'm tired when I get off work. Ain't it nice Ernie wants to help? You thought it would be a good idea, remember?"

The glare Sonny shot Ace was pure hurt. "I thought you liked my cooking."

Ace winked at him, kindness in the crinkles of his eyes and the corners of his lean-lipped mouth. "Course I do. But we're glad Ernie's here and we're grateful for his help."

Sonny's sour look should have given Ernie indigestion. "I've noticed you say 'we' a lot. Why do you say 'we' when you're really talking about how you want *me* to be?"

Ernie knew his eyes flew open, because Sonny hadn't shown that amount of self-awareness in the past two days, and he could tell Ace was surprised too.

And then he looked proud.

"You're right," he said. "I shouldn't try to speak for you. But sometimes... sometimes the thing that comes out of your mouth ain't the thing in your heart. Sometimes it's like my only job in the world is to hear what your heart's saying and translate that for the world. Do you want me to stop doing that?"

Ernie's own heart stopped, gooped up by the tension in the room.

Sonny swallowed unhappily. "I just... you don't like his cooking better than mine, do you?"

And translating Sonny's heart for the rest of the world must really have been the thing Ace was best at. "Of course I do, Sonny—he put garlic breadcrumbs on it. It's delicious. But I don't like *him* more than I like you. They're two different things. Maybe, if you're nice to him, he'll show you different ways to cook stuff on our day off, and you can make it too."

Sonny glared at him suspiciously. "You won't *start* to like him more than you like me, will you? He's awfully sweet."

Ace hid a smile. "He is. But I'm more of a fan of surly, ornery, and bitchy. I'm not falling for Ernie instead of you. Can't happen."

Sonny gave him a flat look and then rolled his eyes. "I'm not always ornery."

"And I'm not always breathing. So now that you can deal with his mac and cheese, try the chicken he made with it."

Sonny settled down into his seat and took a bite, then let out a sigh of defeat. "Yeah. Fine. He can fuckin' cook. Hooray. Can he rebore the engine of a brand-new Jaguar that just blew out the gaskets in the fuckin' heat?"

"I'm betting not. Your place in my heart is safe and always has been."

Sonny couldn't hide *his* smile, not even a little, and Ernie felt like it was safe to speak.

"I learned to cook in a bakery," he said, hoping this worked. "Do you want to help me make donuts on your day off?"

Sonny's eyes got as big as a child's, and his body wiggled like the little dog he was feeding chicken to under the table. "Could you? Like, a real person makes donuts? We could do that? They don't just come in boxes?"

Ernie looked him in the eyes and smiled, seeing the young in Sonny, the part that had seen the world in darkness for so long that seeing it in light was a revelation, every day.

"Course," he said gently. "I'd love to. You could make some for Ace."

Because it was clear that the light of revelation came directly from Ace.

Sonny smiled, then looked vaguely ashamed. "Sorry I was mean about your mac and cheese," he said, taking another bite. "It's not bad."

That night Ace did the dishes and Sonny took the dog out for a walk, keeping him on a leash because if, God help them all, the little goober should run past the house and past the garage, the cars barreling down the road were going too damned fast to stop. Ace had Ernie stay and "help him" even though he didn't let Ernie do more than sit at the table and drink a soda.

"Thank you," he said quietly. "For being patient with Sonny. I'm sorry he took your cooking wrong."

"He usually cooks," Ernie said, feeling like he should have seen this at the beginning. He was supposed to be gifted, right?

"Yeah. But we've been working extra hard in the shop lately. It's weird. It's like people will actually have their cars towed here to have him work on them."

Ernie cocked his head, reading the unspoken truth. "He's a genius with them," he said softly. "He's a genius with them, and you just sort of let him be a genius."

Ace shrugged. "Not much else I'm good at. Now, we usually have ice cream for dessert, but if you write me a list of stuff, I can buy you anything you want."

Ernie's breath caught. Not much else Ace was good at? "Burton thinks you're awesome," he said, faith in every word. "Why do you think he thinks that?"

Another laconic shrug. "I got no idea. He's just nice to us is all. We don't talk much, but we're friends. I'm gonna go out and check on Sonny and Duke—sometimes our world begins and ends with that dog's crap in the evening, so—"

"Ace!" Ernie said, because this was important. "You hold the whole garage together!"

"Yeah, Ernie. Me and three other people. We're the equivalent of going out and saving the fuckin' world."

Ace sounded bored, and Ernie subsided, feeling young. It was true—Ace and Sonny had a small life of safety here, but Ernie could *feel* the truth. This tiny eye of safety was as big as the sky to them.

Ernie hadn't met Alba yet—but he smelled her when he went into the little cashier's cubicle. He smelled girl's body wash, and saw a backpack of books and notepaper and a used laptop he was pretty sure Ace had rebuilt for her so she could do good in school. He smelled fierceness, and he read intelligence in every entry in the books.

He *had* met Jai, their employee. Had, in fact, had a little dinner ready to go in a plastic container for him before he'd left for the night. Jai was a giant of a man with a shaved-bald head, a black goatee, and a white smile meant for devouring children, and he turned that smile on Ernie.

"This is kind," he'd said, nodding sharply. "Too bad you are not...." He looked at Sonny and grimaced. "I like the yellow hair," he said with dignity, and Ernie had taken that to mean something else entirely.

"I'm Burton's," Ernie said, hoping it was true. Burton hadn't texted him yet, and conscious that anything Ernie said could be distracting Burton at a key period in time, he hadn't pushed it. He figured he'd give Burton a week before texting again.

"Burton is good man. You could do worse. Thank you for the food. I'll go shopping for you, if you need to."

So Jai had given Ernie's second offer to go shopping—but he figured Ace was his real benefactor, and he probably approved of taking care of Jai.

Ace was the general caretaker on all fronts here, and his interaction with the erratic and capricious Sonny had just proved it.

Ernie filed the thought away. After Sonny got back with the dog—who ate his little treat and went into his crate with the ease of a creature who liked his routine—Ace and Sonny cleaned and organized the auto bay while Ernie was looking at accounts. Ace worked efficiently, with that steady-eyed attention to detail and practicality that had marked him from the first.

Sonny moved from thing to thing, erratically, paying attention to all the tasks, from replacing the tools to making sure all the diagnostic machines and air compressors were clean and well cared for. Ace didn't prompt him, didn't correct him, just kept working. By the time he was done, Sonny was done, having accomplished all the smaller tasks at about the same time Ace finished the one big one.

When they were done, Ernie called them over.

"See," he said, pulling up accounting software on the laptop Ace had given him. "You're doing okay, but if you ordered more regularly, I could get you discounts on your most-used items and maybe get some tchotchkes for you—key chains and stuff—to advertise. How 'bout once a week you take a look at the inventory, and I'll see what we can order when."

"Sure," Ace said, at the same time Sonny said, "We don't need no—"

Ace looked at him and arched an eyebrow. "I'm being an asshole," Sonny muttered. "Sorry." He turned and stalked back toward the house, and Ace pinched the bridge of his nose.

"He seemed okay with me being left here," Ernie offered tentatively, still confused after dinner, and Ace gave him a droll look.

"I don't know, Ernie, what do *you* think is wrong with him?" Ace asked, eyebrow lifted.

Ernie had tried to stay out of Ace's and Sonny's brains. It was impossible to do completely—he'd already read their darkness and their light. He knew Ace was the center and Sonny was the skin that bound him, but the specifics—those he'd avoided.

"He's jealous," Ernie said promptly. "You said it yourself. He's afraid of me taking your affection. But you told him—"

"A couple of times. It's going to take a couple of more. *You* can walk into a room and know who's bad and who's good. That's a blessing. Sonny was...." Ace's face closed down, and Ernie felt a steel wall clang between what Ace knew and what he wanted Ernie to know. "Sonny was betrayed by any safety he ever knew. He... he got confused with a lot of shit you don't want to think about. So he's gonna need me to tell him repeatedly, and you're going to have to understand that. He was kind to you that first day. Remember that moment?"

Ernie nodded, because the moment with the dog and Sonny as he'd lain on the bed crying had seemed propitious.

"That was the best I've ever seen Sonny Daye. So he's got it in him, and he's got it in him for you. Just... it's gonna take more than one good moment. You've had a couple today, whether you know it or not. We'll keep working."

"Mm."

"Mm?" Ace arched a skeptical eyebrow.

"Mm...." Ernie sighed. Ace looked like he expected people to do what he wanted, and that weight of expectation was a powerful thing. Ernie had slept with a lot of people because of that weight and had understood—even as their sex shielded him from the worst of the stuff in people's heads—that he was a willow, bending in the wind. Ace was a powerful storm wind.

"Mm, I am not used to being with people," he said baldly. "I'm used to sleeping with men—but that's not what you want from me."

Ace's eyebrows went straight up. "No, sir, it is not. But I think you need to ask yourself a question, son." Ace was three years older than Ernie, but this didn't seem the time to bring that up.

"Which question?" For once Ernie couldn't anticipate the answer. It was like this particular man's experience and solidness in the world made him as impervious to Ernie's gift as the storm wind would be to Ernie's willow.

"What do you want from *us*?"

Ernie blinked.

"You came here and offered to help—and damn, we're grateful. And you're useful and smart, and I will use that. And you've spent two days trying to be friends with Sonny, and the only friend he's ever really had is Jai, and they don't even speak human being together, so you're also sort of a first. So I welcome all the good you're trying to do here—don't get me wrong. But you were stashed here among strangers by a man you may be in love with but you barely know. So before you give up on Sonny, before you start poking around in his bear trap of a brain, ask yourself—what do you want from us?"

Ernie hadn't put it into words before. "I…. My parents died when I was seventeen," he said, feeling raw. Nobody really asked him about this. Even Burton had known. "I… I didn't have a place until the Navy brought me in illegally, I guess, and tried to get me to… to be a witch for them. Didn't work out. And then they cut me loose. I… used clubs and crowds and sex and drugs to silence the shit in my head—to keep me safe from it. But…." Oh God. Ernie felt his head clog again. He hadn't cried since Burton left. Before that, he couldn't remember the last time he'd thought about this… this silly, sad, stupid thought. "I ain't—" He had an education. Ace said "ain't." Dammit—he really was a withy reed! "I haven't had a family in a long time. I… I read so clearly. I came here and I read you and Sonny and Jai and Alba—even Burton and the girl you took to your parents. You're family. And you've been kind to me. I really want to fit in."

Ace was looking surprised—and a little grumpy.

"What?" Ernie asked anxiously.

"That's just really… healthy," he said, sounding stunned. "I mean… like so damned emotionally healthy. It's a refreshing change," he declared, standing up from the desk. Unexpectedly, he turned his head and hollered. "Sonny! Get back here! I know you didn't go to the house!"

It was Ernie's turn to be surprised when Sonny stuck his head around the door to the auto bay. "Ace?" he asked tentatively.

"C'mere. We're gonna give Ernie a hug, and you're gonna see it's all okay."

"Why's he need a hug?" Sonny asked suspiciously, but still he advanced on the small office like there might not be snakes in there.

"He needs one so he knows where he fits here. You need one so you know he's not a threat. Don't worry. My family wasn't a complete shitshow. I have faith this will work out."

Unbidden, Ernie had a vision of Ace as a little kid, blood on his face and a stubborn expression, while a plump woman with a once-pretty face and fluffy blonde hair fussed over him.

I ain't a baby!

No, but I don't like seeing you hurt.

She'd hugged him, and for a moment the guarded fierceness that made up Ace Atchison melted, and there was comfort and warmth.

Before Ernie could recover himself from that, Ace was wrapping his cannon-shot arms around Ernie's shoulders, and with a little bit of urging, Sonny was holding him almost uncomfortably tight with arms like tree roots. For a moment Ernie was tumbled about in their thoughts, in their pasts, and he couldn't breathe. *An animal held him down and violated him until he bled. An ugly clown grinned at him with a big red smile where his throat should be.*

Ernie fought not to scream.

And then he pulled back, felt the strength there, the control that held these other terrifying moments in check.

Felt it surrounding himself.

Relaxed into the hug.

Became a part of it.

Ace backed off before it could get awkward, but Ernie was left feeling like he'd used to feel when he'd awakened in a pile of bodies. As though, for a little while, he'd been shielded from the terrors of too many minds.

He blinked owlishly at Ace and Sonny. "Thank you," he said gruffly. "That... you guys have demons. But you beat them back. That's what I got around my shoulders. The strength to fight the demons."

Ace blinked back. "You know, if you go walking out into the desert tonight, take Duke. He can't fight anything for you, but he'll be a good alarm system."

Ernie nodded, and Ace stepped back and grabbed Sonny's hand. "C'mon, Sonny. Let's go have some ice cream."

It was the first gesture Ernie had seen between them that indicated they were anything other than work partners, and even though Ernie had known, from the moment he'd arrived, that they were lovers, he suddenly understood the twin-headed snake that was strength and control.

His whole life he'd been an open nerve, had used other people's bodies, used chemicals, to protect himself.

But now, after a hug from Ace and Sonny—one they weren't entirely comfortable giving, he'd felt that too—he realized he had some things to learn.

He finished up what he was doing in the office, waiting until the lights in the little house went off. The night before, he'd stayed out to familiarize himself with the garage and to give the guys inside a chance to be together without him.

He did the same thing now, except he let himself into the quiet and found Duke's crate, where the little animal lay curled up in the corner of the very large cage in the living room. Ernie wondered if Duke wouldn't be happier in something smaller, but he could see Sonny's visible reluctance to leave him in a cage at all.

In the other room the mattress creaked, and Ernie heard movement, a murmur, a gasp.

Oh.

"C'mon, Duke," he whispered. "You and me got better things to do right now."

He called softly and held out the leash, and Duke uncurled and allowed himself to be led outside to the fall desert.

It wasn't hot—pleasant, in fact, in the low sixties—and Ernie grabbed Sonny's sweatshirt, hanging by the door, to wear outside. He figured that would make Sonny less batshit than wearing something of Ace's—and Ace's stuff was way too stretched out in the chest and arms, because damn.

Ernie ventured out into the desert, staying parallel to the road, and allowed the quiet to seep through his bones.

Magical.

That was the only way he could think about it.

No questing minds or restless hearts going *beat-beat-beat* against his own. He could hear the murmur of them, out across the highway, back where the suburb actually lay, but it was far enough away that only Ace and Sonny were a bright spot in the black velvet of his mind, like embers in the dark.

But that meant they weren't close enough to hurt, weren't personal, and Ernie took a big breath.

Realized it was the first time he'd been free since he was a little kid. His parents hadn't known about the gift—not really. But they'd had a way of anticipating him. Maybe they'd been gifted themselves. When he'd become overloaded with too many people, they'd taken him someplace quiet. When school had proved a nightmare—too many voices, too many problems, too much anxiety, too much fear—they'd schooled him at home. His father had changed jobs so they could live in a smaller house in the country instead of a bigger one in the city. His mother worked as a consultant, so she could do most of her work from home. Ernie had always known he was blessed, and after his parents had passed, he'd realized that the bulk of his blessing had come from his parents' *lack* of worry.

Our son's a little high-strung—this just works better for the family.

He's taking a little longer to mature, but he's such a kind boy—he'll find his way.

Kindness had been an asset, a character strength, a thing they were proud of. Ernie's clairvoyance, his ability to read the hearts of people with just their presence, had never been a problem, because his folks surrounded themselves with the nicest people they knew.

Even when taken into the coldness of his lonely barracks and then cut loose into the chaos of a small city, he'd protected himself the best way he'd known how, having full faith that sanctuary was out there, somewhere, waiting to be found.

It wasn't until Ace and Sonny had hugged him, let him see their darkness personally, that he made the truest realization.

They were only sanctuary because they'd had the strength to become their own haven. While their kindness—and for all Ace's talk of Ernie's usefulness, it *was* a kindness—was welcome, Ernie needed to build his own fortress, become his own source of strength.

Such a simple concept. But then, the withy reed was always so in awe of the oak, it never occurred to it to grow.

Ernie picked his way across the desert, enjoying the quiet happiness of the little dog, until the night grew chill and he could feel time passing in his bones.

He stopped for a moment and turned his face to the stars—

And was awestruck.

Even his parents' quiet country home had been closer to civilization than this place out in the desert. He was far enough away from Victoriana that he could see it glow, a boil of light pollution, waiting to burst into day, but here....

All stars.

Vast and indifferent and intense—not a scattering, but a pile of them, pulsing under the black velvet shroud of night.

For a moment he just glutted himself on the quiet, and then, unbidden, came a vision of Burton.

He was sitting in a bar, eyeballing a pair of twos and a pair of jacks over a poker table. The guys he was playing with were... bad. They glared at Burton, angry because he was winning, angry because he was harder and smarter than they were, angry because he was black. But Burton sipped his beer and gave them zero fucks, because after he won this hand, he was going to best them in a fight and get introduced to their commander, some guy with a name like a hamster, and then he'd see if maybe he could find the people who'd been paid to take Ernie's contract.

The thought of Ernie constricted his heart, and he fought off a wave of loneliness that made Ernie himself want to cry—but not so much that he missed the guy on Burton's right, slipping an ace out of his sleeve.

Ernie yanked himself away from the vision and pulled out his phone.

Burton, the guy with the scar is cheating and has a pair of aces.

He sent the text immediately and tried to slip back into the vision. He couldn't—the phone was his anchor to the here and now, and he had no idea how to reach out and find Burton in the vast infinity of space again.

Then the phone buzzed.

Thanks. Good call. I don't want to know how you knew.

Ernie clutched the phone to his chest. *Burton.*

For a moment he wondered if he should text back and, for that matter, *what* he should text back.

And he remembered his resolution to become his own haven.

He needed to be Burton's haven too.

I was walking under the stars and they were just so beautiful. So I looked up into them and lost myself in infinity and my heart found you. And you were in the middle of a poker game and needed help. I hope that was okay.

He turned around and picked his way back, wary of the creosote brush, the succulents, the saguaro as he placed his Target waffle stompers very carefully on ground he could see. He had maybe a mile to go when the phone buzzed again.

I like hearing from you. You talk poetry.

Would you like me to write a limerick about your body? Ernie giggled to himself.

No. But I like poetry.

Ah. So he was going to pretend it hadn't happened. Sort of. But the poetry thing was promising.

You brought me to a shelter thinking it was earth and wood, drywall, siding, straight pine beams, fresh paint. But two souls live here, a lion and a rabbit, both of them protecting anyone in their environs. And I became folded in their strength and would like to grow strength of my own.

He caught his breath as he hit Send. Poetry was naked and raw, and he wondered if this was how Burton had felt in that hotel room.

You're stronger than you think, kid. Gotta go. Stay safe and strong. Makes me happy to think of you there.

And then he was gone—Ernie even felt Burton's attention turn away from the phone to something more pressing.

Listening to Fish

THE COM room was like any com room Burton had been in during his career—people in various capacities, communicating with different places, monitoring different operations, generally a nest of spiders keeping track of what was going on in the outlying places of the web.

Except this web wasn't supposed to exist.

"Hey—Oscar! They at it yet?"

Burton looked up, answering to his cover name without hesitation. Calvin Oscar, ex-Navy SEAL, at your service, sir. The fake ID was already established with Jason's unit—Burton knew that activating it would serve as a tacit flag to Jason that he was active and had found something important. He'd kept both phones—the one he was turning on again in four months and the one he'd called Jason from when he'd made that decision—and he was fully aware that Jason Constance could find him at any moment.

The thought gave him comfort in this nest of snakes.

"No," Burton answered, sounding bored. "One of 'em's still gone."

He'd been working in this abandoned military base outside of Barstow for the last few weeks—ever since Ernie had given him the unexpected tip that had helped him win the game, the fight, and the initiation into Corduroy, the assassin's guild he'd held in such contempt when they'd tried to kill Ernie.

Ernie had texted him once a night ever since. Sometimes Burton could respond—Ernie never asked important questions, like where was he or who was he working for. He asked things like *Is it getting cold there yet?* or *I had a teddy bear as a kid, and it gave me a lot of comfort. Would it be totally dumb if I had Ace get me a teddy bear?* Burton had told him not to bother Ace about that last one—and had sent Ernie a bear from his own account, something huge that was supposed to be the softest stuffed animal on the planet. Ace would have gotten him something small and spare and necessary.

Burton wanted the kid to be spoiled a little.

He'd saved Burton's ass at least three times in the last two weeks.

The first time that phone had buzzed, he'd been a little bit annoyed, had checked it on sufferance, wondering what sort of terrors the kid had

58

imagined. But the directions had been so specific, and Burton had grabbed his fellow player's wrist immediately—and shaken out the card.

And then snapped his wrist.

After that night he'd kept the phone next to his heart, almost like a talisman.

There's a man a mile from you under a sign of a giant bird. He's waiting for you with a gun.

Well, the guy wasn't waiting for anyone anymore.

This isn't a test. The man with the scar plans to kill you and say it was accidental.

Yeah, well, accidents happen.

Burton, after the "accidental" crushing of his fellow Corduroy employee's windpipe, programmed that particular phone with a buzz pattern of three sharp bursts, because he didn't want to be too obvious about checking his phone, dammit, but that kid hadn't steered him wrong yet.

Burton had no idea where he got his information—and he hadn't asked either. He'd just taken it on the same faith that he'd taken "There's a good donut shop in this town," or "Ace and Sonny are good."

Twenty hours in a hotel room didn't sound like grounds for throwing away a lifetime of stone-cold reason, but it had saved Burton's life a lot of times so far, and it was only logical Burton respect the holy shit out of that.

And it didn't hurt that Ernie kept texting poetry.

I see you, lines and shadows, dramatic blacks and browns, glowing like the night. Your heart's a brilliant diamond pulsing beneath your skin. Will it soften?

Yes. Oh God, kid, yes, his heart was soft, tender and quivering, just one more word of sweetness, black shapes on a white screen.

He stayed sharp for the warnings from Ernie—but the poetry made him tremble. He'd had no idea it was a vice until those random words, usually a comment on Ernie's day, his feelings, what was growing inside him, pranced across Burton's screen, and Burton was back in that hotel room, merging, becoming one and holy with a man he'd met less than a day before.

Maybe that's why the poetry.

Poetry was magic, and Ernie was magic, and as far as Burton could tell, it was the magic that had gotten his heart into the mess it was in.

On the nights he couldn't respond, Burton felt lost. Bereft. Like a child who'd forgotten how to call out for his parent.

And this undercover assignment was killing him.

He'd made it into Corduroy, had even made it onto the military base—but that's where he hit a wall. Corduroy was working with Karl Lacey—who had managed to pull off the one and only successful Bob's-in-the-bathroom scam Burton had ever seen. One day he and Jason were going to get very drunk figuring out how Lacey had managed to convince the Navy that Lacey was in San Diego while he was running his own little fiefdom a hundred and fifty miles away.

Right now what mattered was that Lacey *had* done it—but he hadn't done it alone.

Burton had won that fight after the poker game and had been taken to Rufus Hamblin, a dapper little man who showed up in a goatee and a really pricey suit and shoes worth more than what Burton's father made in a month. And his father was an engineer.

Hamblin had put Burton on provisionary status—Burton was good enough to monitor coms and to help with general day-to-day, but he wasn't getting any assignments, no matter how good Calvin Oscar's fake jacket looked or how many off-campus kills he was supposed to have. (Burton had credited Oscar with some of his own kills, the ones out of country, because that way he could tell believable stories and have them pan out if researched.)

So Burton was in the compound—but the compound was a joint Corduroy/Karl Lacey venture.

Karl Lacey's guys either thought they were still in the US Navy—or didn't give a shit. But most of them still thought they were US military, and it bothered Burton. Bothered him a lot.

Because the things Commander Lacey was having his guys do were not part of the country Burton had been fighting for during his nearly nine-year career.

Lacey had organized a "conformation squad" of some of his worst bullies, some of the people who were the cruelest to their peers, and put them in charge of keeping the rest of the Navy guys in line. Everything from sleep deprivation to KP to physical assault was used to take the few guys who asked questions and put them in their place.

Repeatedly.

Until they shaped up or died.

Being put on coms and forced to spend days on end in a room listening to two guys Lacey wanted monitored would have ordinarily driven Burton batshit crazy. But God, Jackson Rivers and Ellery Cramer were a welcome relief from the pressure cooker of one monster with two masters.

It was supposed to be some sort of punishment—Lacey's "unit" was almost uniformly white, and Burton knew military demographics, and that was not the way it should be. Lacey had shaped his unit just like he'd shaped his "conformation squad," in his own image, and Burton was given a garbage assignment because Lacey thought of him as a garbage human.

Burton took a great deal of joy fucking with the information he gleaned from Jackson and Ellery and passing it on to Lacey in filtered, predigested form.

Lacey had met Ellery Cramer—and hadn't liked him. Referred to him by unflattering references to his religion, his sexuality, and his profession. Burton had started out the job thinking at best he'd be bored out of his skull. A lawyer and his lover, working together and fucking—worst thing that could happen was an inconvenient hard-on or a very public nap.

Wrong. So very wrong. If Burton had been as wrong about anything else in his profession as he'd been about being a fly on Ellery Cramer's wall, he'd be dead.

For starters, Ellery Cramer was a defense attorney—and while Burton had never thought particularly hard about the law, listening to Ellery reason through his cases, try to figure out if his defendants were guilty or not and if they would be better served by a guilty plea if they were or by a courtroom battle if they weren't, proved a healthy instruction in the gray areas of life.

Yes, some people were just evil, and those folks deserved to be punished.

But that was only a percentage of the folks who broke the law.

Ellery seemed to know that, and Burton listened to the goings-on in his office like he was watching the courtroom channel or, hey, first-run episodes of *Law & Order*.

And his boyfriend? The PI?

That guy was a *trip*.

Snarky, sharp, cocky, and wounded—Burton had never met a man so in need of... well, someone. Someone to organize his life, someone to boss him around, someone to fight so he did the right thing, and someone to make sure he took care of himself while he did it.

Burton had gotten the assignment right after Thanksgiving, and Jackson was still on medical leave from what Burton gathered to be something that had nearly killed him.

Listening to Ellery badger the guy about his health was like a window into a mother's soul.

"Jackson, what are you doing?" Ellery's voice ran through his phone, so Burton pulled up that feed. Ellery's work phone was tapped, and his home in general, but apparently Lacey could only spring for so much tech, and listening to Hamblin's guys grumble about spending what they had on these two made Burton wonder why they hadn't killed Lacey outright yet.

"Sleeping," Jackson said, but he sounded out of breath.

"Bullshit. My neighbor buzzed me and said you were running around the neighborhood looking like death. What did we agree on?"

The solid silence on the other end of the line told Burton that fireworks were coming.

"Jackson?"

"We didn't agree on shit," he snapped back. "The doctor said wait until I felt better—"

"And how do we feel now?" Ellery asked sweetly.

Burton had looked up pictures of the guys. Ellery had a plain, sharp-featured face with big brown eyes, a pronounced nose, and heavily gelled dark brown hair—and he didn't look sweet, not in the least. He looked, if anything, sharklike.

Lacey knew what Ellery looked like and despised him.

But Rivers?

Burton had found pictures of Rivers online—and doctored them so nobody in Lacey's company could spot him in a lineup.

It was like Ellery's concern was catching, and Burton wanted to be in on the conspiracy to protect the guy.

Because Lord knew he wasn't up to the job himself.

"Peachy," Jackson wheezed, and Burton could hear him fighting for breath. His heart—apparently it had stopped during whatever had happened before Thanksgiving. Burton almost wanted to shout *Go to the doctor, dumbass!* through the phone lines.

"Are you by the machine?" Ellery asked, and Burton could see from his station that Cramer was pulling up client files and studying them while he nagged his boyfriend. This guy was nothing if not efficient.

"No."

"You lie, because I called you on the house line. Are you by the machine?"

"Yes." There was a note of resignation in his voice.

"And your heart rate is...."

"Five hundred beats per minute. I'm dead. Make sure you only get takeout for one."

"Don't fuck with me, Jackson," Ellery muttered. "Not today. I'm bringing takeout for two, so if you don't eat it, remember we have to watch it rot in the fridge."

"I cleaned the fridge. Will never happen."

"We have a cleaning service!" Burton couldn't actually hear Ellery banging his head against his desk, but he was pretty sure it was happening.

"Well, yeah. But she kept nagging. The fridge was too full to wipe down, so I just chucked all the bad stuff and put it in the trash and—"

"So I didn't have to see you hadn't been eating, and then to make yourself feel better about not eating and lying to me—"

"It's not lying technically when you can look in the fridge too—"

"You went for a run, when you're not okayed to run yet, and now you're probably light-headed and clammy and sitting at the table wishing you were prone. Am I even close?"

Silence.

"I'm totally right, aren't I?"

"I was trying to get hungry," Jackson mumbled. "So I could eat and you don't have to nag."

Burton heard the pleading whimper in Ellery's voice, and he was suddenly beset with the terrible, terrible sense of wrongness. He should not be here listening to these two men have this argument. Whatever was going on with Rivers—and it was bad—this was not a thing for strangers to hear.

"Baby... could you just... maybe you could just talk to someone?"

"I miss running," Rivers said plaintively.

"I know you do. Maybe have someone over for company?"

"That's entertaining. Come watch me rot? No. I'm taking an online course in electronic locks. I'll just finish that and find another one."

"Not every course you take has to relate to work. You know that, right?"

"Like what?"

"Like poetry? Literature? History? Computer engineering? Law?"

"Ellery, I work for a law office."

"I know, asshole. I'm just saying—take a literature class. They're entertaining, if nothing else. You're stuck at home for another month, if not two. Maybe do something that doesn't... I don't know. Hurt. Think of that?"

"Maybe." But it sounded like Rivers was thinking about it, and Burton was relieved for both of them.

It would suck to be Rivers, home, obviously worrying himself sick about something, and restless. But it would suck even worse to be Cramer, losing his shit about his boyfriend without a damned thing he could do to fix it.

Cramer let out a relieved sigh. "I'll be home in an hour—"

"That's early."

"Wow. You sound so excited. Gee, Ellery, isn't it great that you get a chance to get out early—"

"Don't dick with me, Ellery. And don't shortchange your job for me either. I'll be fine."

"Maybe I miss you. You ever think of that?"

"Hunh."

Burton grimaced. This was not a good word in their relationship.

"I'll take that as a no." Ellery's dry humor came out in full force. "Well, I do. I'll be there in an hour. Maybe we can drive to Old Town and look at the Christmas lights. It's Friday—I mean, don't *you* want to go out and do something fun?"

For half a second, Burton expected another "Hunh," but Jackson surprised him.

"God, yeah. I'll shower."

"Excellent. I'll join you."

Rivers's laughter, low and dirty, effectively signed him off, and Burton breathed a sigh of relief as he heard Ellery start packing shit up. He switched the feed to the office, not surprised when he heard the door to Cramer's office open.

"So—was he running?"

Burton kept his face bored and his breathing even, but this here was one of the biggest lies he'd told Lacey so far. Rivers, it seemed, had an extensive support network around him—a woman he called his sister but whose relationship seemed more complicated than that; her boyfriend, who was also renting out some property Jackson owned; the woman's twin brother, who lived up in the hills; and a group of young kids getting out of jail for drug offenses—all turned their gaze to Jackson Rivers like he was the light in their sky. Burton had looked the guy up, and his jacket was impressive—hunting down killers, saving policemen, turning state's evidence. But listening to the way people talked to Jackson made Burton wonder if there wasn't more to the story.

Either way, he didn't like the idea of people messing with Jackson's family—so he hadn't told Lacey shit about them.

"Yeah." Cramer's voice lost the tones of disgust and irritation that he'd used with Rivers. "Didn't go well for him."

"He hates being left at home." Jade Cameron's voice was warm and maternal—sometimes. "You're just lucky your neighbor hates Jackson."

Cramer chuckled meanly. "I think the old bag crushes after him. Seemed to think he was obscene in his running shorts."

"It's forty degrees outside!"

Burton shivered, and then Cramer surprised him—as he often did—with a slice of biting humor. "You could probably see his nipples through his shirt—most excitement she's had in years."

Jade let out a *hmmph*. "Bring him by for dinner tomorrow night."

"Deal. Thank you."

But Burton didn't hear any movement.

"Jade?"

"He's… not getting better," she mumbled.

Cramer sighed. "He won't talk about it. Any of it."

"I wouldn't want to talk about it either," she snapped. "But he's got to. It's…. God. I need him to get better. You understand that, right? For one thing, all those goddamned kids next door—the only thing keeping them from using again is him over the headset playing *Overwatch*."

Burton didn't know what Cramer was doing, but at this point he was massaging the back of his own neck.

"I am aware."

"And Mike has never had a friend like Jackson—it's like he worries about him, all day, every day."

"I know that too."

"And why wouldn't he talk to you? Or come home when he was lost? Or, for Christ's sake, go running when the doctor said not to—"

"*I don't know!*"

Burton actually breathed with him. In through the nose, out through the mouth. This man didn't know it, but Burton was doing Lamaze breathing because this little family drama had become a part of his bones and blood.

"I'm sorry," Cramer muttered. "I'm sorry. I don't know. All I can tell you is what my mother said—"

"What does Lucy Satan have to say about this?" Jade asked, voice all attitude.

"My mother, *Taylor*, says it's going to take a long time before he talks. That even if he's said something once, he's going to have to talk about it two or three times, maybe, for it to sink in. And I can tell you what I know, which is that if he had his druthers he wouldn't have told either of us a damned thing about those two days. He'd let us wander around thinking that everything in our lives is hunky dory and there's nothing to worry about. So we're lucky. We know just enough to worry. And that's all I've got for you."

Breathe in through the nose, out through the mouth. This time it was Jade's turn.

"I'm sorry. It's probably worse on you."

"It has its moments," Cramer said grimly. "Running in December. For fuck's sake, my balls shrivel just thinking about it."

"I didn't know sharks had balls," Jade said sweetly, for form. "I'm just messing with you. Keep doing what you're doing. I mean, he's not dead. That's saying something."

Cramer grunted, and finally Burton heard the door close. He yawned and stretched and looked around to see if anyone was nearby. He sort of wanted to go pee while Cramer was commuting home.

"So are they fucking *now*?" Patrick Manetti asked, leering.

Burton rolled his eyes. "No, jackass. Cramer's driving home. We got no coms on them in the car, and Rivers is on the computer, looking up classes. I'm gonna go take a piss—feel free to listen. Maybe you'll hear one of 'em jacking off and your day will be complete."

"Gross. No, man, I'll leave that homo shit to you."

"Just sac up and do the fuckin' job," Burton growled before he stalked away. He was pretty sure that would ensure that *nobody* picked up the com to listen, a thought that filled him with relief. He'd killed people in cold blood—bad people, but still. No remorse. All the sympathy of an alligator, and he had no regrets. And he'd still rank listening to these two people— who, by all accounts, had done nothing more than stop a serial killer on brains and guts alone—as one of the top three worst things he'd ever done.

And listening to them make love....

He suppressed a shudder, saving it for when the bathroom door was shut and he could have a modicum of privacy.

Of course, he'd no sooner sat down than his phone gave three short bursts up against his thigh.

Have you met them yet? The shark and the broken fish?

Burton's breath stopped in his throat and his bowels turned to ice.

Yes, he typed numbly. *They're good men.*

I know. You're watching out for them, right?

Yeah. I'm monitoring their coms. It's invasive as fuck. Finally—somebody he could say that to!

I'm sorry. It must feel really dishonorable.

It does. It's so personal. I hate hearing them talk to each other when they think no one else can hear.

And their sex gets you horny.

Burton pulled in a sharp breath. Oh God. It did! It so did! And it occurred to him that he was talking to the one person in the world who might understand.

Which only makes it worse!!!!! He was going to have to flush soon and walk back in there. Oh God.

Well, it's a good thing you're the one listening. Anybody else wouldn't respect them like you do.

Burton stared at the screen hungrily. God. He needed to hear that. He'd been undercover before, had posed as an arms dealer, a crooked narcotics officer—once, God help him, as a coyote so that he could trap the real monsters who left people to cook in the desert. But he'd dealt directly with the bad guys, the scum, the dregs of the earth, and deception hadn't bothered him in the least.

Doing this, listening to two nice people make love, felt so horribly dishonest.

I do respect them, he typed simply. *They're really decent people. The shattered fish*—the description fit perfectly—*needs time to recover from his wounds, but he won't let himself have it. I keep wanting to butt in and tell him to just give it a rest.*

Burton's hands were shaking, clammy with the relief of confessing this strange intimacy to somebody.

Ernie's next text was a shot of the sky in the desert, the last light of the winter sun lingering in the powder blue of the horizon, fading into a shiny obsidian blue-black, the stars as crystal on his phone as they probably were in person.

That's beautiful. He swallowed. Suddenly that peace, that sense of freedom, the heat of Ernie's body next to him as he let his spirit soar, was the only thing he wanted in the world.

It's like you're here with me.

Except Burton wasn't. Burton was hiding in the bathroom of an abandoned military base, getting ready to go listen to two men who didn't deserve to have their privacy invaded, and lucking out because the other thing he'd be asked to do would be to carry out a hit on a possibly innocent victim.

He'd just typed *I've got to go* but hadn't hit Send yet when Ernie's text came through.

I miss you. I don't know if that helps or hurts. But I think I have to tell you.

Oh hell. *I dream of your skin, your heat around me, the shyness of your smile. About how a thing I've done a thousand times was brand-new. Like our time was a cloud, and we'll never find it again, and I'll spend my whole life searching the heavens for that exact same cloud.*

He hit Send, thrust the phone in his pocket, and flushed, going to wash his hands. His phone buzzed against his thigh, and again, and one more time, but he couldn't be seen mooning over a text, not in the bathroom.

He waited until he got to the hall and gave his phone a businesslike glance.

I'm waiting.

Here on our cloud.

Poetry. Me. We're here.

Burton couldn't afford a deep breath, or a harsh swallow, or even a fond look. He put the phone back in his pocket and kept his expression neutral, barely nodding as he passed Leavins, Lacey's favorite new boy, down the hallway.

Leavins gave Burton a sideways glance and muttered a racial slur under his breath.

For a moment, Burton's heart rate sped up, his anger reaction kicking in on instinct. But none of that showed. He kept his respirations even and lifted a disdainful eyebrow.

Just that, with a careful roll of his eyes, and he kept walking.

He was prepared for Leavins's kick behind his foot, using his forward momentum to roll, coming up and whirling to give a chambered kick to Leavins's shin. Simple and effective—Leavins went down like a dumpster of rotten squash.

"You fuckin' asshole—what was that—"

Burton placed the toe of his boot up against Leavins's lips. "You were so close behind me that you could have been wearing my pants. Next time you want to fuck with me, make sure I know it's not you. Except now I *will* know it's you, so if you want to get someone else to fuck with me, remember, *I'll always know it's you*. Always. You enjoy that. And maybe drag your sorry ass to the medic and see if he knows what to do with a bruised bone. But make sure he doesn't have a sharp object in his hands when he sees you—he tried to remove a sprained wrist last week with a scalpel."

Poor Saunders—he wasn't the brightest bunny in the forest. Somehow he'd gotten on an admiral's shitlist, and Lacey had co-opted him as a medic. The kid maybe knew how to put on a Band-Aid—and that was only with instructions. Burton had needed to walk him through using an Ace bandage, and he didn't have really high hopes for the patient's survival after he left the room.

If Saunders himself wasn't the only morally decent person in this entire clusterfuck of an operation, Burton would feel sorry for anyone he had to treat. As it was, Burton was mostly grateful. If shit went sideways, Saunders had accidentally decommissioned three operatives in the last week, and those were men Burton *wouldn't* have to fight.

But walking away from Leavins right now, Burton wasn't counting him among the guys out of commission. This fucker.... Burton had seen guys like this—usually at the other end of his scope. The idea that Lacey was actually *training* men to be like—oh hell, Burton didn't even know his rank. He was on a supposed military base, and Burton didn't even *know this guy's rank*. Somebody was going out of his way to create assholes like Leavins to be bigger assholes with *no respect for protocol*, and it offended Burton to the pit of his balls.

And it made him want to protect Ernie and Ace and Sonny even more.

He was it. He was the guy standing between the people he cared about—and that was starting to include Rivers and Cramer and all *their* people—and this fucking viper pit of twisted delusions.

He could practically feel Leavins sighting a target on his back, even as he turned the last corner to the com room.

Once there, he spotted Patrick Manetti at his coms, listening in. Sonuva*bitch.*

Manetti spotted Burton and pulled the headset off. "You were gone a while. Thought you'd miss something."

Burton regarded him with ill-concealed dislike. "He was driving home. Did they plan world domination when he went for Thai takeout?"

"No," Manetti grunted, handing the headset over. "It's just taking a damned long time for you to find something. Lacey's looking for a way to jam these guys up—why aren't you finding it?"

"Because all they do is fight and fuck!" Burton shot back unfairly. But he didn't want Lacey's people to move on them too soon, and he *didn't* want them to know Rivers could barely run around the block at the moment. "That's not my fault!"

With a grunt, Burton pulled the earphones on and scowled until he caught the thread of who was speaking.

Oh. They were listening to the home setup now. Cramer had just gotten in.

"I got your favorite," he was saying as Burton caught up. "Pumpkin cur—oh my God. You look awful."

"I just got out of the shower. Jesus, sue me for forgetting product."

"Goddammit, Jackson, is there any way I can talk you out of—"

What followed was a muffled sound—one Burton was getting used to.

"Mm…." Cramer was the one breaking off the kiss. "This isn't going to make me stop nag—mm…." And some more. Apparently it *did* stop him from nagging, which might explain why these guys went at it like rabbits on Viagra.

"What are they saying now?" Manetti demanded, and for the first time in his undercover career, Burton almost lost it and belted someone for non-cover-related reasons.

"They're kissing." He stood up then and raised his voice. "For anybody wondering, Rivers and Cramer are about to have rabid homosexual sex. I assume there will be oral/genital, oral/anal, and anal penetration by both digits and penises. Does anybody need to listen to this for information or arousal purposes, because I can put this shit on speaker now if you all are that hard up."

Fifteen or so people in the com unit, and they all turned to stare at him with wide eyes—some of them more interested than others, even though they all claimed to be straight.

But none of them wanted to *admit* they were interested. He was relieved at the first actual look of disgust he got, and then the others, until the entire room had rolled eyes and waved him off.

And then he was left alone with two guys getting naked, in spite of Cramer's best intentions.

For a moment Burton was able to put his brain on "skate" and just listen to their sex noises like he was listening to white noise. Then Cramer gave a grunt and spoke.

"No—no—not on your knees out here. Dammit, Jackson—we've got a perfectly good bed."

The image of Burton—*Jackson*—on his knees before Ernie—*dammit, Ellery!*—seared itself into Burton's brain, and he had to fight to keep his breathing even.

"But I was mid-blowjob here!"

"Well, you can be mid-blowjob again—just on the bed."

Their conversation moved down the hallway, and Burton switched the feed to the bedroom, where they were still bitching at each other.

"But you were digging it!" Jackson was saying, sounding defiant. "I mean, I know my way around a BJ, and you were liking that BJ—"

"Yeah, I was digging it. You were giving me your best professional-quality blowjob—it's top-notch."

Burton's antennae pricked up at the term "professional-quality," because he'd learned in bed those were never good words. But Rivers—Rivers was a different breed of alley cat.

"Then what's the problem?" And Burton could also hear the thread of hurt in his voice. Oh… damn. This was a tough one.

Fortunately Cramer could talk his way through an ion storm.

"C'mere," Cramer demanded throatily. "C'mere and kiss me like you mean it."

"I always mean it." Burton pictured the man in the jacket *he'd* gotten, not the one he'd given Lacey. Arms crossed, green eyes snapping, stunning face full of distrust.

"Yes—but sometimes you mean it like you mean it, and sometimes you mean it like you want my attention on my orgasm and not on you. I'm not sure who taught you about sex—"

Rivers cleared his throat, but Cramer kept right on going.

"*Besides* her—but the person you're with is supposed to be paying attention to *you*. I mean, I get you're supposed to be God's gift to manwhores, but you've *got* me. Maybe use me a little in this whole two-person interaction!"

Rivers's chuckle, wholly filthy, had Burton solidly on his side. For a moment.

"You want me to use you?" Flirty, throaty, wholly sexual, Burton could admit it—if he hadn't had those hours alone with Ernie, almost a month ago, the guy might have made his knees a little weak. "Hands and knees, counselor, and watch me use you."

Judging by the squeaking of the bed springs, Burton reckoned Cramer was no different, but then, God help them both, the guy started talking.

"You think... oh God... rimming me isn't using me... oh wow... you're good at that... dammit, Jackson...."

He tried. Burton listened, keeping his face stoic, as Rivers apparently licked Cramer into submission.

And then fucked him into the mattress.

Their moans, harsh and unapologetic, filled his head, and he kept his shoulders back and his crotch under his desk to hide the unmistakable sign of arousal.

"Goddammit," Rivers panted. "*Come.*"

"*You. First.*"

Burton's eyes popped open, and he almost chortled. That was just sneaky! He'd never realized how much power people wielded over each other in the bedroom until he'd heard these two guys negotiate their relationship while literally balls-deep in each other.

"*Augh!*" And that there was Rivers, losing a game he hadn't known he'd been playing. His orgasm was followed quickly by Cramer's, and then... oh no. A pain sound, as Rivers collapsed on what was apparently a bum shoulder.

"God, Jackson, are you okay—"

"Fine, counselor," Rivers slurred, sounding out of it and fond. "No worries. Overdid it."

"Yeah, I know." There was some rustling then, and Burton imagined the two men righting themselves on the bed. Maybe they were snuggling under the covers. That would be nice. Kind. For all their snapping at each other, these moments were always rooted in kindness. "You overdid it all day," Cramer said softly, his voice muted. "Care to tell me why? I mean, running *today*? It's vile outside."

"My head was a sort of shitty place today," Rivers admitted grudgingly. "AJ was at work, Mike was minding the gas station. Just... needed to do something."

Cramer grunted. "Wanna share?"

"Nope," Jackson said promptly. "Starving. Wanna eat." Everything Burton had heard between them told him this was a lie.

"Fine." Cramer sighed. "Just... you know. I'm here."

"Yeah, well, you get a front-row seat to the whole damned show. I'd rather tonight be the comedy romance version, 'kay?"

There was a weighted silence then, and Burton found himself holding his breath, torn between two instincts. *Don't let him get away with that emotionally evasive bullshit!* vied neck and neck with *God, maybe give the guy some space. You've been up in his business all fucking day!*

"Okay, fine," Cramer conceded, and Burton couldn't decide if he was relieved or disappointed. "But only because I've got news."

Suddenly he had other things to worry about.

"What sort of news?"

"I did some research into our friends from Victoriana—"

"Ace and Sonny?"

Breathing: optional. Panic: operational. *Ernie Ernie Ernie Ernie....*

"Yeah. More particularly Ace. He's the only one I've got family on. His parents live in Bakersfield with various grandchildren, including his brother's widow and her two kids."

"What happened to the brother?"

Cramer grunted. "Suicide. Before the second kid was born. I don't have details why."

Burton blinked slowly. He'd had no idea. His heart ached for his friend, the solid guy he'd seen in the field, the fiercely protective guardian and lover of fragile Sonny. Burton had always known his own childhood and family had been blessed.

"Well, from what we've seen of Ace, his family's probably not a lot of talkers. But poor Ace. That would suck." And Rivers—whose jacket told Burton he had *not* had a blessed childhood or family or anything of the sort—still had compassion. Ernie's shattered fish was garnering Burton's admiration here.

"Yeah. There's something else—a girl his parents are fostering. I can't find *any* paperwork on her before she showed up at the local high school. Russian by the name, but no family listed besides the Atchisons, and no place of origin. It's... it's *just like* Sonny, actually, and I gotta tell you—"

"Ellery, we said we weren't going to—"

"But maybe his past is why Sonny ended up in Galway's unit, right? He was an easy target—"

"Stop." The vulnerability and defensiveness disappeared from Rivers's voice, and what Burton heard now was a decisive man capable of making hard choices. "We're not going there. We're not investigating them. *They* are not the problem."

"Well, no, they're not, but the things we don't know make them vulnerable—"

"Did we not have this talk? Everything points to them being victims. Just because they have a past doesn't mean anybody else has a right to it. *I've* got a past—do you want assholes probing down *my* secret holes? Yes, they're vulnerable. That's why we haven't approached them yet—we don't want anybody else poking around in their nest. It's wrong."

Burton caught his breath and thought maybe his heart restarted.

"What kind of perversion are they up to now?" Manetti asked, leering.

Burton managed not to startle. "Arguing over takeout," he said, keeping his voice the right side of bored. "It's making me hungry for decent food."

"Closest decent food's in Barstow." Manetti shrugged. "I mean, you haven't left the base in a month—even in the real military, you get to go off campus and eat a steak, right?"

Burton blinked slowly. He'd wondered how many of the people in this unit thought they were actually working for the United States government. Saunders the hapless medic did. The very young, obviously prematurely promoted drill sergeant did. Lacey had told his lies selectively, maybe. The Corduroy people seemed to have a conspiracy not to disabuse the co-opted naval personnel of their real circumstance.

The whole sitch made Burton want to vomit.

But Manetti had a point. Burton got off duty when these two went to bed. That was part of getting the shit job, but that was also....

Convenient.

A plan started to form, even as Burton listened to the change of conversation.

"It's not wrong if it helps us stop Lacey—"

Rivers must have made a gesture then, because Cramer trailed off.

"Ellery, I know you're used to going for the jugular—and it's served you well. But do you remember why we didn't press these guys in the first place?"

Cramer let out a breath. "Because the asshole I was defending at the time was way the hell worse."

"Exactly. Lacey is way the hell worse. If I could *run around the fucking block*, I'd be flying down to question Lacey's men—"

"Yes, Jackson, I definitely want you around all the sailors in San Diego."

Rivers guffawed, wiping away some of the bitterness that had tinged his voice. "Why would I go for sailors when I've got my own shark in a suit? But that's not the point or the problem."

"What's the point?"

"The point is, if we have to ask them questions, we will. But we don't have to break their privacy. Their military record is fair game. Any spots on their record—"

"Ace has a sealed juvie record—"

"So do I."

A pause, while both Burton and Cramer digested this.

"Fighting?" Cramer asked, sounding curious and nothing more.

"Yeah. Some asshole of Celia's groped me in my sleep and caught my elbow in the windpipe. They were going to prosecute for attempted murder, but Jade and Kaden's mom stepped up. I was eleven."

"Jesus…," Cramer breathed.

"It's not the only thing there—just the thing that made the biggest splash. I'm just saying, before I decided to be a cop there was plenty of evidence suggesting I'd go the other way. Ace has a solid record in the military—and he's got a giant Russian bear and a smart teenager who'd all throw themselves on a grenade for him. We *could* investigate him, but I'd rather investigate Lacey. What do you have on *him*?"

"Besides three divorces, two kids in rehab, and one on her third baby before she's eighteen?"

"Oh dear God…." Rivers muttered. "See? *See?* That's the kind of scumbaggery we want to know about!"

"Yeah, fine. Come talk to me over Thai food—"

"I was only kidding before. I'm not—"

"Eat or I'll sit on your throat and shove it down your face!"

"—not gonna pass that up!" Rivers saved in a hurry. "Sounds delicious!"

"Worst. Liar. In. History."

They bickered down the hallway and to their dinner, and Burton wrote down a couple of fake notes while he listened for some stuff that not even Jason had been able to uncover.

Lacey had monetary difficulties—his personal finances were crap. Even worse—at least as far as Rivers was concerned—was that he appeared to have no personal *connections* anymore.

"It makes a man… disconnected," Rivers said through a mouthful of Thai food. "A man with no human connections is less likely to make human decisions. It makes him more dangerous and less predictable."

It was a solid observation—Burton concurred. He found himself wondering if this little illegitimate operation had its roots in Lacey's last failed marriage, in the alienation of his children. He could see those things acting as a trigger. If Lacey had lost faith in the military at the same time—

"His budget was slashed," Cramer said, reinforcing what Burton had just been thinking. "Those contracts he had pulled from my mother's company were really important. He went after us, and the Navy damned near demoted him. Which serves him right on the one hand—"

"But makes him super dangerous on the other," Rivers finished.

Burton had to agree. He listened to them reason their way through a situation that should have been above their pay grade and beyond their ken and had the wistful notion that he could be friends with these guys. As they cleaned up dinner and sat in front of the television, talking desultorily and petting their cat—who purred so loud Burton's second-rate equipment picked it up—Burton wondered if this is what it felt like to put a child to bed. Like you'd seen them safely through another day.

Then Manetti got his attention and looked urgently to the door of the coms unit, and Burton's illusion of safety shattered.

"What's he want?" Burton muttered.

"I dunno—maybe you're not listening hard enough," Manetti muttered back. "Whatever. Remember, you work for Hamblin, not him."

Burton had been recruited by Timothy Norton, a former Green Beret gone merc. He'd never officially met Hamblin, but he had to concede now he felt a little bit protected. Hamblin's people were solid mercenaries—Corduroy might not have been legal, moral, or ethical, but it *was* organized. Burton had saved Norton's ass in that poker game Ernie had helped him with—Lacey might hate him for the color of his skin, but he wasn't going to shoot him without cause.

"You coming, Oscar?" Lacey looked and sounded like every boy's wet dream of a commanding officer. Tall, patrician features, prematurely gray hair that gave him an air of handsome experience rather than age.

His voice had echoes of an East Coast upbringing—and all the warmth of a rabid skink.

"Sir?"

"I need a debrief on the two subjects. My office—now."

"Sir, yes sir."

It was a military response, given laconically and without respect. Burton was good undercover, but no Marine was *that* good, given how badly this guy had violated every oath of honor and protection the US military had to give.

"You got a problem, Oscar?"

Burton looked around, where none of the men in the coms unit were pretending to look away. "My guys just went to sleep, sir. I got no problem at all."

They were, in fact, talking quietly back in Cramer's bedroom. This was often where they hammered facts out, although sometimes their bedroom was more of a personal sanctuary than that. Burton turned the feed way down on the pretext of adjusting the dial and set the earpiece down.

"Would you like to listen yourself, sir?"

Lacey's expression twisted with distaste. "No, thank you. Have you heard anything important?"

"Let's see. So far I know that Rivers likes to run in December and green curry is his favorite Thai food. I also know he barely graduated from high school and Cramer's such a control freak he won't let him so much as surf the net without his permission. Neither of these guys is scary, Commander, but I'll listen to them fuck like bunnies as long as you need me to."

Burton's lies spilled off his tongue so easily, he was *almost* unprepared for Lacey's hand flying toward him in the perfect backhand.

Almost.

Burton caught him midair, squeezing Lacey's wrist in his fingers and meeting his eyes with all his formidable ice.

"Was there something else you wanted?" Burton asked, as though they weren't having a furious struggle between Lacey's desire for the slap to land home and Burton's determination to break his wrist before that happened.

Lacey snarled—and then backed off. "No, boy. But you'd better find something out damned quick. We can't afford to be listening in on these guys without some payoff. According to your boss, you've got more valuable skills than that, and we need to start making you earn your keep."

Burton figured his chances of staying alive were a lot better if he read that last bit as *We need to start making you walk into as many dangerous situations as possible until you get taken out*, but he wouldn't give this fucknut the satisfaction of translating.

"Any. Time. Sir."

Lacey glared at him and turned on his heel, and Burton slaughtered him with his eyes until he'd exited the coms room. As soon as he was gone, all the usual activity resumed, and Manetti turned to him with a reluctant grin.

"That was great! Seriously—but you should go tell Collins at the front that you're going out for a little breather now. I mean, if you don't get out of here, you're gonna rip that guy's throat out next time he comes over here and starts to talk shit. Not that any of us would care, but it'll be a lot of blood to wash out."

Burton nodded and killed his coms for the night. "They should be sleeping until six, when I'll be up to do this again." For a moment Manetti looked like he was going to offer to take Burton's morning shift, probably just because he may have been a trained merc but he wasn't a complete douchebag, but Burton couldn't let him do that, no matter how grateful he was for the offer. "With my luck they'll probably wake up with a quickie— my God, they need to give it a rest."

Manetti grimaced in distaste, and Burton took his enigmatic ass toward the front of the office.

"Oscar? You need something?"

Kevin Collins, a short, tough, grizzled veteran with sparse once-blond hair, had been an Army grunt for his entire career before he'd been recruited by Corduroy—but he'd been smart, fearless, and bloodthirsty. The mercenary life suited him, and if Corduroy had been the tiniest bit selective about who got set in its sights, Burton might consider the guy worth his time. As it was, he had to remind himself that Collins was the commander who sent three guys after Ernie, and God knows how many Ernies had been blown away under Collins's watch.

"I need off campus for a bit," Burton said, casual. "If I don't get some decent chow and anywhere but here, I'm gonna take that guy out the next time he sniffs around my com, and that's bad all around."

Collins nodded once and checked his own readout—he was tracking two operatives in South America, from what Burton could see—and then looked back at him. "Good job not taking that asshole out here and now. As long as you're back at your unit tomorrow, I don't give a fuck where you are. Go get fed, go get laid, whatever you need."

Burton nodded and gave a terse "'Preciate it" before he strode out of the room. He had plans, dammit—and he certainly didn't need that guy's permission to implement them.

He was halfway through the admin building when a slightly built man in a superexpensive silk suit and shiny black wingtips began to pace him at his elbow.

"You are upset?"

Burton threw a glance down at the slight form of Mr. Rufus Hamblin, European businessman, mercenary, and CEO of Corduroy. "Lacey's got a stick up his ass about something," Burton spat, hoping it would be in character to speak so disrespectfully of an officer by this point.

"Well, yes. The investigation you're listening to has cost him some important military contracts. He'll need to make a trip in January to see if he can get some of that back." Hamblin sounded unruffled by the prospect of Lacey's empty pockets.

"Aren't you worried?" Burton would have asked it even if he were a legit member of the organization. "What happens if he can't?"

Hamblin shrugged. "We signed on with him because he promised us the perfect soldier. I've seen some of them operate. They might be the real deal. But if he can't provide for us, we shall move elsewhere. I make it very clear that this is a for-profit enterprise, much like the pirate ships of old, yes?"

Burton's mouth twisted, and he hoped it passed as a smile. "Well, Captain sir, I need some shore leave or I'm throwing that guy off the port bow."

To his relief, Hamblin laughed. "Understood, young Calvin. Go, do what you must. Your duties will be here in the morning. Do you have transportation?"

He did.

He'd traded in the SUV he'd been driving when he'd found Ernie for a battered Ford F-150 Extended Cab. He kept camping supplies in the back—bedroll, sleeping bag, water, and rations—and figured he'd tell people he was an outdoorsman if he needed to.

Truth was, he hadn't been sure if he'd have to disappear or not, and he was prepared to live in the desert and off the grid for at least a month.

He hadn't lived this long by taking chances.

He pulled out his phone, remembering Ernie's schedule. The picture he'd taken at sunset was from Ace's back porch—Burton had seen a corner of the garage and a couple of cars sitting in the dirt-packed parking lot to the sky. But that had been hours ago. Ernie liked to wander in the late-at-night, when other people were sleeping.

Where are you?

Walking. Why?

East or west of the garage?

West, about three miles. Why?

Burton thought about it—time and distance and accidents and collisions and Ernie's pale skin under his hands.

Keep walking that direction. Stay in sight of the road.

Am I in danger?

Burton swallowed. *Only from me.*

No danger. Drive safe.

Burton had been walking a high wire for a month, the taste of Ernie's kisses the only balance that had kept him from falling. He'd fly the damned truck before he wrecked it now.

Pain Shield

"YOU'RE GOING out early," Alba remarked without looking up. Her glossy dark hair bobbed from a ponytail behind her, and she was wearing an OD-green T-shirt neatly tucked into her jeans. It looked much laundered and much loved, and Ernie had a bittersweet moment of wondering if it had belonged to Ace once.

He could smell the first love emanating from her in gentle waves, but no bitterness. She'd learned to live with it, to maybe accept that there would be other boys.

As first crushes went, Ace wasn't bad.

"You're here late," Ernie told her, smiling. She was a good girl, working hard through her senior year in high school. He'd heard Ace and Sonny talking about the money they were going to use to get her through junior college and then state and had helped them rake the books to give her a raise.

Good but smart—and observant. Ernie was good at staying away from the sharp side of her tongue.

"Yes, I'm in your spot," she said unapologetically. "You saying this is my fault?"

Ernie tried to control the restlessness in his legs that made him want to bounce. He'd captured the picture for Burton and finished their text, and the buzzing that had haunted his skin only got worse. Something was going down tonight.

"No," he said, keeping his voice as neutral as possible. "I'm sorry— just as well you're there tonight. I'm not feeling much good at anything."

She tilted her head perceptively. "Jai is out of town, getting him some. You could always go with him."

Jai stood nearly seven feet tall. A ginormous Russian bear, Jai shaved his head to a sheen, kept his goatee sharp, and had a smile that was… disturbing, at the very least. Ernie bet he could roll down his window and say, "I have a penis to match my foot size," and have guys diving through his windows. Ernie was just grateful that he *did* have the gift—he wasn't sure if he'd be so comfortable around the guy if he hadn't felt the solid core of… well, not exactly *good* that emanated from the guy. It was more like solid, no-bullshit dedication. Jai was dedicated to Sonny and therefore dedicated to Ace. He was dedicated to Alba, and therefore, anybody that they were dedicated to, Jai would protect.

Ernie fell into that category, but so far the guy hadn't been forthcoming about his personal life.

"How do you know he's going to get laid?" Ernie had to ask.

Alba shrugged. "Last night, when we watched movies. He sat far away from us. Usually he lets me lie on him. I figure he's just itchy. Needs to get it out of his system."

Ernie thought about that. "That's pretty clever," he said. "But you lay on me instead, and I'm pretty itchy."

She rolled her eyes. "Yeah, but you got it bad for only one guy. Jai hasn't found his guy yet."

Ernie clenched his nether regions and nodded. He needed to start walking or he'd let himself relax and stain his shorts.

"I'm just missing him is all," he confessed. His body was screaming *dance dance dance*, but Alba was so damned smart. Ernie wasn't going to give her any reason to believe tonight's wander would be different than the others.

Ernie used to go clubbing prelubed. An openmouthed syringe, a little prep in the bathroom, and all the other guy needed was a rubber.

That night, as he'd awakened in long shadows of late afternoon in the winter, his body had tingled like someone was rubbing mental fingers all over his skin, over his nipples, along his thighs, between his crease. He'd startled in the shower, feeling hot breath on his neck.

He'd taken that picture of the desert for Burton and had practically felt the rasp of his fingers as he felt the face of the phone.

He'd decided to go walking early, and before he'd hooked the leash on Duke's collar, he'd visited the bathroom, wondering how sure his instincts could possibly be.

He didn't have the syringe—but as he'd shoved fingerfuls of lubricant up his own ass, he'd shivered. God, if this turned out to be nothing more than extreme need and not a premonition of any sort, he was going to have to order himself some adult toys, embarrassment be damned.

His stomach cramped with the hunger for possession.

The last month he'd slept restlessly, dreaming of rough hands on his skin, of the taste of Burton's tongue in his mouth, of the glory of his come.

81

It was early December, but all Ernie could think of was Burton's big ol' Christmas tree right up his chimney.

And if only his need was as simple and as crude as sex.

Six years.

His parents had died six years ago.

That year in the foster system, he'd been adrift, a prisoner in his own detachment, a bit of lint in the wind. The year in the military, he'd been the same lint in a cage of space. Nobody wanted to talk to him. Nobody wanted to touch him.

He'd been dropped in an alien city and forced to protect himself. He'd done it with bodies, with buzz, with just enough drugs to mask the *beat-beat-beat* of minds on his own.

He didn't need the bodies or the drugs out here. Ace and Sonny and Jai and Alba were family—they cared about him and gave him a structure and a framework he badly needed. He didn't crave the clubs or the bodies or the mask of buzzing minds—he had good people around him and the sky at night to keep him grounded.

But... but Burton. Burton had touched him—had *known* him, had known the real him. Ernie had been new to Burton, but Burton had been a whole vast other planet to Ernie, and now Ernie was going to go out under the velvet black sky of winter and... oh God. Please, let them touch again.

But Alba was looking at him with pity. "Not everybody gets a happy ending," she said, sounding absurdly old. But then, she'd been working for Ace and Sonny for two years now—maybe you got old fast when your first love really was everything you've dreamed of but in love with someone else.

Ernie summoned a smile from sheer hope. "But sometimes you get a happy dream," he said. Then he gave the lead a little pull, and the dog—who'd curled up at his feet because he was a good dog, yes he was—hopped up and started quivering. Duke adored Ace and Sonny, but his walks in the desert were the highlight of his day.

"Dream happy on your wanders tonight," Alba said gravely. "I'll dream some for you too. My uncle was a *brujo*, you know. Maybe I got the gift too."

She was pulling his leg, and he grinned. "You don't need the gift when you're as smart as you are," he said, bowing. She laughed, delighted, and waved him on his way.

"You are a terrible flirt, and if you weren't gay, my mommy wouldn't let you anywhere near me. Go."

Ernie nodded and managed to saunter out into the world.

He'd been walking for nearly an hour, the chill of the desert at night making him glad he'd worn jeans and a thick hooded sweatshirt, when he felt his cell phone buzz in his back pocket. He pulled it out and checked, shivering all over again when he saw Burton's message.

I'm coming for you may not have been written in words, but it was screaming in every character on the screen.

He kept walking west, keeping about twenty feet from the edge of the road. He'd walked this path often enough that there was a worn strip through the brush where he'd trodden, and he knew that snakes and scorpions would be off somewhere else, somewhere warm.

Approaching headlights were few and far between, but Ernie knew the raised chassis of an SUV or a truck, and he suspected Burton would be in something big, something with power. Not that car—*zoom*. Nope, Mercedes. Not that one—*putt-putt-putt*. Nope, Toyota. Not the *chug-chug-chug* old Crown Vic, and not the *whiiinnne* of the unlikely Tesla. But there, looming from over a mile away, Ernie could see it. He paused, pulling Duke's leash short, and waited.

The car overshot him, and for a moment his heart fell, his disappointment in his gut instinct almost as acute as his disappointment it wasn't who he thought it was. Then, about fifty yards down the way, it made an abrupt left, crossed the vacant oncoming lane, and bumped through the desert until it came to a stop at a man-made hill where once somebody had tried to mine something and had left a pit and a hillock instead.

Ernie was running toward the truck before it even came to a stop.

As he ran, Duke excited but silent by his heels, the door opened and Burton got out, left the door open, and stretched his arms up to the sky. Then he leaned against the bed of the truck, smiling, as Ernie ran toward him.

Burton looked relaxed, but he was ready when Ernie leaped into his arms and wrapped his legs around his waist.

Their lips crashed together in a cataclysm of want, and every thought in Ernie's head shorted out, because oh heavens to fuck me, here he was, he wasn't a dream, and he was plundering Ernie's mouth, his neck, his senses, like he had a God-given right to be there.

Duke's yapping brought Ernie back to his surroundings, and he looked at the little dog in dismay. Then Burton reached into the front seat of the truck and pulled out—

"Is that a hamburger?" Ernie asked breathlessly. "You brought a hamburger to a booty call?"

Burton chuckled. "I got food for all of us. That's just the plain one I brought for Duke so he'd leave us alone."

With that, Burton whistled to the little dog and set the burger on a bag on the floorboards. He'd folded a blanket up on the seat and had a little bowl with water on the floor too, and Ernie hopped out of his arms for a moment and grinned.

"You thought of everything," he said, surprised.

"There's even a bedroll in the back," Burton rasped, unhooking Duke's leash as he ate and *thunk*ing the door shut on his little den. "He'd better not crap in there."

"He won't," Ernie squeaked, seeing Burton's granite-carved profile in the moonlight and trying to catch his breath.

Burton turned back toward him. "You ready, kid? I am ready to be rough and hard and unmerciful. You got that in you tonight?"

"Bring it on, Cruller," Ernie told him, his whole body shuddering in relief. Then Burton took his mouth again and relief was the last thing on his mind.

Augh! But Ernie was lost in his kisses, lost in the width of his shoulders, the brawn of his arms. Then Burton shocked him, falling to a crouch in front of Ernie, dragging Ernie's jeans and shorts with him.

"Oh God," Ernie breathed. "Burton, what are you—"

Burton licked him, tentatively, and then grinned up into his face. "I been listening to those guys and thinking about this. I kept thinking it was them that made this seem like all I ever wanted, but it wasn't them. It was you."

His lips and tongue were still rough, still unskilled, but Ernie didn't need someone who'd done this a lot. He needed someone who only wanted to do this to *Ernie*, and that's what he had before him.

He sucked hard and pulled back, head bobbing while Ernie cupped his shaved skull in his fingertips and held on. Burton's hands were busy as he worked, and Ernie widened his legs, feeling the lubricant sliding between his cheeks as he did.

Burton's fingertips hit the slick and he pulled back, surprised.

"I woke up needing you," Ernie said by way of explanation. "Needing you so bad. I just prayed it was the gift and not my need. And you're here, and you're gonna make it okay."

Burton nodded. "Only me, right?" he asked, his voice threaded with a vulnerability Ernie hadn't heard before.

Ernie had no way to do this but with his heart on his sleeve. He cupped Burton's cheeks between his palms and made sure Burton could see him nod. "Only you, Lee. Since I first knew you, it's been only you. It might not be anyone else again."

Burton nodded, a fluttery little smile shaping his lips before he pulled Ernie between them again.

Ernie cried out, knees going weak, the buzz that had ridden his skin all night taking him over from the inside, growing, swelling, exploding outward. Orgasm overtook him, and he screamed with it, sobbed with it, and Lee swallowed convulsively, like he was trying to take Ernie into his very soul.

Ernie tugged at his shoulder and he stood, mouth parted slightly, glazed with Ernie's come, and Ernie kissed him hard and fast and deep, taking everything he hadn't swallowed, tasting himself in Lee Burton's mouth like it was wine.

Burton pulled back first and rested his head against Ernie's. "Do you want to climb in the ba—"

Ernie broke out of his arms just enough to turn around and lean forward.

"Fucking now," he demanded roughly.

Lee didn't disappoint him. Ernie didn't even hear him fumbling for his pants before he felt him, hard and huge at Ernie's entrance, demanding to be let in.

"*Now!*" Ernie begged, feeling tears start. He needed. He needed. "I'm empty, dammit. *Fill me.*"

And he did. Shoving rudely in, no finesse, no skill—just want, naked and raw and real, just the same as Ernie's, needing Ernie's heat like Ernie needed the flesh inside him.

Burton popped inside and slid in to the hilt, and Ernie would have screamed *Yes!* if he'd had any breath at all.

Instead he whimpered.

"More. Please." And Lee didn't let him down.

Hard. He'd promised hard. He'd promised hard and rough and unmerciful, and Ernie could accept nothing less. Lee pounded inside him without pause or gentleness, but Ernie had gotten gentleness, had gotten care.

He needed a good hard fucking, needed something bold and vivid imprinted on his body, and Lee Burton was the man to do it.

Harder and faster, Burton grunted half-formed obscenities as he fucked, and Ernie moaned. "Yes! God yes! Yes! Keep going! Keep going! Oh God, please!" while Burton built to a thundering crescendo inside him.

Ernie's own cock grew hard again, flopped against his thigh uselessly, but Ernie couldn't reach for it, couldn't do anything but cushion himself against the bed of the truck with his arms and hold on.

His second orgasm, pulsing through nerve endings, dragged out of him by the pressure inside, took him by complete surprise. He gasped, a quiet little hum next to Burton's primal scream echoing through the desert.

Burton came, scalding inside of him, while Ernie rested his head against one fist and pounded through his own climax with the other. When Burton finally stopped, collapsing against his back, Ernie could only cling to the side of the truck and try really hard to breathe.

The soft touch of Burton's lips on the back of his neck brought him to reality again.

"Mm...." He turned, Burton sliding out of him with resistance. Burton moaned softly, and Ernie took his mouth in apology. This kiss was gentle, soothing, their raw hunger for each other a low pulse in the background but not rearing back and screaming for attention.

Not yet.

Burton pulled back and sighed, wrapping his arms around Ernie's shoulders and pulling him tight against his chest. "Want to see if the dog left us dinner?"

"Sure."

"We can lie on the bedroll and look at the stars...." Something plaintive in his voice told Ernie he'd suddenly realized this wasn't a nice restaurant and a fancy hotel.

"That would be beautiful," Ernie told him, closing his eyes and rubbing his lips along his chin, his jaw, his cheekbones. "There is not a thing in the world I could want more than that."

"I missed you, Ernie. You're the voice in my head now, the one that keeps me sane."

Ernie chuckled, the sound free in his throat. "I was thinking the same thing about you. How weird is that?"

"You're the damn psychic, man—you tell me!"

They both laughed then—but they kept holding each other, half-naked, shivering in the desert breeze.

FINALLY THEY pulled up their pants and rescued their food—Duke wasn't looking particularly hungry, but Ernie had cleaned up after him when he'd raided the trash can before and knew he wasn't to be trusted. They hopped up into the back of the pickup and stretched out on the bedroll, under the sleeping bag. Ernie rested his head on Burton's arm, and they looked out at the stars. Duke curled up in the corner by their feet, seemingly content to just *be* and not to be the center of their attention.

They talked.

Ernie had gotten used to finding conversation superfluous with lovers. Really, all he'd wanted was safety from the voices and all they'd wanted was climax, and words were irrelevant.

But Burton had been stuck being somebody else for the past month—*Calvin Oscar*—and Calvin Oscar had to listen to men give kill orders to innocent people and had to listen to his coworkers bully the weak and get rewarded for it and had to fight racist assholes in the hallway walking back from the bathroom and then just keep on going after he'd won the fight.

Burton needed to be *Lee Burton* right now. Just for this moment, under the stars, Ernie in his arms.

Lee Burton wanted a cat. He thought Duke was okay and someday wanted a big dog, but also, he'd seen Ernie with his menagerie of cats and enjoyed their company. He missed his family—had, in fact, been planning to go home that Christmas since he'd had nothing hanging over his head, but then Ernie had literally fallen onto his cock, and suddenly his world was complicated again.

When Lee Burton had been in college, his favorite date had been dinner and a movie, even if it seemed average and pedestrian, because he liked to hear other people talk about movies and he still got excited when the good guy won.

Lee Burton was genuinely distressed that Ernie had been all alone since he was a teenager. He listened to Ernie's stories of Ace and Sonny and Jai and Alba avidly, like a favorite TV show or family back home.

"They're trying to send her to college?" Burton asked.

"Yeah. They've got some money they've set aside for her, but every time they look, it seems like tuition is going higher. They want her to go somewhere after the local junior college—somewhere with dormitories, far away from Victoriana."

Burton *hmm*ed. "You're doing their books?" he asked.

"Yeah."

"Okay—next time you're there alone, text me their account numbers. I'll beef it up a little."

"You'll *what*?" Ernie pushed himself up on his elbow. "How do you—"

Burton had no shame. "It's how I paid for my little brother's tuition. We get access to money, Ernie. My *major* was computer science. A little bit of embezzlement here, a little bit of magic there—"

"But that's stealing!" Ernie felt like his entire concept of right and wrong had been reversed.

"It's stealing from criminals," Burton said with an unrepentant shrug. "I took out three terrorists funded by drug cartels last year. I did it by following the money. By the time I was done, I had every passcode I needed to clean those guys out, and I didn't."

Ernie blinked. "You *didn't*?"

"I didn't need to. I took a modest payout into a hidden account and moved on. I'm not in this for the money—but it comes in handy when you're establishing a cover."

That made sense. It even explained the truck. "Or helping friends out in need," he said, things fitting into place again.

Burton nodded and then grinned, his smile gleaming in the night. "Of course, when Ace is racing, I usually bet on him. *That* has made me a pile of cash right there."

"He and Sonny talked about it," Ernie told him soberly. It had, in fact, been a sore point between them. "Sonny's still scared."

"Mm." Burton pulled off his sweatshirt and wadded it up so they could both use it as a pillow. "Get back down here. I'm cold."

They situated themselves again, Ernie on his side so he could drape over Burton like a robe, and Burton spoke again. "Sonny is right to be scared. Ace quit racing for a really good reason."

"Too dangerous?"

Burton gnawed his lower lip. "It's not the danger—not completely. What *I* do is dangerous. But if something goes down, I know I'm the only one who has to deal with it. My folks'll grieve, yeah, but I'm not so much a part of their lives. But Ace goes, and Sonny...." Burton shook his head. "Sonny will lose his shit. He will not be okay, and nothing anybody can do will make him okay. Ace'll drive that car fast whether he races or not—but if Sonny's not by his side, he's taking a bigger risk than just their lives."

Suddenly Ernie couldn't breathe.

"I… I gotta go," he mumbled, trying to pull out of the bedroll. It got tangled around his legs, and he ended up squinched up by the corner of the truck with Burton rolling over and trapping him flat.

"What in the hell?"

"I gotta go," he repeated almost tearfully. He was picturing it. He could sense that big void opening up, a black hole in his soul and the sudden knowledge that *Burton didn't exist* anymore, and Ernie, who had spent the last month marveling that he *did* exist, was bereft, a lost star adrift in the heavens. The sky, which had offered freedom and shelter, became a trap. Ernie needed to hide, hide in the cab of the truck, run to Ace and Sonny's and hide in his bed, dig a hole anywhere and cover himself or he'd be trapped in the emptiness of beyond.

"Ernie! Baby—God, tell me what's wrong?"

"*What would happen to me?*" Ernie shouted, an open nerve as he always had been.

"You're safe—you're with Ace and Son—"

"But it only works because you're out there," he said, voice breaking. "It's everything I've ever wanted, but only if I know you're breathing the same air. I can deal with you not being by my side, Lee, but you've got to be here in my world! Don't you understand?" He stopped struggling to be free because, just like when he'd been locked in his military barracks, he understood it was fruitless. He'd learned how to fire a gun and how to fight there—but it had been for form, to give him structure, something to do, not because he was effective at it.

Just holding the guns had given him hives they'd needed cortisone to get rid of.

Ernie's best defense was to become liquid. Water. A mirror to hold to the world but not a force that could change it.

He stared up at Burton with that helplessness, that knowledge that he was at the mercy of the sun and the wind and the earth, and Burton did a shocking thing.

He kissed him.

Not hard—but *thirsty*. Pulling Ernie into his soul like Ernie would nourish him, keep him soft, keep him viable, keep him *alive*.

Ernie couldn't help but respond, to give him the only thing he had, the well of sweetness, of gentleness, that had been languishing at his heart, waiting for another person to come share in what he had to offer.

"Sh...." Burton kissed his cheek, his tears, and Ernie tried to breathe, but it came out shaky. "Sh...." He kissed the other cheek, and Ernie nodded, like that would somehow make it okay. "Sh...." One more kiss, this one on his forehead.

"I'll be careful," Burton promised, his voice as broken as Ernie's had been. "I'll be careful. I promise. I was trying so hard to not have anyone who'd miss me. You snuck up on me, kid. You snuck up on me, and I'm still looking behind me wondering how I have this person in my life."

And Ernie got it—he'd been afraid because he was water, but Burton had been afraid that he'd drown.

"Sh...," Ernie whispered, taking his lips again, and together they fell into a deep well, the kiss never ending, not even when they were naked again, their bodies moving silkenly under the sleeping bag, spending their sex over each other's fists.

BURTON DROPPED him off at Ace and Sonny's in the small hours of the morning, long before dawn but long after Ernie usually came home.

"They'll be worried," Ernie murmured, holding Duke close. "I usually knock on Ace's door when I come in."

"Ace texted," Burton told him, surprising him. "After we nodded off."

"Not me?"

Burton grimaced. "I think he was trying to give you your space. But that doesn't mean he wasn't worried."

Ernie smiled fleetingly, warmed. A long time he'd lived without a safety net—it was nice to have one again. "Are you... is this going to get you in trouble?" he asked, because the question had haunted him, but he hadn't wanted to ruin the night.

"No." Burton shook his head without equivocation. "I was pretty much granted shore leave as a reward for not beating the hell out of one of my commanders." He grunted. "Prick."

But something else was bothering him. "What?"

One of those laconic shrugs seemed to be Burton's equivalent of *That ice cube is an iceberg the size of Mars. Don't hit it.* "Your shark and your fish—they're on the radar. I'm trying to protect them, Ernie—I swear I am. But it's getting hard to keep the heat off."

Ernie grunted. "That's...." He gnawed his lip. "Can they protect themselves?"

"Not… I mean normally, yes. I think they're pretty able. In fact, I think they could help put an end to this op. But the one guy is recovering from some pretty serious injuries. I'd like to give him another six weeks, you know?"

Ernie nodded. "Do what you can. I think, if worse comes to worse, you can warn them—right?"

Burton half laughed. "It would come as a shock to them both, I think, that I've been listening to them since Thanksgiving, but sure."

"What are they like?" The question had been burning in Ernie's mind. He had such a clear vision of them—but it was like the difference between Cruller, the enigmatic soldier, and the man who'd just made love to Ernie until he felt like he could grow fruit trees in the desert.

"They're… well, not nice. I mean, *good*, but the hurt one is snarky and stubborn, and it's a toss-up between whether he's going to kill himself or the bad guys are going to do it. The other guy is a lawyer—he's very… regimented. Just when I think they're going to kill each other, they start kissing instead."

Ernie chuckled. "Sounds… well, not normal, but—"

"But like normal's what they're working toward." Burton nodded, staring thoughtfully through the window of the truck. "You always think that if you retire or stop, you're going to do it cold. You're either going to just retire and settle down and live a regular life, or you're going to catch a bullet quick. You never think of maybe just fighting for normal when you're at home and then jumping into the mix when you're at work. You never think that maybe you can have them both for a while, and then you just alter the balance. These guys—that's what I think they're trying to do, you know?"

"So…." Ernie's heart pounded hard in his throat. "Do you think you just want to alter the balance?"

Burton cocked his head and swallowed. "We'll see," he said cryptically.

Ernie made a hurt sound—he couldn't help it—and Burton was just there, crushing him into the seat, searing his senses with a kiss that felt nothing like goodbye.

His phone buzzed—Ernie heard—and Burton groaned and ripped his mouth away. "We'll do this again," he said, like the words were torn out of him. "God, I'm going to need to taste you again."

"Then you'd better plan on coming back," Ernie told him, needing to hear it.

"Yeah, kid—but you better not prep like that for anyone—"

"Only you. You keep coming back and I'll keep needing you." Oh, it was the truth.

Burton nodded, kissed him hard on the forehead, and pulled away. Ernie took his opportunity to gather Duke and slide out of the truck into the cold.

"Burton—be safe."

"You too."

Ernie shut the door with a *thunk*, and Burton drove away. For a moment he just stood, watching the taillights disappear and wishing… wishing… but it was winter, and even the desert got cold this close to morning. Ernie ventured up the stairs and into the warm little house, giving Duke food and water and turning on the television before he knocked softly on Ace's door.

To his surprise Ace opened it a moment later.

"You okay?" he asked, looking exhausted and worried in a pair of sleep pants and no shirt. Ernie was lucky he wore Burton's mark on his skin both inside and out, because he could have been like Alba, another one of Ace's casualties, if he hadn't already been claimed.

"Yeah. Uh, sorry—I should have texted about—"

Ace shrugged. "You didn't know how much you could tell us. I know. I gave Burton an earful about worrying us shitless, but you were just…." Ace squinted at him in the dim light from the television and then opened his eyes really wide. "Getting laid," he said bluntly. "Jesus God, it's a good thing you're our resident vampire. You even got the bite marks on the neck. A shit-ton. You may want to hit Alba up for some makeup to cover those—just saying."

Ernie covered his face with his hands. "I have never in my life—"

"Had sex? Because, boy, you are a walking advertisement for why whisker-burn is a good thing."

Ernie kept his face covered. "You know, I've been coming home by myself for a while now—"

Ace grunted. "So. You're coming home to us now, and we're in your business. You and Burton. We care about you both. You break each other, we're picking up the pieces. Be careful."

Ernie scrubbed at his eyes. "Sure."

"Bullshit. Just saying—if it goes sideways, we'll be here. I promise."

Ernie looked at him through his fingers. "Even Sonny?"

"Yeah. Even Sonny."

"Thanks, Ace." Ernie nodded and then was taken completely by surprise when Ace ruffled his hair like he was a little kid.

"Get some sleep. Your schedule is cattywampus as it is." Then Ace went back to bed, and Ernie flopped down on the futon so he could watch some TV. His body was buzzing from the sex, from Burton's marks on his skin, from the conversation that gave him all the hope. But while most of him was buzzing and cold from excitement, a teeny part of him was warmed, solidly, simply, and kindly, by the fact that he'd come home in the wee hours of the morning and somebody gave a shit.

If Burton had given him nothing else, he'd given Ernie somebody who gave a shit.

But he really had given him so much more.

Christmas Star

JASON, I need something. Burton was on the secure line, the one only Jason knew about.

What?

I need you to help me fake a death.

Target?

Incoming.

Burton sent the entire jacket and then put that phone—recently charged—in his pocket and flushed.

Three days before Christmas, and he had a job to do.

He'd managed two more trips to see Ernie, making Friday night his unofficial night off. The last time he'd gone off campus, Collins had said, "Tell your girl if she wants a real man, I take Sundays off."

"So does she!" Manetti had joked, and Burton rolled his eyes.

"My piece doesn't stray for anyone," he said mildly, but it rankled. Not that they assumed it was a woman—normative thinking was something he was used to capitalizing on—but that they were joking with him like a buddy.

God, he hated everything they stood for.

"That's too bad, Oscar, 'cause you're gonna be out of town Sunday. I was looking forward to something new."

Burton bit back the retort that his "midnight ride," as Ernie had dubbed it the last time, might be a little too new for Collins's little mind and concentrated on the being "out of town."

The last time Burton had been "out of town," he and Jason had needed to have a quick conversation on whether or not Corduroy's target was *also* of interest to the US government.

Burton had lucked out last time. The guy had been a pig—not that being a pig usually marked someone for death, but this guy was a pig who made his money selling political information to US enemies and was in the process of turning that money into black market diamonds.

And he sold opioids on the side.

Burton might have taken him out for free, no recommendation needed, just because he didn't want that guy breathing the same air as his little brothers, or Ace and Sonny… or Ernie.

Especially Ernie.

Burton's kid might be completely legal and very adult, but he'd been ripe for the picking before Burton had come along.

Or ripe for the pushing.

Anything to help with the voices in his head—he'd said that before, and after feeling the waves of peace rolling off him in the desert, Burton had felt in his bones how much he'd meant that.

So Burton's taking out his last target was—as far as Burton was concerned—doing the world a favor.

But this next trip out of town was not.

Name: Troy Angelo Gonzales

Age: 23

Height: 6-4

Weight: 170

Nationality: Dominican American

Occupation: Computer Nerd

Crime: Accruing enough cryptocurrency by legitimate game play to unbalance a startup

The owner of the startup wants him dead.

Burton was at his com when his special Jason phone went off.

Are you fucking kidding me with this guy?

Nope. Next assignment.

Hamblin or Lacey?

Hamblin doesn't do chump change.

Burton had been watching the power dynamics of the two leaders, and while he detested them both on principle, he had to admit—Hamblin didn't dick around.

Hamblin did small countries and large cartels. He displaced stupid men from their pedestals and corrupt men from their fed-up families. He didn't do the Ernies of the world—that had been a Lacey move. Burton's last job had been a Hamblin hit.

This one was Lacey, through and through.

And worse than that—Lacey was just doing it to jerk Hamblin's chain.

Burton had heard the convo the morning after his first midnight ride. It was funny that they put him in charge of monitoring unsuspecting victims and didn't think to wonder that he'd bugged their own damned office.

"The new com guy... what's his name?" Lacey had asked—fortunately on a Saturday when Rivers and Cramer were out running. Rivers was up to three miles without passing out—Burton was impressed.

"Calvin Oscar," Hamblin replied dryly. "He's the only black man on the base—you'd think it would be easy to remember."

"That wasn't my idea," Lacey sneered.

"No. You would rather have that poor pale hamster in the medical bay who can't find his own shoes as opposed to a man like Oscar, who could find the shoes, tie them, fly them up in a helicopter, launch them, parachute down to the ground and *shoot* them, all while being wasted in the com room listening to lawyers fuck. But that's your part of the operation—by all means, don't let my opinion bother you."

Burton bit back a grin. Dammit. After being surrounded by Collins and Manetti—and yes, Saunders, the poor hamster in the med bay—it was good to at least listen to someone smart and snarky again.

Seriously—Rivers and Cramer would never know that they saved his life by not being rampant dumbasses, and that was the truth.

"I won't," Lacey snapped—which just went to show he might be long on ambition, but he had a very little brain. Hamblin may have been more amoral than Burton and his handler combined, but he was also damned smart. For starters, he'd objected to the fucking Corduroy symbol being flown above the military base, which was, as far as Burton was concerned, a good enough reason not to blow the guy away.

And a really good reason to slip plutonium into Lacey's oatmeal.

"So," Hamblin said, sounding bored, "what is your objection to Calvin Oscar?"

"You let him off base."

"He's my man. They're not prisoners here. He'd more than earned a night away."

"But you have no idea where he went! How do you know—"

"I don't," Hamblin said, and Burton could hear the shrug. "The same way you don't know if your men are loyal. I pay well, I recruit for intelligence, and I try not to piss off my men. We work a dangerous business here, Lacey—if you want guarantees, perhaps you should sell insurance."

Burton pictured the smaller man inspecting his manicure. Hamblin's operative mood seemed to be ice, and Burton wished Hamblin had been recruited by the good guys. He and Jason could have been an unstoppable force, for sure.

"Do you think Collins would bug him?" Lacey speculated, and Burton rolled his eyes. *Lacey* had tried to bug him, but Burton had his own personal bug detector as an app on his phone. It had taken him thirty seconds to find the thing and five seconds to put it in the bed of another pickup truck parked at the burger place. That Lacey didn't confess to trying now made Burton wonder how long before this operation crumbled on its own steam. Lacey wasn't competent—and he knew it on just enough of a gut level to not trust anybody who was.

Burton had said as much to Jason, but in the meantime, they'd both agreed: Lacey's list of targets was as important as the operation itself. They needed to know where Lacey was making his contacts, because there were plenty of people who would pick that list up without compunction and execute the hits. In the meantime Burton was on for protecting as many of the nonsanctioned hits as possible.

He was just glad he was the one behind the trigger for this hit, because it had been rough cluing Jason in to the other targets. They'd had to take out an asset, and Hamblin was still pissed—and still wary—that one of his men had gone down. He apparently hadn't forgiven Lacey for the men who'd disappeared during Ernie's hit—Lacey had sent five guys when one should have done, and three of the five were gone.

"He would if I asked him," Hamblin was saying, pulling Burton back to the conversation—and back to the com room, where everybody thought he was listening to Cramer and Rivers fucking some more. "But I won't ask him."

"I'm sorry?"

Burton choked back a laugh, because Lacey *should* be sorry, the incompetent fuck, but watching him get all pissy around Hamblin was a lot of fun.

"My. Men. Oscar could be a CIA plant—and that's on me. But if he is, I'll tell you this—he's a CIA plant because you have done something to catch his attention, and that's on you. All I asked for—*all* I asked for—was men. You've given me a few operatives that have proven very valuable, but you've also given me a few psychopaths who need a short leash."

"Like who?"

"Leavins is unstable, bigoted, and a pain in my arse. He can be your pet from now on, but I don't want him in my stable. Same with Adkins, same with Gleeson. And there's also the *twelve* you sent into the field that didn't return after you called them back. Twelve operatives out of twenty jobs. That's not very good odds, you realize that, right?"

"Those aren't my only men," Lacey said with dignity. "And I'll be damned if you get your paws on any of the others before you pony up some funds."

"I gave you my cap," Hamblin said, unperturbed. "You have about two million more before I stop paying out. Choose wisely, Lacey. Everybody needs to work inside a budget, even your bloated military."

"That's insane! With the scope of our operations in Africa, South America—"

"I can send Oscar out to take care of this target, and he'll be back in two days, the target will be dead, and nobody will even know he was in town. Again, I recruit for intelligence, not skin tone."

"Well, lucky you—I'm sending out Leavins, Gleeson, and Adkins to make sure he does the job."

"Do so on your own dime. I'm not authorizing payment for three men to follow up on the one man who can do the job."

"Goddammit!"

"Sure. We are all damned by God. I've made my peace with it, but you apparently need more cash."

And with that the conversation had ended, and Burton needed to scramble back to his original monitoring of Cramer and Jackson.

And a short time to figure out how to fake Troy Gonzalez's death, because that kid didn't deserve to be shot any more than Ernie had.

God.

Burton confided in Ernie during his next midnight ride. And the next one, when Ernie had wanted to know if he'd make it to Christmas—even just for an hour, because Sonny and Ace had asked after him. He hadn't asked because he expected Burton to be able to be there, but so Burton would know how important it was, the thing that kept him away.

"I get it," Ernie said patiently. "You're so much more than just me." He swallowed and gestured to the desert around them. They were huddled in the back of the truck, because even the desert got damned cold in December, but their skin was touching, and Burton could swear he'd never been more comfortable. "I… I mean, this feels like *everything* to me, but you… you've always had a bigger plan."

Burton closed his eyes and stuck his nose in the hollow of Ernie's neck and shoulder. "The problem with pulling back too far," he said, lost in the universe of Ernie's smell, "is that the things you see close up can be way more wonderful."

Ernie *hmm*ed and sighed. "You mean me."

Burton's sex was growing heavy and full again, and his fingers started to pulse slightly against the skin of Ernie's abdomen. "I used to be able to look at the whole sky," he confessed breathlessly, frotting up against Ernie's hip. "And that was all I needed."

"And now?" Ernie took Burton's hand and put it blatantly on his own cock, which was already wet with arousal again.

One want washed through Burton, and he couldn't fight it. "I need to taste you," he said thickly and disappeared under the cave of the sleeping bag to take Ernie's hard organ to the back of his throat again. He'd just pulled it in, sighing happily at the bitterness from Ernie's last climax when Burton had been buried inside him, when Ernie's hot mouth took his own cock inside.

Burton groaned and tried to think, tried to reason, but he couldn't even see for the need.

He needed Ernie's come more than he needed to breathe, but it was hard to think, hard to breathe, hard to *suck* when Ernie was pleasuring him, fondling his testicles, skating nimble fingers to his backside.

But he had to… he had to… he had to take care of….

Oh my God!

Ernie's finger pushed inside to the first knuckle and worked around just enough to stretch. Burton broke off what he was doing to cry out, his head pillowed on Ernie's thigh, his body shaking, nothing in his head but the supernova cascading through his nerve endings.

"Ernie," he sobbed. "Oh God… oh…."

Ernie pulled him in deeper and added another finger, and Burton came apart.

He didn't just orgasm, he lost himself, an explosion of stars taking its place in the surrounding heavens, and when he came to he was shaking, whimpering, completely wordless and empty.

Ernie had scooted around in the sleeping bag and unzipped the bottom so they were upside down on the bedroll, but Burton's head was tucked against his chest, so that was all right.

"Wow," he said when he could find a word.

"So," Ernie asked, arching against him, still hard, "do you feel very small now or very big?"

"Both," Burton whispered. Ernie's erection pressed deliciously against his abdomen. "Want to see?"

"Mm-hmm...." And it was Burton's turn to scoot down and take him into his mouth again, content and more than content, and then, after Ernie had cried out and spilled on his tongue, down his throat, he was replete.

By the time he dropped Ernie, he thought he had a handle on the world.

"Don't worry about Christmas," Ernie whispered against his neck. "It's a construct. Think of me. I'll feel it."

"I'll think of you," Burton whispered back. His stomach cramped. He wanted to say more. How could he not say more? But he was leaving—and like every other time he left, there was a possibility he might never come back.

How could he not say more? How could he have let it get this far as it was?

TWO DAYS before Christmas he was in Chicago, sighting through his rifle scope on a little apartment closer to the projects than the river, but in decent repair when all was said and done. Troy Gonzalez sat at his window, working on his laptop, apparently planning how to cash out all his cryptocurrency and buy a house in the suburbs to support his wife and unborn child.

Burton felt bad for the guy—such a simple want, really. And he'd earned the money legally, fair and square, during his free time from his job as an IT guy at a local bank. Jason could get the kid and his family protective custody, and they could get them a small house somewhere *besides* Chicago where Troy could have a new name and a new job—but he couldn't let Troy keep the money. As soon as the hit was faked, they were going to have to close down Freedom Tuba, the cryptocurrency company, anyway. All the money Troy had earned would be useless—but he'd still be alive.

Burton scanned the area restlessly, not liking the feeling in his gut. He'd monitored Lacey and Hamblin again to make sure Lacey wasn't sending another shadow after him like he'd first planned. But just like with Rivers and Cramer, there were lots of opportunities for the two of them to discuss relevant business when Burton *wasn't* listening.

The idea of one of Lacey's bullies scoping out Troy Gonzalez and his pretty wife, Tisha, made Burton itchy.

He checked on Troy again, trying not to smile as he watched him bob and weave to the music through his earbuds. At first Burton had assumed he was listening to R & B tracks, but after two nights of monitoring in between bouts of setting up the decoy plan, Burton had caught some strains of American musical theater through the boy's system.

Hamilton today—but yesterday it had been *Jesus Christ Superstar*, and Burton was still humming it. The kid reminded him a little of his younger brother. The hair shaved on the sides and growing into spring curls on the top of his head was James's style, and so was the narrow face and high cheekbones. But the build and the moves were all Ernie, liquid and boneless, like he was slinking through life. Troy's wife adored him, and the day before he'd caught them dancing, the choreography pure AMT, which was where their jacket said they'd met.

He liked to think that he wouldn't have completed this contract even *if* he'd never met Ernie, but Ernie had pretty much clinched it. Burton could never take out another target on his handler's say-so alone—he was about to become a royal pain in the ass.

Burton scanned the area again, startling when he caught sight of a flash in a window two floors below him, to his left. What in the fu—

Leavins—he saw the dark egg-shaped buzz cut first and the hands pumping a bullet into the chamber next. Oh fuck.

Fuck, fuck, fuck—

A shot like this, at a shallow angle, should have taken him a week to prep. He had seconds. He swung his stock around, eyeballed Leavins's *rifle stock*, for sweet fuck's sake, and fired.

Ten floors up, nobody heard the shot, but he watched in satisfaction as the gun disintegrated and Leavins leaped back, cradling his hand against his middle and looking around wildly.

Burton swung the rifle around again and saw....

Oh no.

Oh no oh no oh no....

Gonzalez was down.

Burton scanned through the window, saw the boy's face contorted in pain, saw his shoulder and arm soaked in blood. Oh no. Oh hell. Goddammit.

Jason, we're fucked. Lacey sent a shadow. Target is wounded but still breathing, and I tipped my hand to the shadow.

Breathe.

Burton breathed, hating himself for the panic. But dammit… this was a good kid. This kid hadn't spent his life trafficking drugs or guns or hurting people. He was a *theater major*, for Christ's sakes, and an IT guy and a husband and a father and….

He breathed again.

Breathing, sir.

Ambulance is coming. We'll pronounce him DOA and take him then. Do you have a cover story?

Yes, sir.

Well, he had one *now*.

Then we're solid. You deal with the bad guys, I'll take care of the good one. Deal?

Yes, sir. It's easier when they're bad guys.

But not ever easy.

No. Not ever easy. Burton could admit that now when his adrenaline was up and his heart was raging in his chest. He scowled through the scope at Leavins and made sure he had the weasel's attention. Leavins had binocs now, covered in blood from his injured hand, and Burton extended his middle finger slowly and unmistakably.

Yeah. Burton and Leavins were going to have unfinished business until Leavins was dead and Burton was standing on his throat. It was never easy—but bad guys needed to be taken care of.

It was his fucking job.

THE NEXT day he was in Lacey's office, rolling his eyes so far back in his head he was afraid they were going to pop out.

"What in the fuck do you mean by injuring your own goddamned operative when he was executing the duty that *you* plainly failed to—"

"I don't answer to you," Burton said, crossing his arms and standing hipshot. Every fiber of his being screamed against the breach in protocol—but goddamn if he was going to let this… this *cockroach* lecture him on duty.

Lacey turned purple, spitting in his rage, and Hamblin laughed softly.

"No, you don't, Oscar—you answer to me. And while this is more entertaining than Christmas dinner, perhaps you could explain yourself?"

"The target wasn't military—"

"So?" Lacey snarled.

Burton looked at Hamblin, head tilted, and waited.

"So why would he get shot in his own apartment building, through a window, ten stories up," Hamblin supplied, as though talking to a child. "Were you *trying* to skywrite 'This is a hit!' or did you think people wouldn't care?"

"It's fucking Chicago—kids like that are getting gunned down on street corners—"

"Not musical theater majors and not in this neighborhood," Burton said evenly. "Or did you think brown people just walk around with their heads exploding like it's a skin condition or something?"

"Nice neighborhood?" Hamblin asked curiously.

"Not quite upscale, but that's where he was heading," Burton told him. "Judging by his finances, he was looking to invest that cryptocurrency in a house in the burbs. And now that winky-fingers there took him out through his window from across the street, the cops are going to be looking into that too. Now *I* was going to take him out at the 'L' today, a bump, a trip, the third rail, too bad, so sad, such a nice lad." Actually, a well-dressed corpse donated to medical science had been going to take the fall, and one of Jason's people had been going to hustle Gonzalez out to meet his pretty young wife at an undisclosed safe location. As it was, they'd had to declare Gonzalez DOA and make the switch in the morgue, where he'd been revived and stitched up sans his left arm at the shoulder. Such a horrible fucking waste—but at least the kid was breathing. "See," Burton continued, letting his fury show, "I could do that because I studied his jacket, knew his patterns, and knew when he was going to be there and how many people would be there and where to take care of it where nobody would see. But *this* asshole has to shoot him *through a tenth-story window from across the street.*"

"How was I supposed to know!" Leavins snarled, cradling his bandaged hand. From what Collins had let slip, the asshole had almost lost his finger, and Burton was only sorry it was *almost.*

"Never pays to shoot early, does it?" he taunted, gratified when Leavins swung at him—with his maimed right hand.

Burton caught his fist and squeezed, smiling when sweat immediately popped out on Leavins's brow. Leavins gave a whine and his knees buckled, and Burton kept up the pressure, right up until the guy looked like he was going to puke.

"Do it on my shoes and I'll kick you in the jaw so hard it snaps your neck," he said pleasantly, letting the fury boil through him. "Don't ever… don't fucking *ever* fuck with my op again."

He let go of Leavins's fist and leaped back just as the other man lost his cookies all over the chipped tile of Lacey's floor.

He met Lacey's eyes steadily as Leavins finished heaving. "Are we done here?"

Lacey looked at his pet bulldog, sniffling on the floor, and recoiled at the smell. "You may go," he said, his own fury barely contained.

Burton turned on his heel and headed for the door.

He was halfway down the corridor, heading for the bathroom so he could wipe off his shoes, when Hamblin caught up with him, running a little.

"Sorry about that," he said, sounding genuinely regretful. "That's one soldier I couldn't take as ballast, I'm afraid. I don't know why Lacey thought having him shadow you was a good idea."

Burton swallowed a retort and remembered that this man was supposed to be his boss.

And that he wasn't stupid.

"The whole op was a bad idea," he said, judgment dripping from his voice.

"Well, yes, but then we can't always choose our targets, can we?"

Burton paused at the door to the bathroom and waited, saying nothing to the obvious rebuttal.

Hamblin let out a sigh and dragged a hand through his oiled, combed-back hair—the first time Burton had seen him look less than put-together in his five weeks here at the base.

"Look, Oscar? I know you're pretty disgusted with Corduroy so far, and I have to say, taking Lacey up on his deal seems like a worse idea every day. I'm just hoping...." He grimaced. "Just, this thing is going to fall apart—or it's not. And Lacey's going to end up dead—or he's not. But either way, I will eventually take my men and go. I know you just got here, but would you consider coming with us?"

Burton swallowed. "I have no loyalty to Lacey," he said through a dry throat, because that was the truth right there.

"Well, my loyalty runs out with his money and his troops. I'll hold a space for you when this whole op goes tits-up."

Well, as far as assassins went, it was a fair offer. "Thank you, sir, that's kind."

"Just keep using your brain—and don't kill Lacey until the right time. No matter how much you're tempted."

Burton let a smile slip through. "Roger that."

"Thank you, Oscar. I think we can do some great things together."

Burton nodded. "That remains to be seen."

"Well, thank you for letting me try."

Hamblin turned to go, and Burton opened the bathroom door, desperate to get the smell of vomit off his boots. Before he could achieve his objective, though, Hamblin bought his soul for a few short sentences.

"Oh, and Oscar? Take the next three days off. Didn't you say Rivers and Cramer were going somewhere for the holidays?"

"A friend's house in Crescent City," Burton lied. It was actually closer, in the Sierra foothills near Tahoe, but they talked about the mountains and the water often enough and vaguely enough that he'd been able to carry the deception.

"They'll be there for three days?"

"Yes, sir." It was five, with a day near a shooting range, because Rivers had been promising to teach Cramer how to defend himself.

"Good. You take three days off and come back a new man. I promise you, Commander Lacey and his pet gargoyles won't seem nearly as killworthy when you return."

Burton had to smile. He wasn't sure about them not being killworthy, but it was, in fact, a kind gesture.

"Thank you, sir. I'll leave tonight."

"Where *do* you go when you head out, Oscar? Your trips are just long enough to be anywhere." True—they were three hours from LA, San Diego, even five hours from Vegas. Burton wasn't going to tell him he went less than an hour east toward Victoriana.

"Barstow," he said, because that was in the same general direction. "I've got a girl there. No strings, but regular, you know?"

Great. He'd just confessed to sleeping with a prostitute. After hearing about Gonzalez's arm, he didn't think he could feel much worse.

"Well, if you're paying for that, tip her well. You're always in a much better mood when you get back." Hamblin nodded, like he hadn't said anything offensive at all, and turned and left.

Burton could finally get the puke off his shoes, but God, the rancid conversation was going to linger a lot longer.

HE WENT to the coms room to check in on his guys, relieved when all he heard was the ambient sounds of outside traffic. Even the cat had been taken to Jackson's sister—or the girl he called his sister, whoever she was—and their pricey but cozy house was empty.

Burton felt like he could leave with a good conscience, which was why he wasn't paying attention as he left the base, a small duffel packed over his shoulder.

But he was angry, running on adrenaline, ready to take someone's head off.

The first blow against his kidneys pissed him off enough to do just that.

The fight was hard and furious, filled with the thud of flesh against flesh and the crunch of bone, and when it was done, his three opponents were barely able to drag themselves upright.

No-neck Gleeson he'd expected, and Adkins's giant forehead was not a surprise—although his newly located nose might actually grow bigger before it healed—but Manetti....

"Aw, geez, Manetti," Burton said, surprisingly disappointed as he kicked the guy in the ribs once for good measure. "What in the fucking hell."

"They said you turned on your own guy," Manetti moaned.

"My 'own' guy blew the op," Burton told him, disgusted. "Bunch of fucking amateurs—no wonder Hamblin came to this shithole to find new people. Unfortunately—" Another kick, this one aimed at Gleeson's kidneys, may the fucker piss blood for another week. "—he found shitty fucking people."

He was not unscathed. In addition to bruises on his chest and arms, he had a cut under his swelling eye from a well-timed punch, and he'd be pissing his own share of blood from bruised kidneys too. He'd have to stop and clean up, he thought vaguely. He wouldn't want Ernie to worry.

"Blew the op how?" Manetti panted. Well—professionalism. Of course, Manetti was one of Hamblin's men—Burton expected it from him.

"Ask him," Burton told him, tired in his bones. "But wait until he's done throwing up, and by all means, don't expect the truth." They'd jumped him as he'd been walking around his truck, and he looked at them dispassionately as he took the last few steps to the door. "I'm backing out in thirty seconds. If you're not clear, you're roadkill."

He revved the truck loud and obnoxiously so he could watch them scatter from his rearview window.

Ernie was beating like a pulse in his stomach. He needed that purity, that sweetness—even Ernie's complete understanding of who and what Burton was.

Ernie was the only one who knew.

Halfway to Victoriana he stopped to fill up the truck and remembered to scan for bugs. He found two, at two different frequencies, and was tipped off enough to pull a more sophisticated scanner from his glove compartment and find another one. Goddammit, Lacey kept whining that he couldn't afford to car-bug Rivers and Cramer, but *Burton* he could bug?

When he was sure the truck was clean, he walked to the truck stop adjacent to the regular fill-up station and found the biggest, burliest, most pissed-off trucker in the place and asked him if he was going to Vegas. And then told him why he wanted to know.

"You want me to what?" the guy said, smiling through not so many teeth.

"I want you to carry these with you," Burton told him. "I'll pay you. When you get to Vegas, I need you to go to the sleaziest joint you know and put them behind the toilet."

The guy chuckled meanly. "Why not just flush them down?"

"Because I want them to have to reach behind it. They're not smart enough to wear gloves."

The trucker guffawed. "That's beautiful. Who pissed you off enough to do *that*?"

Burton liked the guy—he hadn't blinked at Burton's black face in a mostly white place, and he'd smiled and laughed with his whole heart.

"Bunch of racist assholes who're supposed to have my back," Burton said with a sigh.

"They give you that shiner?" And to his credit, the man sounded concerned.

"They did."

"Don't worry none. I've got the perfect place."

Burton grinned and put out his hand to shake. "Thank you, sir. Let me buy your gas."

"I won't object to that—but trust me on this, kid. I'll make them sorry they ever came to Vegas."

Burton handed over a wad of the disposable cash he'd told Ernie about and considered it money well spent.

It wasn't until he was pulling into the little gas station in Victoriana, making sure to go around the garage to hide the truck, that he remembered he'd been planning to stop to buy presents, and that he'd forgotten to clean up the cut under his eye.

It didn't matter.

Ernie had burst out the door to the house, Duke at his heels, before Burton turned off the engine.

In the Shade of the Cliff, Beneath the Sky

Two DAYS before Christmas, Ernie woke up early—still-daylight-in-December early—and tried not to crawl out of his skin. The thing that had woken him up sounded like a shot in his head. He couldn't sit still. He couldn't concentrate. He and Duke took turns pacing around the little house while Ace and Sonny were working when a wave of wrong crashed down on him.

He rushed to the bathroom and lost his breakfast, then cleaned up and tried to pinpoint the wrong.

At first he thought it was Burton—that was always his fear, Burton. But while Burton was angry and unhappy and sad, he wasn't hurt.

A flush of nausea, a prickle down his spine, sent Ernie out into the midday.

"Alba," he cried, running for the cashier's window, "you don't work today."

She looked up from her schoolbook and took in his expression, his worry, and the intensity of his eyes. "I don't work today," she said decisively, folding up her book. "Ace, I don't work today."

She turned on her heel and headed for the little Nissan Sonny had fixed up for her, pausing only to give Duke his customary treat so he'd stay and not follow her to her car.

Ace was under a minivan, changing the oil, and he shoved out on the dolly as Alba got in her car.

"What's doing?" he asked, serious. Ace did that, took people seriously.

"Bad guys," Ernie muttered. "Bad fuckin' guys. They're—"

"Sonny!" Ace called. "Get your ass in the house with Ernie and the fuckin' dog. Fuckin' now!"

"But Ace—" Sonny complained, right up until he saw Ace's expression and took in Ernie's flop-sweating body. "Come get your gun," he said instead.

"Jai?"

"I'll deal with it until you get back." Jai smiled, giant teeth gleaming, and unzipped his oil-stained jumpsuit. He reached around the back until he pulled out his own piece and then repositioned it, grip out, in his belt.

Ace nodded and took off at a full sprint for the house, Ernie and Sonny behind him.

He disappeared into his room, and Ernie heard the sound of a lock being turned in a wooden drawer, and then he was back in the kitchen.

"Sonny, take care of Duke," he said seriously, squeezing Sonny's shoulder. He winked at Ernie. "Ernie, maybe turn on the TV in Burton's room and watch it there."

Ernie nodded like he was reassured, but he and Sonny both jumped as the door slammed behind him.

Sonny was the one who locked it, and then he went to the laundry room to degrease his hands and take off his jumpsuit.

"Anything good on in the day?" he asked.

"Kids' cartoons," Ernie said, thinking. "I used to watch them all the time when I woke up."

A smile split Sonny's face. "I like those! Do we have more now that we have some cable?"

"Yeah—Ace got Nick. We're good."

"Do they have *SpongeBob*? And the little fairy guys who grant the wishes and fuck shit up?"

Ernie nodded, bemused. He often forgot how much little things meant to Sonny. "C'mon. We'll sit and watch cartoons and let the guys work."

They'd no sooner situated themselves on Burton's bed—Duke quivering between them—and found something distracting on the television when the wave of nausea swept Ernie again.

Sonny stiffened, and they both heard the whine of an engine badly out of alignment as it *thump-putt*ed into the garage.

"Sounds like an SUV," he muttered. "Been beat to shit. Probably overheating."

Ernie closed his eyes and breathed through his mouth. "They're bad," he whispered. "Bad. Drugs and murder bad."

Next to him, Sonny started to shake. "Ace is out there," he whispered back.

Ernie grabbed his hand more to reassure himself than to reassure Sonny. "We gotta trust him," he said, suddenly thinking about Burton. "Ace and Jai, they're smart. They're mean. They'll take care of us."

Sonny nodded and squeezed Ernie's hand. "Ace wouldn't go down without taking some of 'em out first."

Ernie focused on the television for a moment—and on Sonny's hand in his. They were both sweating uncomfortably, but neither of them let go of the other's cold, clammy hand.

Two hours later the bad was still there, and Ernie took a breath. "I should start dinner."

"Are the drapes drawn?" Sonny asked. "Did we draw the drapes?"

Ernie stuck his head out of the room and saw that, yeah—in his fit of restlessness before he'd snapped, he'd drawn every drape in the house, including, fortunately, the ones in the bedroom.

"Yeah. If I keep my body away from the window, I can put some water on the stove for spaghetti."

"Tomorrow we're having fried chicken," Sonny said, "and Christmas we're having ham, which is enough to serve all of us including Alba, who comes over in the afternoon when we sit down to play games. Last year she brought Scattergories, which made me feel dumb as hell, but she also brought Monopoly, and I could play the shit out of that, I tell you. But we got green beans for tomorrow and salad for Christmas and I forget what's going for today—"

"We've got frozen peas, Sonny. It'll be all right." Ernie swallowed against impatience because he knew what was going on in Sonny's head.

Sonny was two people in his head. One of them was in the bottom of a deep well, so far down he almost couldn't see daylight. And at the top of the well, shining like the sun, was Ace, reaching down to help him out.

The other person was outside the well, holding hands with Ace, rooting him on to save that little kid in the well—but only vaguely aware of his own power to help that little kid.

The thing was, both of those people in his head were dependent on Ace to get him out of the well.

So if Ace was in danger, the bottom of that well went black, and the Sonny at the top of the well had to talk about all things under the sun so the Sonny in the bottom didn't panic.

All the things that made Sonny's world normal, all the day-to-day-living things that any regular person would take for granted, were all the things Ace gave Sonny on any given day. Sonny had to talk about them or they'd go away.

"Frozen peas are really good, but I don't like them as much as corn. Corn is good, especially with butter, but Ace says he can't have too much butter 'cause he'll get fat, which I wouldn't mind 'cause he's so solid, but he's really health conscious, says he needs to be around forever. I figure I got white-trash bloodlines, I'll be here for-fuckin-ever, and he says he needs to keep up with me. I think he's about three years older than me, maybe two, but I'm not great at math so I don't know. I figure we won't never know, but he's the one that takes care of me so I'm guessing he'll—"

A noise outside caught Ernie's attention, and he grabbed Sonny's elbow to shush him.

And Sonny went limp.

He didn't sag or lose his knees or anything, but his entire body just *relaxed*, and the terrified conspicuous chatter came to a standstill.

In Sonny's head, the little boy at the bottom of the well curled up and dreamed of the day he could live in the sunshine with a lover and a dog and a thing to keep him occupied that he loved to do, and the man at the top of the well calmed down because the boy was safe.

Tentatively, Ernie let go of Sonny's elbow, relieved when he stayed standing but just looked at Ernie tranquilly, waiting for direction.

"Sit at the counter, Sonny, and I'll make spaghetti and frozen corn for you."

"I like the corn," Sonny said quietly.

"I know you do. Come keep me company until the guys come in. I think Jai's going to be eating here tonight too."

The noise that caused Ernie to touch Sonny in the first place sounded again—a car engine, in much better repair.

"They sound about done," Ernie said softly.

"Yeah. Ace and Jai can work miracles together, I guess."

Fifteen minutes later they heard the car pull out, and fifteen minutes after that—about the time the spaghetti was done and Ernie had Sonny working on the corn and setting the table, Jai and Ace came inside.

They were grimly quiet as they stripped off their coveralls and unlaced their boots. Jai took Ace's coverall into the laundry room. "I'll leave it to soak—plenty of bleach," he said, and Ace nodded.

Sonny stood, paralyzed, looking at him wistfully, and Ernie realized he wanted to touch Ace—hug him, pat him, something—but they rarely if ever did that when someone else was watching.

"Turn on the Christmas tree lights," Ace told him quietly. "It'll be nice to see something cheerful."

Sonny nodded. "Uh, the, uh, customers are gone?"

"Toward San Diego," Ace muttered. "Jai, did you write it down?"

Jai rattled off a license plate number casually, like he memorized them all the time. "You think we should call now?"

Ace shook his head. "An hour and a half," he said, like he was thinking. "Even if they're driving balls-out for San Diego, they're not going to get there any sooner—not with this traffic. We'll call the cops then. You wanna make the call?"

Jai shrugged a massive shoulder. "I have a phone that would work nicely."

Ace's mouth twisted. "Of course you do. But good. We'll eat some dinner, let them get good and far from here, and call it in. You want to shower first?"

Jai nodded. "Da. I've got clothes in my car."

"I'll get 'em," Ace said. "You get under the water, ASAP."

Jai went to do just that, and Sonny looked a little desperately at Ace. "Ace...?"

"They used the bathroom," Ace said, voice thick with disgust. "We had to power hose it out—which reminds me, we gotta buy some of that good-smelling shit and some flowers, like, tomorrow, or Alba'll be pissed. But they left drugs and shit—and shit too—in there, and it was gross. We were careful and all, but I'd just as soon not touch anything with that crap on my body." Ace looked apologetically at Duke, who was whining at his feet. "Not even you, buddy. Sorry. Just can't take the risk."

"Then I'll go get Jai's clothes," Ernie offered quietly, stunned from his inaction. "Sonny, keep setting the table."

Sonny's eyes went to half-mast again, and some of that frantic need to touch Ace went away. "Sure thing," he said.

Ace's eyes widened, and he looked at Ernie askance.

Ernie shrugged. He couldn't very well say *I witched him into submission*, but essentially that's what he'd done.

Ace nodded thoughtfully. "I'll come with you."

Sonny looked up and smiled, not exactly happy but calm.

The door shut behind them, and Ace said, "What did you do?"

"I... I touched his arm. I... was thinking he had to hush it, sort of, you know, calmed him down." It had happened before, when they'd first met, but Ernie hadn't been aware of what a drastic change he'd made.

Ace frowned. "We... we need to only do this in emergencies," he said. "And this counted, but...." He took a deep breath. "Sonny... he's getting better at controlling himself, you understand? If he thinks someone else is doing it for him...."

Ernie thought of those two versions of Sonny. The one on the outside of the well hadn't been completely passive, and he wondered what Sonny had been like when he *hadn't* seen a way to help himself. How much darkness would it take before the child at the bottom of the well turned feral, snarling and scratching, even at the hand reaching into the darkness to help?

"If he can't help himself, he loses hope," Ernie said, understanding. "I get it. Emergencies only."

Ace nodded. "Good. Thanks, Ernie. And thanks for calming him down too. I was worried about him."

Ernie's mouth quirked up. "Not me?"

Ace half laughed. "Son, you can take care of yourself. Anybody can see that."

Ace swaggered off to Jai's little Toyota, and Ernie thought for the umpteenth time that Ace was, what? Four years older than he was? Maybe? But maybe one man's years were another man's decades—or maybe some men were just born old.

ABOUT AN hour and a half after Jai and Ace first came in, Ernie felt a sort of transitory nausea—like what you felt when your bowels hadn't been working and suddenly you had to go really, really bad.

He'd shuddered and looked at Ace weakly as Ace slouched on the couch, Sonny next to him. "They're in San Diego County now," he said, seeing the sign in his head. "You've got about an hour before they do something really bad."

Ace nodded casually, and Jai threw him a burner phone. Ace had already looked up a crime tip line, and he was about to dial when Ernie said, "Give me the phone. You've got a twang in your voice, Ace. I sound like a college kid—nobody can pick my voice out of a crowd."

Ace shook his head. "I can deal with police, Ernie, and you can't. I can take the country out of the voice, don't you worry none."

Which hadn't sounded promising, really, but Ace worked hard to keep his voice flat and uninflected, and mostly he succeeded. He placed the call and then unpaused the action movie they were watching. Jai grunted in satisfaction.

"You think the cops will catch them?"

Ace nodded. "I hope so—that was a lot of fuckin' guns and a *lot* of fuckin' coke."

All of them shuddered, and about an hour later that coiled nausea uncoiled, leaving Ernie feeling tired and limp.

"I bet the cops have 'em," he said softly. "If you want, I can look it up on the computer."

"Think Burton would know?" Sonny asked, one of the first signs of real animation they'd seen from him since Ernie touched his elbow.

"Burton's busy," Ernie said, not wanting to think about that other source of anxiety. "Don't worry. We'll find out from the cops if we need to."

Turned out it was on the eleven o'clock news.

They all watched in relief as an aerial view of the burgundy SUV Jai and Ace had worked on got pulled over by the police. The copter had captured the subsequent shoot-out and wounding of two of the men—and the death of the other two.

Everybody breathed a sigh of relief—and Ernie had a moment to give thanks for people who could be just as cold-blooded as he was about saying "This person isn't good for my people. He can go now" and have "go" mean death or simple relocation—it didn't really matter as long as they were gone.

Still, it was reassuring to have Jai stay the rest of the night, sleeping on the futon in the living room rather than going home. Ace gave him the morning off so he could go get a decent nap and get ready for Christmas Eve.

Ernie hadn't had a family for Christmas since his parents died. The first year he hadn't really wanted one. He'd had a small but happy family. There hadn't been grandparents or aunts and uncles and cousins, but he'd been the center of his mom and dad's world, and the thought of spending a Christmas any other way but with them had left him heartbroken. After that there had been nobody, not even when he'd been sleeping his way through the Albuquerque club life.

But this year he had people, and a sort-of boyfriend, and a dog.

He drew a small salary for the work he did for Sonny and Ace, and with a little help from Burton, they'd established a bank account and an alternative identity. Elmo Caldwell. At first Ernie had been dismissive—like *this* was going to keep him safe?

They're not looking for you to come back, Burton had texted. *And at this point nobody knows about Victoriana, and I'm working hard to keep it that way.*

Ernie had needed to think about that one. *The shark and the fish?*

Yeah. They're trying not to stir things up there too, but I'm not sure I can put them off much longer.

I'm so excited to meet them! It felt like a foolish thing to say, but Ernie couldn't help himself. He'd been dreaming about the two of them, circling in a small, perfectly clean, neatly kept fishbowl. Ernie wasn't sure if they were going to eat each other alive or start some really amazing fish sex in his dreams, and he always woke up before he found out.

Well, I think you may catch them by surprise. Maybe don't mention we know them from beforehand, you think?

Well, no. That's not circumspect. Ernie felt no disappointment about that—he knew that sometimes what the gift gave him was a sort of television voyeurism. He was fine with that—people didn't need to know he knew everything. But he *was* excited about meeting them. It was like hearing about cousins for your whole life and wondering if the real thing would measure up.

But right now it wasn't the fish and the shark he was thinking about. He was thinking about Christmas with Ace and Sonny and Jai and Alba. And Duke, his walk buddy. He'd ordered presents for them all, little Amazon packages that Ace had left outside his bedroom door before he'd awakened in the evening. He'd wrapped each one as it came and set it under the little tree they'd put next to the TV. Other presents had shown up there—some from Jai, some from Alba.

One day about a week before Christmas, Sonny and Ace had gone shopping at Walmart in Barstow—a place that gave them both the willies—and two hours after they got back, Sonny emerged with an armload of packages that went under the tree. That morning, when Ernie had come in from his walk, he found Ace up, finishing the last of his wrapping.

It was small—but then, Ernie hadn't been used to big. He'd been used to being a vital member of a really small group, and being that person again…

Felt important.

He wondered if it was important enough for Burton, who was doing things like saving the world and stopping rogue assassins and whatever it was that had knotted him up so badly in the past two days that Ernie felt like he was holding Burton's hand across Middle America.

He wanted so badly to have more than a night's time with him, to just *ask* him—but he'd been so reserved about Christmas, about whether or not he could make it.

Ernie had resolved not to hope. He toned down the "Burton radar" in his head so he couldn't feel Burton so close and know he wasn't coming. It wasn't until they were sitting down to Christmas Eve dinner, talking excitedly about what to watch on television (another thing Ernie had only started doing since he came to live with Sonny and Ace, because it was something better done in company and boring to do alone) when he felt it.

It was like the light of a nova sun shining down on the little house behind the garage.

"What?" Ace asked, like it was the third or fourth time he'd said something. "Ernie, what's that look? Where'd you go?"

They all heard the crunch of tires on the gravel in front of the garage.

"He's here," Ernie whispered, his heart shining in his chest. "He's *here*."

He was out the door before the truck had even parked.

Burton held him so close, so tight, his bones creaked. He couldn't breathe. He couldn't see.

And he didn't care.

Ah God! All that strength! All that goodness surrounding him! It was the best, the only thing he could have asked for, and for long minutes he just let it surround him.

Finally Burton drew back, and Ernie got a good look at him.

"You're cut! You're bleeding!"

"Shit—I forgot to wipe that off." Burton grimaced. "Hazard of working with assholes—I'll clean up and—"

"We have dinner," Ernie said, excited in spite of himself. "Fried chicken. And they let me bake cookies. I've been baking cookies for a week. Well, not yesterday—yesterday was kind of fucked—but cookies. The sugar kind with the icing that you like best—"

Burton stopped and held him at arm's length for a moment, grimacing. "I did not tell you that."

"But I'm right, aren't I?"

And then he pulled Ernie back against his chest. "Yeah, but that's spooky."

"Well, so am I. I thought you'd be okay after whatever happened yesterday—I didn't know there was more bad shit."

"Me neither. This sort of snuck up on me right before I left the base."

Ernie grunted. Right when he'd sat on his "Burton radar," as it were. "I was trying not to feel you," he said glumly. "I thought you couldn't make it, and it hurt." He brightened a little. "But man, once you hit that last mile, it was like a spotlight in my eyes. I couldn't have missed you if I'd been underground."

Burton grunted right back. "Which is funny. It felt I was being pulled like a string," he said with a sigh. "But what happened yesterday?"

"To you? I don't know. But it was bad. I could feel it—it woke me up around four o'clock." It had been what alerted him to the bad guys, actually. "It's a good thing it did, because there was some other shit to sort, but *you* were not having a good time."

Burton's groan actually surprised him—it sounded emotionally honest. "No, no, I wasn't. But it's nice to have someone who knows I wasn't, thank you. So what happened to *you*?"

Ernie shrugged. "Nothing so's you'd notice. But come in. Wash up. We've got dinner and TV and presents and...." His shoulders sagged. "It's all really normal. I mean, I hope that's okay. You went out and did amazing, dreadful things, and this is all very—"

"Normal." Burton held him close and kissed his temple. "Kid, you don't know how wonderful normal is until you're stuffed to the gills with amazing and dreadful, you know what I mean?"

"No, but you're going to tell me, right?"

"Not tonight, Ernie."

Ernie took a deep breath.

And decided to let it go.

"Merry Christmas, Burton."

"Merry Christmas, kid."

"Thanks for making it home."

"Thanks for making it *a* home."

"Thanks for making it *my* home."

"You mean that?"

"Yeah. Let's go sit down to dinner."

IT SOUNDED very idyllic, but an hour later Burton was supremely unamused.

"Ace, you did *what*?"

"We fixed their car," Ace said, unperturbed. "Ernie, is there more of that apple pie you made? That was spectacular. I might eat the whole thing."

"You got four gangsters from... from... from...."

"Ukraine," Jai said, on his fifth piece of chicken. Ernie had noticed that he never said no to more food. "They did not speak Russian."

"They didn't speak much English either," Ace said, mouth full of pie. "But they definitely spoke gun, so that was no good."

"You will explain that." Burton glared at him, and Ernie hid a smile. He was trying to be pissed off about the incident, but he'd eaten fried chicken like a champion and was wearing ice cream on his chin. Once they'd washed the blood off his cheek, he looked like he was in permanent dad mode.

Ace shrugged—an overcasual gesture that actually set Ernie's teeth on edge, because to someone who knew him, it meant he was about to tell a whopping lie of omission.

"It means as long as they saw we were carrying too, they weren't going to give us any trouble," Ace lied.

Suddenly Ernie was wondering how Jai and Ace had gotten out of yesterday's pickle without bloodshed.

"But Ace," Sonny said, coming more fully out of his zone. "How do you fix a car with one hand on the gun?"

Ace and Jai met gazes, and Jai shrugged. "We took turns," he said. "Ace held gun, I changed out coils. I held gun, Ace changed belts. We needed help, we made them hold things. Hey—they were the ones who came in armed."

There was silence at the table, and Burton opened his mouth to say *They were going to kill you*, but Ernie shook his head firmly, darting his gaze to Sonny and back.

"You were lucky," Burton said instead. He swallowed hard. "We were all lucky."

His eyes locked on Ernie's face then, with such heat and intensity that Ernie had to look away.

"Hey," Ernie said, a weak attempt at a joke, "I was lucky you were the one sent to shoot me in the first place."

There was a gasp around the table, and when Ernie looked up, Burton was hiding his eyes in his hand.

"What?"

"*That* was how you two met?" Ace half laughed in disbelief.

Oh. Oh hell. "I'd forgotten you didn't know that."

Burton's weak chuckle curled warmly in his belly.

"Well, of course he couldn't shoot you," Sonny said rationally from the other side of the table. "You're… you're *Ernie*. People don't go around shooting people like Ernie. It makes as much sense as shooting Duke."

If Duke hadn't been the most important thing in Sonny's world next to Ace, Ernie might have taken exception to that. Instead he smiled fondly at Sonny and went for reassurance. "Of course he couldn't shoot me. He's a good guy."

Sonny nodded. "I know it. Anybody else want any dessert or dinner? I'm gonna start putting stuff away so we can have it tomorrow."

"Feel free to raid the fridge after you and Ernie get back from his walk," Ace said casually, standing up to help clear the table. "But don't stay out too long, okay? I'd really love to fall asleep before three a.m."

"Burton needs to sleep too," Ernie said, surprised at the authority in his voice. "We'll be back while you're still watching TV."

Ace smiled. "We sure would like your company," he said, sincerity ringing from his voice.

"It's a deal," Burton said. "But first, Ace—a word?"

Ace grimaced. "Course, Lee." He set the dishes in his hands down on the counter and kissed Sonny's cheek in a rare public show of affection. "Leave some of it for me, okay?"

"Sure, Ace." Sonny nodded, and Ernie started packing up the last of the leftovers. He knew what Burton wanted to talk to Ace about—and he wasn't sure how to make it better. But God, he was sure glad Burton was there.

Fighting For

BURTON COULD still feel the adrenaline-bleed from the fight and the endorphin hit from when Ernie had run out the door. He could feel the sugar hitting his bloodstream from dinner and from the desserts Ernie had poured his heart into, and the dopamine and testosterone from the promise of Ernie's sweet body next to his, in a bed no less, with the lights off.

He knew these drugs his body produced—had mastered them to an extent, knew how to counter them when they were a hindrance and use them when they weren't.

What he *didn't* know was which drug was responsible for the heart-dropping, stomach-sick rage pounding through his bloodstream.

"How did you—" he began, but Ace cut him off with one of those maddening shrugs.

"We took turns holding the guns," he said, like he and Jai hadn't sat out here and repaired a vehicle while worried for their lives. "I watched Jai's back, Jai watched mine. The boys stayed inside with the drapes drawn. I'm pretty sure even if the worst had gone down, they would have been safe."

Burton nodded and tried to calm his shaking down. "You could have been killed," he rasped. They *all* could have been killed. "Why didn't you—"

"Ernie said you were out of town," Ace told him matter-of-factly, nothing to see here, sir, just Burton's entire existence, threatened by gangsters from fucking nowhere. And Burton would have been… would have been…. "He didn't want to bother you with it, and, you know. Since we called the authorities and they took them out, there wasn't anything to bother with, right?"

Burton nodded, eyes closed. "Nothing…. God, I'm pissed. I don't even know why!" He didn't like admitting it to Ace. Hell, he didn't like admitting it to *anybody*.

"'Cause your boy was threatened," Ace said, unperturbed.

"And my friends." Burton felt compelled to say it. This was his third Christmas at Ace and Sonny's, and while Ernie had made it his best, it was still the only place he could think of to be right now. A group of gangsters passing through, deciding his friends were too much of a liability, and Burton could be adrift here in the desert. Just him and Duke, probably, mourning the nucleus of their world.

"That's kind," Ace acknowledged. "And speaking of friends, how deep under are you? Because you look like hell, Lee, and not just from the fight."

Burton grunted. "I hate undercover," he said, thinking Ace might be able to figure he wasn't speaking at random. "I hate it. You think these guys are okay, some of 'em. You think they're your friends. But they're not. They're just fuckin' killers looking for a reason to kill."

"Mm. I'm glad you're one of the good guys, yes I am."

Burton managed a limp smile in his friend's direction. "You know as well as I do that guys like me—"

"Us," Ace said unequivocally. Well, Ace had done his share of bad things for a good reason.

"Us," Burton acknowledged. "Guys like us aren't really good. We're sort of—"

"We have pure intentions and a certain moral flexibility," Ace said, so innocent and self-righteous that Burton's smile grew a few watts brighter.

"That's a nice way to put it."

Ace chuckled. "Well, you either learn to live with the things you've done, or they weren't worth doing in the first place."

Burton nodded, letting his hands fall to his sides and staring out into the chill of the winter desert. "I almost failed," he said softly. "I... I almost let someone innocent get killed. I'm... I'm not okay with that."

He heard Ace's deep inhale. "I almost let Sonny get killed—"

"That wasn't your—"

"Let me finish. The one person I care most about in the world and he was knifed, right in front of me. And I was helpless until I wasn't. And that's all I got, Burton. All I'll ever have on that subject. 'Almost' can fuckin' kill us if we let it. You got a boy in there who lights up brighter than Christmas when he hears your tires in the driveway."

"He's not mine," Burton said automatically.

"Well, don't tell him that—because if you *almost* keep him, that would be an even bigger tragedy than *almost* letting the bad guys get away with being bad guys, you think? Don't let the almosts break you down. Sometimes you gotta be helpless—I get that more than most. But you obviously defended yourself, so I'm going to think helpless was not your gig. It never has been. So you were helpless for once—but not for long, because it was *almost*. You're feeling helpless about those drug dealers here at the station—but you left Ernie with me, and I coped, so it was *almost*. Son, you've got a whole lot of blessing you are *almost* taking for granted, so maybe when that boy comes out here, you give thanks for him instead of dwelling on the almosts, okay?"

Burton felt his jaw drop open. "I am two years older than you, Jasper Atchison—"

Ace rolled his eyes. "I've been watching your lover break his heart over you for two months. It's aged me."

"I haven't broken his—"

"He misses you, idiot. I understand he's got the witching and he thinks he's all self-contained, but those nights when you stop by and give him the cosmic booty call? He comes home and Sonny and I dream of sadness for the next two, three nights. Just sadness—the color, the texture, puppy-in-the-goddamned-rain sadness of watching you go. He sees stuff—I get that. But he also *projects* stuff, and unless you find some way to reassure him that you and him are going to be okay, you're going to lose him, because nobody can be that sad all the time—nobody. So before you go dwelling on *almost*, start thinking about what it would be like if you almost had a soul mate but you let him go because he wasn't what you expected, and then tell me how you feel."

Burton stared at him, completely off-balance. Dammit, he'd been planning to yell at *Ace*—he hadn't expected it to be the other way around.

"He shouldn't have been dragged into this life at all," he said at last.

"But he was." Ace's implacable practicality would be the death of him. "Wasn't your fault, and here he is. And you know what? I think here suits him. He can calm Sonny down like nobody's business. We like him here. We like *you* coming here to be with him. But you will hurt him if you keep him at almost length, you hear me?"

"I don't know—"

"And if you break up with him on Christmas, you and I will have words, and by words I mean my foot up your ass."

Burton blinked. He could kill men with his bare hands, but he suddenly did not doubt Ace's ability to lay him out in the dust with that much protective rage.

"I wasn't going to break up with him," he said defensively.

"Good. I didn't think my buddy Burton could be that much of an asshole. Was there anything else you wanted to talk about?"

Burton tried to salvage his dignity. "Is there anything he needs? Or wants? Besides me, I mean."

Ace thought for a moment. "He needs a pet. I'm not sure if Duke is up to being second dog to another animal, but Ernie has an open heart. He needs a thing to care for that's exclusively his."

"That's not a fish," Burton sighed, thinking of their fish and shark, who were, for the moment, safe.

"Fish are only okay pets," Ace said decisively. "Can't pet a fish."

Burton laughed. "Send Ernie out?" he asked, feeling pathetic. "If I go back inside I'm going to sit down, and I won't make it out for a walk."

"Fair enough. I'll tell him to take it easy on you, old man."

"I'm twenty-eight!"

"Not the way you're going. Like I said, don't stay out late."

And with that Ace went back inside, leaving Burton to contemplate what he'd said.

Don't dwell on the almosts. Be grateful for what you have. Treat your lover right.

Ace Atchison might not ever be more than a small-business owner and a grease monkey, but he sure did seem to have a handle on the world.

Ernie trotted out a few moments after Ace went in, the little dog on a lead. Burton smiled tiredly.

"I'm starting to think that dog's more yours than Sonny's," he joked.

Ernie shook his head, all seriousness. "No. I'm like his nanny. He lights up when Sonny walks in the house. Sometimes, when I get in after they've had sex, Sonny will open the door and whistle for him so he doesn't have to sleep in his crate alone that night."

Burton chuckled. "Ace said you need a critter of your own."

"I'd need to move," Ernie said, taking Burton's hand and tugging him into the darkness. "But not far. I do real work for them at night—Ace says so, and I believe him. And I like sitting down to dinner with them—although I think some nights they'd like to be alone, but they're too nice to say so. But, you know. Close enough to walk at night."

Burton looked around the desert and thought about the small housing development nearby. "I'm pretty sure land's a steal around here."

"Yeah, but water rights are a bitch to get—Ace was telling me, and he let me help him with the paperwork that he has to do once a year."

"Hunh." It was a word he'd borrowed from Jackson Rivers, and he liked it.

"What does that mean?"

"Means I can pull strings for them. Means I need to think about water rights if I want to build out here. Just means I'm thinking is all."

To his surprise Ernie pulled away from his hand.

"What?"

"Don't talk about that unless you mean it," he said woodenly, and that quick, Burton knew Ace was right about him breaking his heart.

"I don't ever want to toy with you," he said, chest tight. "I just... I don't know how to think of a long-term thing."

"Then think about coming back to me." Ernie allowed him to take his hand again. "Just that. Just plan on coming back to me whenever you leave."

Burton tried to blow it off. "Course I do!"

And Ernie's scowl knocked him flat. "You're still bleeding, dammit! Lee, I get you've got to go, and I get you've got bigger things than me out in the world, but you've got to promise you'll bring yourself back intact!"

And Burton got it. He'd avoided it big-time, but Ernie just smacked him in the face with it. No matter how hard he'd tried to tell himself it was only *his* life, Lee Burton's life, that he was risking, he was risking Ernie's heart with every close call.

"I...." He swallowed, thinking about Troy Gonzalez and his pretty wife and the baby who almost grew up without a daddy. "I almost let a good guy down," he said after a minute. The cool breeze of the winter desert washed over his face, and he kept his eyes closed, imagining every word as a star. "I was supposed to hit him, but he was like you—innocent to the core—so I made arrangements to fake it. But there's two guys—one of them's a pro and the other one's a wannabe. The wannabe doesn't like me—he sent a backup guy, and the backup guy almost took my mark out." Burton took a deep breath, remembered the blood and Troy's tiny wife's terror as she screamed for help. "I... I called for an ambulance and thought it could have been you. It could have been me, finishing the hit on you, and I wouldn't have missed, and God, how can I make any more hits when I won't miss...?"

He tried to haul his emotions to a screaming halt, but he couldn't. He was just so damned mad. The military had been his crucible, his home, and his god, and the fact that Lacey was using it to put hits out on people like Ernie felt like such a terrible betrayal. And Ernie was supposed to be *safe* here, dammit, and a part of him knew that there was no such thing as safe—and that if watching Troy Gonzalez get shot had proved anything, it had proved that—but this wasn't rational, this wasn't a thing that could be proved, this was *Ernie* and—

Ernie, who was cupping his cheeks and pulling him into a hard, grounding kiss.

Ah! God! Burton devoured him, took great gulps of Ernie into his soul, drank him like… like nectar.

He tasted salt with the nectar, his own tears, and kept kissing because he didn't want to cry, he just wanted to keep feeding his soul with Ernie's warmth and his strength and his passion.

The kiss climbed, amped, became frantic and life-giving until Burton pulled away and cried out, for a moment confused into thinking it was orgasm, but it wasn't.

It was sobs.

Pissed off and worried and needing the man in his arms like the desert needed the sky, he fell apart in Ernie's arms and cried like he hadn't cried since that bad intel in Fallujah when he'd come apart on First Lieutenant Jason Constance with a dead child in his arms.

EVENTUALLY THEY wandered back in, passing up the rest of the walk entirely. Ernie just dried his face and kissed his cheek and murmured, "Family. Mindless TV. Normal." And that was that.

Burton found himself falling asleep in front of *A Christmas Story* like every other family in America, including his parents.

He'd sent them a card this year, and suddenly, Ernie leaning on his shoulder, he had a wish to see them, to introduce them to Ernie. He wasn't sure if they'd care or not that Ernie was a he and not a she—he'd always been so invested in a career in the military, even from middle school, that he hadn't thought much about who he'd marry. He'd assumed it would be Ariana, but even that had been sort of a blurry, half-formed idea.

Roger and Anita Burton, and his little brothers—would they look at Ernie and see someone good? Someone pure-hearted?

Burton swallowed. When this was over, maybe he should write them and see.

The movie ended, and Ace and Sonny, who had leaned on each other easily during the movie in a way Burton didn't often see them touch, stood up and wished them good night. Sonny called to Duke, who trotted in after them, and Burton heard Ernie exhale in relief.

"What?" he whispered.

"It means they won't be having sex tonight. They're really loud."

Burton snickered. He'd been there when they'd had sex—they actually weren't that loud, but maybe Ernie, attuned to every thought, every breath, every emotion in the house, heard them louder in his head than they were to Burton's ears.

"I am sleeping on the futon," Jai announced. "I'm going to take off my pants now."

He pushed up from his spot on one of the pillows on the floor, and Ernie and Burton got up quickly.

"Going to bed now," Ernie said brightly. "Wait just a second! We don't need to see your undies!"

"Who says I don't go without?" Jai baited, and Ernie let out a little squeak.

"'Cause you don't want to be shown up by me, big man," Burton said easily and was rewarded by Jai's belly laugh.

"You only think so. But go to bed. You make me lonely just looking at you."

And that was probably the truth.

Ernie tugged his hand until they were in Burton's room, and Burton looked around, surprised.

It didn't feel so much like his room anymore.

"What did you do to it?" he asked, trying to put his finger on it. Ernie had hung a quilt up on the west-facing wall, over the window, which was probably a good thing. In the summer it didn't matter how much they cranked up the swamp cooler, this room got stifling, and the quilt would help. There were heavier drapes on the north window too, and Burton realized they were probably there so Ernie could sleep, but it was more than that.

Ernie had ordered a shelf for Burton's doodads, the ones Ace and Sonny had bought, and he'd put up a picture—on photo paper—of Ace and Sonny, and one of Ace, Sonny, Jai, and Alba, like a family picture.

And there was a more colorful comforter on the top of Burton's tan quilt.

And the place smelled....

Like cedar and pine. Like rich earth.

Like Ernie.

"It's your place now," Burton said, feeling an absurd drop in his stomach. It had been his church.

"No. I just keep it for you. Don't worry. It's still got your mark on it."

But Burton didn't see that—not at all.

And he was reassured by it.

"You're here," he murmured, pulling Ernie to him in the still-dark room. Between the quilt and the blackout curtains, he could barely see Ernie's outline, but that was fine. Better. He worked in the shadows, did things best left to the dark.

Ernie's touch was his light in the darkness.

As they fell upon each other, he closed his eyes and saw daylight, the long hills and outlines of the desert.

Ernie's pale face, peeking out of the shade, a small moon in the shadows, shedding a thin silver glow.

Fish and Shark

BURTON HAD always treasured his time at Ace and Sonny's. When he stayed for longer than a day, he often made his way out to the garage, grabbed a spare jumpsuit, and went to work. Ace and Sonny had needed to train themselves on the diagnostic machines that modern mechanics relied on, but Burton could reprogram them to work better, to be more efficient, and to deal with new engines without needing the pricey upgrades.

It was good to remember that he had legit job skills, and that he could be a useful human being who didn't kill other human beings.

Of course, the garage was closed for Christmas Day, and while they had some business on the twenty-sixth, Jai, Alba, and Ernie all convinced Ace and Sonny to take the twenty-seventh off and go somewhere.

Burton could see Sonny lighting up like a halo at the thought of going to the ocean, even in winter.

Burton and Jai worked hard that day—a lot of other people had the same idea of traveling over the holiday. By the time they closed the garage, Burton went inside to find that Ernie had cooked dinner for him, and Sonny and Ace's snug little home had become theirs, a fairy-tale cottage gifted to them for but one night.

Burton took good care of himself in the shower before he sat down to dinner.

"Turkey gravy and mashed potatoes," he breathed, enchanted.

"And steamed chard with lemon," Ernie added virtuously.

"And bacon." Burton arched an eyebrow at him.

"Well, I don't think we have to eat healthy until the second of January," Ernie replied, eyes twinkling. "Can you survive?"

Burton bit his lip and smiled uncertainly. "I... this is... this is wonderful," he said.

"But...."

He shook his head. "No buts," he said. "No reservations. You're just... you did this super nice thing for me. I... I didn't even get you a present."

Ernie grinned. "Well, you *sort* of got me a present."

Burton had to laugh. Two nights in a row of sleeping next to each other—in a bed—and making love and talking quietly.

"You deserve that every night," he said throatily. "Every night, you deserve to know someone will be there."

"But military couples deal with it all the time," Ernie told him simply. "It's not perfect—I get that. But you're saving the world, Lee. And, you know, all I did was make dinner."

Burton took a bite and smiled. "It's perfect."

"Thanks for coming for Christmas."

Burton grinned wickedly. "Many, many times."

Ernie grinned back. "Plus however many we do tonight."

Well, many, many more, actually.

But even more important—even scarier—were the moments in between the lovemaking. The silent, breathless moments of Ernie sprawled on his chest, exploring his skin with dancing fingertips, so content it radiated off him like a cat's purr.

Burton fell into those moments and found peace there, smelling his skin and shivering under the gentleness of his touch.

Each breath of peace was a plate of armor he pasted on his soul to defend himself from the grim job ahead.

"How much longer?" Ernie asked the next morning as Burton loaded up his truck.

"A month, maybe." He wasn't sure what told him that, except, "I really can't keep faking it for Rivers and Cramer. Lacey's going to move on them soon, and I'm going to have to show my cards." He sighed. "Also, the money is running out. I know in the middle of the month he's planning to make a trip to the capitol—there are some lobbyists he wants to talk to there who will take his requests to Washington."

It was so frustrating! The bug in Lacey's office was helpful, but as of yet he hadn't been able to get a bug into Lacey's *quarters*, which would have been *more* than helpful. Burton had the feeling that Lacey met with his pets—Adkins, Gleeson, Leavins—in his quarters, or even somewhere else. That attack as he'd left had been pretty coordinated, and he hadn't caught wind of it at all. Also, Lacey had sent Leavins on a flight without backup, and that took planning. He was definitely doing his talking somewhere else.

But Ernie caught what he wasn't saying. "Wait—if it's that close, doesn't that mean it's going to get more dangerous?"

Well, shit. Kid never had been stupid.

"Try not to worry?" he said gamely, knowing that was some class-A bullshit right there.

Ernie just shook his head and held Burton's cheeks between his palms. "You know how you can't figure out what to do with me?" he asked, cutting to the heart of Burton's uncertainty with a few words of truth.

Burton closed his eyes, remembering how they moved in the dark. "Sometimes I know exactly what to do with you," he confessed.

"Keep thinking about how to make that happen as often as possible," Ernie whispered. "And then you'll know what to do with me."

Burton growled and wrapped his arms around Ernie's shoulders with all the possession in his soul.

"I just want to protect you," he said brokenly. "Just want to keep you safe."

"There's nowhere safer than right here. Remember that while you're saving the world."

Burton had to close his eyes or Ernie's big, fathomless brown infinity pools would capture him inside Ernie's soul and never let him go.

It was hard enough tearing himself away from Ernie's final kiss so he could hop in the truck.

"Don't forget about me," he said absurdly.

"Stay safe while you're saving the world." Ernie bit his lip like he was holding his sadness in, and Burton nodded before shutting the door. He was halfway back to the damned base before he realized his eyes were leaking, and he felt like a fool because a grown-assed man shouldn't cry over leaving a lover behind, particularly not one in Burton's line of work.

But Ernie was fragile, and Ace and Sonny didn't get back until that night, and even after they got back, the world was the world.

And Lee Burton knew exactly how perilous that world really was, and the thought of his lover adrift in it without a Burton for protection gutted him as nothing ever had in his life.

THE BASE was dead quiet over the holidays—apparently all good assassins got time off for Christmas. The guys who thought they were still in the military had been granted leave, and Burton came back to a diminished staff. He used the time to cull through Lacey's email, looking for some hints as to what was coming next.

He didn't have long to wait.

He's hitting up lobbyists on the twelfth.

His text to Jason—in the bathroom once more—was more than a little bit panicked.

Needs funding?

Yeah. Almost has them locked. Has three he can't buy—WILL TAKE THEM OUT.

The order was for the seventh—which, Burton assumed, was when his pet rabid bulldog got to use his digits again.

Names?

Burton sent the names and followed with *Has home addresses. Make families disappear.*

Really?

Because that was pretty ballsy, taking out the families, right?

Yeah. There'd been hints in the emails, back and forth from Lacey to the lobbyists, that collateral damage was the price you paid. *They're one more threat from giving up.*

Why won't they tell anyone?

Burton blew out a breath. *That a commander of the US Navy is threatening them with bodily harm if he doesn't get funding for his secret behavior experiment? Who will believe them?*

He'd once seen Jason Constance shatter his knuckles on a brick wall in frustration. He waited for a primal scream to come over his phone and wasn't disappointed.

AUUUGGGHHH!!!! WHY IS THIS BASTARD SO SLIPPERY?

Because he's coated with the slime of respectability, sir.

I hate you for that sentence. We'll put everybody into custody and maybe put someone in the room—we may not be able to bust this guy yet, but we can protect them.

One more thing, sir.

?

And Burton took a deep breath. It was time. *A lawyer—Ellery Cramer—and a PI—Jackson Rivers—are both onto this guy. They're going to start looking into him when they get back on the 10th. On the one hand, half the jacket I sent you I got from what they dug up on one of his experiments gone wrong. On the other....*

They're in danger too.

They are.

We can't warn them. We can't even tell them we're watching.

Sir?

I have no authorization for this investigation, soldier. And now you know. I've been pulling Bob's-in-the-bathroom since Chicago. I will probably be demoted when this guy is ended—be prepared.

Burton swallowed. Oh. Once he'd broken his original radio silence and told Jason he was part of Corduroy and working on an abandoned military base, he'd apparently destroyed Jason's career. Jason could have turned him in right then and put the op in someone else's hands, or he could have stayed rogue and tried to bring Lacey down.

I won't work for anybody else. Hell, he might not work for *anybody* after this. But at this point he wouldn't work for anybody but this man, who had his back.

I don't want anyone else on my team. Let's get him. Let's tie him up in a bow. Let's make him so neat they can't ignore him. And then we'll keep our jobs.

Sure.

He ended the text convo wondering… just wondering….

And then he went back to his com and his computer and began siphoning money from his active accounts. Not a lot from each one. Not enough to cause eyebrows to raise.

Just enough for maybe a dream.

TWO DAYS later Rivers and Cramer got home. He listened to them bicker as they walked through the door, and then he listened to—amusingly enough—Rivers talking to his cat.

It was almost as personal as what Rivers and Cramer said in bed, although far more amusing.

"Look at you. You're drooling. Motherfucker is *drooling* all over my sweater. You know, this is a new fucking sweater, asshole—you sure you want to… yeah, sure. Make me your personal toothbrush. Look! White fur! Goes with everything! Jesus, you're dumb. Yeah, sure, I'll go for kisses. Push your whiskers back on me, motherfucker, see if I care. Yeah, okay, fine. Scratches. Right there? Right there? God, you're easy. Just a big slutty motherfucker, missing his dick. Hey, don't blame me about the no-dick thing, that's Ellery's fault. He chopped off your balls and your dick disappeared."

"Still not sorry!" Cramer called from the other end of the house.

"Of course you're not! You didn't dream about kittens one day!"

"You want kittens? Let's go to the pound. Let's get some fucking kittens." Cramer's voice grew nearer—and softer—as he spoke. Burton pictured him standing behind Rivers, arms around his middle. Ace and Sonny didn't show much affection in front of other people. Hard men in a hard land. But Cramer had grown up rich, and he seemed to want to shower Rivers with the affection Rivers had never known.

"If we get them before they're fixed, we can adopt them pregnant," Rivers said, and Burton wanted to groan—who couldn't hear the twelve-year-old smirk in his voice?

"Maybe just get one. Not pregnant. You know, to sort of keep Billy Bob company."

Rivers snorted softly. "You hear that, buddy? He wants to replace you."

"I said nothing of the sort!"

"Wants to replace you with another cat who's got no dick. You'll see how it is, you no-thumbs-having motherfucker. Gonna be no-balls to the walls cats-without-dicks. You can have a support group."

"Jackson?"

"Mm?"

"Shut up, put the cat down, and kiss me."

"God, you're…."

Burton smiled softly to himself. They were barely home and ready to christen the bed again.

"Bossy," Cramer whispered breathlessly when the kiss ended. "And I want to ride you like a show pony, so deal with it."

"Fine." But Rivers didn't sound that put out. It wasn't until they were in the bedroom—shocker—and doing things Burton could only dream about since Ernie wasn't there with him, that Burton realized paying a price for things never went away.

A yelp of pain—of legitimate, shudder-inducing pain—interrupted their sex noises.

"Shit! Jackson! Are you okay—?"

"Fine, swear. Let's change position—it'll be fine—"

"Here—just stay there for a minute—"

"No, don't worry—I'll fix it—"

"But maybe the best way to fix it is to stay off of it!"

"Or maybe I just need to push it a little harder—you think about that? *Ouch! Fuck!*"

"Frankly, no—now lie down and let me get you some ice and some ibuprofen."

Burton heard the pause in the action with a little disappointment and realized he'd actually been looking forward to hearing them make love.

Two things hit him then, so hard he saw stars.

The first was that his guys weren't ready. Lacey was going to be in town in two weeks, and Rivers was still not 100 percent.

The second was that he missed Ernie so bad he couldn't breathe.

HE HIT his bunk when the guys went to bed—that was his day. This night he slipped out without even realizing where he was going. He knew Ernie's walks by now, caught him by surprise right after he'd turned back toward Ace and Sonny's.

Until the truck rumbled to a stop on the shoulder, he hadn't even articulated why he was there—not even in his own mind.

It wasn't sex.

It wasn't even worry, exactly.

"What's up?" Ernie asked, trotting up with Duke, a surprised smile on his face.

Burton just shook his head. "Just… just needed," he rasped unhappily. "Needed to see you. Just…. New Year's Eve is tomorrow."

Ernie took his time and fit himself against Burton's body. Felt like he belonged there. "I am aware," he said softly.

"I… I don't know what's coming." He sighed. "I never know what's coming—that's why I got into this business in the first place. But you… you need to know what's coming, and…." Even with Ernie in his arms, he started to shake. "I just want to know you're safe," he whispered. "How do I know you're safe when I don't know if I can be with you to take care of you?"

Ernie buried his face in Burton's shoulder. "Don't you get it?" he asked after a long moment. "I can take care of myself—been doing it for years. And now I've got people who can step in. You've done your *job* taking care of me, Lee. It's not your job I need. I can keep on keeping on… but I need to know I have you before I can think about losing you."

Cosmic booty call, Ace had called it. Burton shooting through Ernie's orbit like a comet, knocking him off his routine, and careening away again. He tried to pull away, tried to form the words *Forget about me, kid*, but Ernie was so warm against him, so giving. He tilted Ernie's face up so he could look in his eyes and end their worlds and kissed him instead.

Sweetly.

Gently.

No endgame in sight.

He just couldn't stop.

He couldn't tell Ernie no. Couldn't tell him it was over. Couldn't end it.

The kiss, fervent and giving, was all he had.

Ernie broke off and leaned his forehead against Burton's, and Burton stroked his cheek with his battered knuckle.

"Why'd you come, Lee?"

"Because I thought I could end it," he said, his chest sore.

Ernie let out a little moan and kissed him harder, his hands going to Burton's belt like he'd pull down his pants right there on the side of the road.

"No," he said, catching hold of them. "That's not why I won't quit you."

"Then why not? Tell me so I can keep doing it! Because you can't just leave me. You can't—"

"Because you're you, Ernie. Because I hear you in my head when I'm alone and you're the only thing that keeps being alone from being horrible. Because you can calm my friend down and keep him from the worst parts of himself when even his boyfriend despaired of ever giving him peace. Because you know I like Chinese food, but only the good stuff."

Ernie nodded and took a deep breath. "Then why even think about it?"

"I'm ready to die for my country, Ernie. But God, wouldn't it be easier on you if you just never saw me again?"

"No." Ernie took a step back and crossed his arms, glaring. "No, it wouldn't be easier. It would actually suck worse."

"There are better, easier men out there—"

"And I've fucked a lot of them," Ernie said brutally. "Is that what you wanted to hear?"

Burton rubbed his stomach. "No. Actually, no."

"Because I'm the only one you really want, right?"

He sighed, conceding. "Yeah."

"We haven't used condoms—I know you're on PrEP, and Ace made me go get tested—"

"He *what?*"

"Twice. Did you want to know that? I didn't tell you. I said it would only be you and you believed me and I wouldn't break that promise. But I figured we should both know."

"I didn't even think about it," he admitted. "I—"

"I'm your only guy and you're covered. Why would you worry about it? My point is, we've already made plans to be exclusive, asshole. You may not have realized it, but we're a thing. I have plans for the future in my head. And I get that us together in a house alone with nothing to do but stare at each other is not in the cards, but...." And now the anger that had sustained him seemed to slip away, water, lost in the damp sand of the winter desert. "But we can find a way."

Burton nodded. He might not even have a job after this.

What would he do without a job?

Ernie was offering him a way out, a person and a place to be. He thought he'd come to break up with Ernie because he had neither of those things.

Turned out Ernie had them both.

He swallowed against the tightness in his throat, his chest. "Kid, do you ever get tired of reminding me who I am?"

"No." Unequivocally. "I will *never* get tired of remembering who you are."

Burton nodded and held out his arms. "I can't stay," he rasped. "I can't... I can't stay."

Ernie ran into his embrace again. It took him until the chill settled into both of their bones and Duke started to yip with the cold to rip him away. He gestured to the truck, but Ernie shook his head.

"I'm a mile away from home," he said. "Just... I gotta pull my shit together before I walk in or Ace'll know." He wiped his cheek with the back of his hand.

"He already knows," Burton said hoarsely. "Ace knows every time. He knew even when I didn't know what this was doing to you. Get in the car, Ernie. Let me take you home. He'll pick up the pieces if you let him."

Ernie nodded without answering and climbed into the pickup. When they got to the garage, he waited until Burton could put it into Park before taking his hand and kissing it.

"Have some faith, Lee," he said, but Burton heard tears in his voice still.

"You too, kid. Don't give up on me."

"Call me Ernie and I won't."

Burton looked him in the eyes. "Ernie, I'll find a way to come back to you, I promise."

He saw a smile glimmering through the sadness then, and it gave him heart. "That I believe."

He slid out of the truck and into the house, Duke at his heels, and Burton thought that he wasn't sure he could do this dance with the dog and the house and the leaving Ernie here while they both slept alone one more goddamned time.

A WEEK into the New Year, Lacey used Hamblin's plane to take Adkins, Gleeson, and Leavins to Sacramento—and Burton didn't like any of it.

"All three of them?" he muttered to himself. "What kind of op is he running?" So far he couldn't get wind of a hit on Rivers and Cramer, because if he *had*, he'd be in the truck trying to beat the goddamned plane to Sac.

"More surveillance," Manetti said next to him, like they were friends again. Burton regarded him neutrally. They weren't friends. They would never *be* friends. But sometimes he needed to take a leak and text Ernie, and Manetti was the one who minded his com, so he was actively *not* an asshole to let Manetti think he was a friend.

"My guys?"

"Yeah. You said the PI was going back to work. He really hates the lawyer guy—it's the Jewish thing, maybe. But I think he's making sure there's nothing leading to us yet."

"We keep hounding them and they're going to find something," Burton snarled. God, those guys did *not* belong here!

"I know, I know. But hey—he's the one squandering his money on batteries." The listening devices had to be swapped out once every ten days. As far as Burton knew, Lacey had a lapdog in Sacramento who went in as maid service for both places, but he didn't know who. The bug broadcast to a relay station hidden behind their power meter, and that, in turn, broadcast to the government satellite Lacey had commandeered as his own—and *that* device needed periodic maintenance as well. This entire operation was expensive and unnecessary, and it was driving Burton batshit that he had to monitor these guys at this point so he could step in and save their fucking lives!

He was almost relieved when the whole thing went south.

It started with the dumbest of accidents.

"He did what?" Burton asked Hamblin, staring at him in shock after Hamblin called him out of coms to brief him personally.

"He'd just paid the maid service that re-ups the bugs," Hamblin said shortly. "Apparently he'd had more surveillance than I was aware of—some of his targets disappeared, and he was running late for a meeting in the capitol and pulled around a car as it approached a crosswalk. He struck a woman— Melinda Alves, mother of two. She was dead at the scene, and he stopped to threaten the witness who saw the accident and then drove to his meeting."

Burton couldn't seem to scrape his jaw off the chipped tile floor, a part of him relieved that the lobbyists were at least safe, but most of him appalled. "He killed a civilian and then just drove away."

"Yes." Hamblin looked away, embarrassed. "He claims to be dealing with damage control?"

"Like witness tampering and…." Burton flailed, because at this point anything was possible.

"I think he was going to have the car that the witness was driving stolen so they won't figure out that the witness didn't do it. That's who's claiming responsibility now—"

"Because why?" Oh God. This did not get any better.

"Because he threatened the woman's family and the lives of the children she was dropping off at preschool before she saw the crime. She was, I believe, the nanny."

"*Why are you working with this asshole?*" Oh dear God. He didn't like Hamblin—but Hamblin was at least an honest mercenary. He took contracts and filled them. Not a prince, no, but not a haphazard killer who dabbled in behavioral manipulation either.

And Hamblin had the grace to look away. "I'm making plans to stop working with him as soon as he returns and we have a bead on how bad this whole thing is," he said shortly. "You are still on board when I split?"

Burton shook his head. "I'll think about it, man, but if he has his assholes take out a hit on the fuckin' nanny, I'm out of here."

Hamblin nodded. "As am I. I've tried to make it very clear that he's to take out no more civilians, but…." He laced his hands behind his head and blew out a breath. "He's not very bright. And once we started contracts together, he's gotten… well, worse is an understatement. More unhinged is like it."

"What made you think this was a good idea in the first place?" Burton had to ask—for his own curiosity, not because it made any difference.

"I've seen good men die because they couldn't do this job," Hamblin said bleakly. "I've seen good men turn bad and hard men turn soft. He… he said he had a training method that made it easier for a skilled man to kill. I… I should have known in November this was a bad idea."

"November?"

"One of his old recruits was in the news—Tim Owens?"

"The Dirty/Pretty Killer?" Burton managed to sound surprised—and was grateful he knew the name the media had given Owens. For Rivers and Cramer, Hamblin might as well have said "The Bogeyman" or "Nightmare in the Flesh." Burton had known about Owens when he and Ernie had met—there was a bolo on the guy in the black ops community, and general knowledge that if Jason's unit found the guy before the cops, they were to terminate him quietly. One more serial killer who suddenly went "dark" and one less reason to investigate the military for—what Burton had believed—a guy who slipped through the cracks.

And then he'd met Ernie and realized Owens had been chopped up into pieces and forced through the cracks.

What had come out on the other side had nearly ground up Rivers and Cramer as a side dish.

"He's the one. Lacey tried to give me a song and dance about Owens being on a prolonged mission, but have you seen the details of the case?"

Burton nodded. "Pretty fucking grim."

Hamblin squeezed his eyes shut. "I'm telling you, Oscar, if I could go back to before I met this guy and ignore him, I would. I should have bolted when I saw most of his training data depended on a psychic." He shuddered. "He sent five guys to take that kid out, and three of them disappeared. I think the damned psychic killed them—and seriously, more power to him. He never should have been in our sights."

Burton swallowed. Those men had claimed to be working for Corduroy. Apparently Lacey had lost the only three of Hamblin's guys he trusted well enough to let them in on the secret. Maybe that really *was* when he'd started to become unhinged.

"A psychic," he laughed weakly. "I wouldn't have given him the time of day."

Hamblin shook his head in admiration. "No, you would not have—for which I'm profoundly grateful. I promise you, if you follow me in company, I won't leave you to waste in the com room listening to lawyers in love."

Ugh. Of all the men Burton had worked with these last three months, why did *this* one have to be so likable?

And so likely to need killing by the end of the op?

"That *is* incentive," Burton told him soberly. "What are we going to do with these guys anyway? I mean, they're not heading this way. The one guy's mother is apparently a big deal in Washington—do you really want that kind of exposure?"

Hamblin looked at him in horror. "She's what?"

Oh. This was interesting. This had been among some of the few truths Burton had let slip through the lies. "Cramer's mother—Lacey's been putting pressure on her by pulling clients. She's a big deal in Washington—reps defense subcontractors, that sort of thing. I thought you knew."

What happened to Hamblin's neatly goateed face then was a study in rage. All expression slid from his eyes, his jaw, his mouth, to be replaced by the steely concentration of a man who had better things to do than punch holes in walls—but punching the holes would have been fun.

"I did not know," he said icily. "Excuse me. I need to go rip some assholes."

"Sir, yes sir."

Burton stood back and let the smaller man by, waiting until the ring of his hard-soled wingtips disappeared around the corner of the hallway. He didn't return to his com immediately but instead went to the bathroom.

Where he texted Jason all about it.

Then he went back to his com, for all the world like he wasn't getting ready to duck the shit about to come off the fan.

Two days later the shark and the fish discovered the bugs and dropped off the map—and right into Burton's worst nightmares.

Broken Fish, Shattered Bowl

ALBA SLAMMED the landline down with undue force, the ring echoing in the tiny cashier's chamber she occupied. The string of Spanish she spewed was not the sort of stuff Ernie remembered from school.

"Anything wrong?" he asked hesitantly.

She eyed him with distaste. "What are you doing up so early?"

He bit his lip, wondering if he should explain. "Things are itchy," he said at last. "The guys Burton was watching have sort of disappeared. It's hard to explain—we got attached."

Her eyebrows went up. "That is very odd," she proclaimed before scowling again. "You lost two assholes, and we just had two assholes call us up out of nowhere and want to talk to Ace. I think we should trade assholes."

Ernie burst out laughing, and Alba chuckled reluctantly before calling to Ace. Ace had just emerged from under a minivan that—according to him—had an interior that looked like the McDonald's apocalypse and an engine that looked like angels wept there. It belonged to one of the women in the little housing development out of sight to the south, and Ace had apparently been helping the owner of the van—a beleaguered single mother—milk the last few hundred miles out of it before she could afford a new one.

"What's up?" he asked, swaggering over in that way he had and wiping the remaining oil from his fingers. "You look like you ate a pickle."

"Pickles are gross," she announced. "No—this is worse. You remember that lawyer asshole that was here, and his cop buddy?"

"Ex-cop," Ace told her, eyes narrowing. "Why?"

Alba darted a furtive look at Ernie, and he was going to take the hint and leave, even though his senses were screaming he needed to be there.

"Ex-cop called up and told us they needed to talk to you. Said it was important. I told him I'd let you know when you got back."

Ace's turn to raise his eyebrows. "Got back from where?"

"From wherever you were when he called and I said you weren't here!" she explained on a huff. "Anyway—you need to talk to him. He said it had to do with shit coming back to bite you in the ass."

"Or on," Ace said laconically. "Either one sounds uncomfortable. Did he leave his number?"

"I wrote it down." She scowled. "I didn't like him. He was way too clever."

"Well, Mr. Rivers has had quite a life," Ace murmured. "I'll talk to him, don't you worry—Ernie, you look like you swallowed a bug. What the hell is wrong with you, boy?"

It took ten minutes for Ernie to calm down enough for him to even get the story out. When he was done, Ace did little more than blink.

"So these guys discovered the bugs—all the bugs—on Sunday, after Rivers got his melon conked?"

Ernie nodded. That had been two days ago. He pulled out his phone and showed Ace Burton's text string—clearly panicked, because oh my God, if Burton didn't know where the guys were, he couldn't protect them the way he could if they came down here.

"The day after," he said, trying to get the timeline sorted. "And he must have spent about three days in the hospital, and another day down here recuperating, and—"

"And they decided we might know something about the guys they're dealing with." Ace rolled his eyes to heaven. "Do we?"

Ernie shrugged. "I didn't think so until they called you and you guys knew each other. But Burton's been listening to them since November. They've been... I don't know. Growing on us. Like we've got a responsibility to them. It's weird."

Ace bit his lip in thought. "It is. Next time you decide to get a responsibility, get a puppy. I know somewhere you can get something sort of adorable and bigger'n Duke. It's like a pit bull/goldendoodle mix—it's about the goddamned ugliest cute thing I've ever seen."

"You want me to get a Golden Dude Bull?" Ernie asked, not sure he'd heard that right.

"As opposed to adopting a lawyer and PI who might not like knowing your boyfriend listened in on them living their lives for the last three months, I'd think that might be a wise choice! Now shut up and go back to bed. I've got to go talk to Sonny and let him think it's his idea I talk to these guys."

Ernie grunted, feeling the wrongness of being up before six in his bones. "You wake me up if anything happens," he said anxiously. "I'm gonna go tell Burton about this."

"Only if you think it won't freak him out!" Ace called anxiously.

Ernie didn't bother to tell him that Burton needed something that wouldn't make him run for Military-Flunkies-R-Us, because right now he was desperate to know how their guys were really doing.

They just called up? Burton asked him.

Yeah. Apparently they knew Ace from something. He wouldn't say what. Mind. Blown.

Ernie chuckled. *Yeah—we may think it's just a little gas station in the middle of nowhere, but apparently it's the vortex of hell.*

And he's here? Down south?

I guess. He wanted to meet with Ace.

Shit.

What?

You remember those guys you had to assess for Lacey?

No. Ernie remembered telling Burton about them, but he couldn't remember specifics. *Not really. Why?*

Galway was one of them—he almost killed Sonny and Ace when they were deployed. Ace got him first. Owens was another. Rivers is still recovering physically and mentally from taking him out. If Rivers and Cramer looked far enough into Owens....

Oh! Ernie got it now. *They found Ace and Sonny. And if they already knew them from something else....*

There was a pause. Ernie wondered if Burton was finding it as hard to breathe as he was himself. *They're going to be looking for the people you're trying to bring down.*

Tell me how that meeting goes, kid. Anything you can get from Ace.

Should I tell him anything else?

Yeah—tell him he really needs to go.

Ernie felt it then. A rumbling storm-cloud feeling, the charge of lightning before it struck.

But it's dangerous. Oh God. *It's really dangerous. Burton—if they go, they'll both be in danger.*

Your gift tell you that?

Yes.

What's it say about them not going?

A wave of blackness rolled over him, so vile it crushed him to his knees.

"Worse," he whispered aloud before texting *Worse.*

Hang in there, Ernie. Have some faith in our guys. You were told to look out for Cramer and Rivers for a reason. We've got to believe you and me can help all our boys get out okay.

Ernie took a deep sobbing breath and tried to convince himself that okay was a thing. *I'm just a flaky dance club kid,* he texted, suddenly so naked he *had* to tell Burton the truth. *Being with you was the best, most awesome, pure and honest thing I've ever done.*

Augh! I'm texting from the frickin' BATHROOM, Ernie! I can't tell you here why there's more to you than that—just believe me that there is, okay?

And oddly enough, that calmed Ernie down. *Okay, Burton. I'll believe you.*

Good. I gotta go. Keep me briefed—I might not be able to text you back, but you need to keep me in the loop.

Okay. I love you.

His heart stopped. He was just so undone. He'd been dispassionate about his rescue because he hadn't *cared*, dammit. His own life had been such a haze of sleep and drugs and dance and just trying to survive in the jumbled roar of the city. But now he'd had peace and he'd stared at the stars and he'd felt Burton's hunger for him as he drove through the dark of night just to hold Ernie in his arms, and he *cared*. And it was amazing and terrifying, and he didn't just care about Burton, he cared about Ace and about Sonny and even about the two guys he'd never met before but somehow he was part of their destiny too.

He cared and he was frightened and he needed Burton to know, that was all.

You and me got business, kid. I'll see you soon.

Well, it wasn't "I love you" back—but it wasn't goodbye either.

Ernie was going to have to be happy with that.

He got up at his regular time and sat with Ace and Sonny over a very tense dinner.

"So," he said casually, "you guys going to Walmart tomorrow?"

Ace swung his head around quickly. "How in the hell did you know it was Walmart?"

Ernie blinked and considered. "I have no idea. Sometimes that shit just pops out of my mouth."

Sonny groaned. "Well, now we *gotta* go!" he muttered. "You got a goddamned witch in the house, what you gonna do, tell him 'No, we're not gonna do what you told us we'd do in the future'? I've seen that movie, and everybody dies anyway. In fuckin' *Barstow*. Jesus God, Ace, why we gotta die in fuckin' Barstow?" Sonny cast Ace a look of pure anguish. "You know I hate that fuckin' town."

"Nobody's gonna die, Sonny," Ace soothed. "And there's Barstow and Barstow, and we're not going to the second one."

"What's the fuckin' difference?" Sonny sulked.

"A better class of Walmart." Ace nodded decisively, like that made all the sense. Then he gave Ernie an assessing look. "But I do think we're both going to go and not just me." He pursed his lips. "So, Ernie—do we tell them? Tell them about you? Tell them about Burton? How much do they need to know?"

Ernie thought about it. "I think... I think you need to see what they want first and what they're going to do about the information. I...." He looked at Sonny sympathetically. "Look, Sonny? I think they're good guys."

"They're fuckin' nosy guys is what they are," Sonny muttered. "I don't know what being good guys has to do with anything—"

"They're good guys," Ernie reiterated, not wanting to fight, especially with Sonny, but needing him to know this. "Sonny, I know you don't get it, but these guys—I've been dreaming about them for months. And... and there's danger tomorrow, for you and for Ace, and there's danger for them too—but it's gonna be worse if you don't go."

"You knew this was coming?" Sonny snapped. "You knew this was coming and you didn't warn us?"

"No, I didn't know this was coming!" Ernie thought hard, because it was a fair question. "I knew something was going to happen with *them*, but I didn't know how they tied into *us*. But I think you gotta go. I just do."

Ace grunted. "I'll tell Rivers tomorrow. No worries. And don't get mad at Ernie about this, Sonny. This is just what happens when you leave unfinished business, that's all. We tried to shoo them away last time, but I don't think they were fooled for a minute."

"That lawyer guy was," Sonny said, voice laced with disgust. "The cop wasn't. He fucking saw everything."

"The lawyer guy was not," Ace argued. "He was just an asshole about wanting to be in our business. The cop was more of a people person."

Ernie had to smile. "What made him a people person?"

And Ace's grunt was pure frustration. "He let his boyfriend talk to me while he went around and talked to all my people. I think he figured out quite a lot doing that."

"You mean he saw past your 'aw, shucks, just a humble mechanic' bullshit?" Ernie asked acerbically. "That must have been a shock."

Ace cast him a sharp look. "Ain't bullshit."

"It so is."

"I don't know what you think I am, Ernie, but Sonny's actually the best mechanic in the shop. About all I'm good for is racing cars *and*," he added with a meaningful look at Sonny, "I don't do that no more."

Ernie glanced at Sonny, who was gazing at Ace with worship in his eyes, as though he bought every goddamned word.

"I know, Ace. Only when we're both in the car, like you promised."

"You buy that?" Ernie asked, to make sure. "That he's just a little ol' street racer?"

"And mine," Sonny said simply. "These are real good fried potatoes, Ernie. I like how you got 'em all crisp in the oil. Mine get mushy, even with onions, but yours are super good."

Ernie pinched the bridge of his nose. "Thanks, Sonny. I'll make you potatoes as often as you like. Ace, you're bigger than this tiny picture you're painting, and you need to—"

"Why?" Ace asked, serving himself some more potatoes and sausage, and then adding some steamed broccoli to his plate like a good boy. "Why do I need to be bigger than anything? This here is the only dream me and Sonny ever had. And it's good. And we love it. Why does it need to be more?"

"It doesn't," Ernie told him, feeling grumpy. "But you at least need to acknowledge that you mean something here. This dream of yours, it's powerful. It's formed sort of a... I don't know. Nexus. Where things cross."

Ace frowned. "Like Rivers and Cramer coming to ask us questions and then have us show up in their investigation later?"

Oh thank God. "Yes. That. Like those guys with the guns and drugs showing up so you could fix their car. Anybody else would have died, but you and Jai aren't gonna be fucked with."

"Like Burton showing up with you," Sonny said guilelessly. "That's weird. I mean, you gotta admit that's weird. You're saying it happened 'cause Ace, he's a... a center. A crossroads. A guy who makes things happen."

Ernie smiled from pure relief. "Yes. And it's important he knows that because it means... well, it means he can get away with shit that some people can't. And it means that some shit is just going to land at his feet that would pass most people by."

"And why's that important to know?" Ace asked, shrugging. "Y'all, it's just a garage—"

"And it's just a meeting at Walmart," Ernie muttered.

"Yup. Me and Sonny, we'll be back before Alba gets off work. You'll keep an eye on her, won't you, Ernie? Tomorrow's Jai's day off."

Ernie huffed out a breath, feeling exhausted by sheer nerves already. "Yeah, fine. I have the feeling I'm going to be going to bed early this morning anyway."

"Good," Ace said pragmatically. "We worry when you're out too late."

Ernie fought the urge to bang his head against the table. "Well, I'll worry about you guys tomorrow. Just, you know, be careful."

"Always," Ace lied, taking another bite of potatoes.

Still, Ernie was reassured. He was reassured while pacing back and forth in front of Alba's cashier stand as she did the midmonth tallies and answered phones and called vendors. He was reassured while greeting the few customers who drove in and telling them the mechanics would be in later that day. He was reassured running across the street and buying him and Alba a late lunch.

He was reassured right up until that thunderhead of wrongness he'd been waiting for all day crashed down on his head and he almost passed out.

ALBA PUT the Closed sign on the cashier's station and helped Ernie into the house, clucking gently. "You magic guys, you get your panties in a twist and it's no good."

"Something's wrong," he gasped. "Alba... I can... I mean, I think you need to go home!"

She grunted. "No. Wait. Somebody's gonna text you. Give it a minute."

Ernie glared at her. "How in the hell would you know that?"

She shrugged. "I'm no *bruja*, but I got a feeling. Is Ace dead?"

He examined that statement. "No."

"Sonny?"

"No. How did you know?"

"Because you'd be sad," she said, like that was a given. "You don't just come here and live and take care of us and give us presents and not be sad. You're scared now—and that's no good. But it's not sad. Here. Take more deep breaths. Hold the dog. I'll make you some tea."

It took fifteen minutes for him to calm down, and just when she set the tea in front of him (the tea that was there only so she could have something to drink when she visited—Ernie made Ace buy it himself) his phone buzzed.

It was Sonny—Ace and Cramer had been taken, and Sonny and Rivers were on their way. Apparently Sonny had convinced Rivers they had a superhero on their side.

Ernie looked Alba in the eye. "Honey, they'll be here in half an hour."

"I'll be gone before they pull up," she promised. "Now text Burton. I think it's time."

Burton, they got Ace and Cramer.

THE HOLY FUCK!!!!

You didn't know it was going down?

I know I'm in the middle of a bad guy civil war, that's what I know. Where's Rivers and Daye?

On their way here. Sonny was freaking out—the only way he could keep Rivers from driving straight after Lacey's men was to tell him about me.

The next pause was interminable. When the text came back, Ernie had to read it three times.

Okay. I've emailed you plans for the military base—they're pretty standard. Text me when they've got a plan. I'll do what's needed.

Wait. What in the hell?

But aren't you undercover?

Not for long. Hang tight. Keep them calm if you can. When you send them to me, make sure they're not insane.

But… but… but….

Lee, you'll be in danger. YOU'LL ALL BE IN DANGER.

Cramer and Ace most of all. I'll stay here and keep them safe. Hopefully I can hand them off to Rivers when it's time. Don't worry about us, Ernie. Hold down the fort, okay?

Burton, can't we just call somebody?

Ernie, if I'm the good guy, I'm who you call. Tell me, what did Sonny say?

He said we needed you to be a superhero.

Then I'm going to be a superhero. 'Cause that's what you guys need. Love you, kid. Just stay safe.

Ernie was never really sure how things went so south after that—or so north after they went south. But he was pretty sure it had nothing to do with his gift and everything to do with the three words Burton texted that he'd never texted and that he must have meant, but Ernie was going to have to look him in the eyes to see if he meant them.

The key part being look him in the eyes.

Shark in the Tank, Ace in the Hole

BURTON ALMOST dropped his phone.

His hands, abnormally cold and clammy in the bathroom, were shaking, and after he rescued the phone, he had to try twice to put the damned thing in his pocket.

Then he realized he really did have to pee.

They had Ace. And Cramer.

Sonny and Rivers were on their way.

Oh Jesus.

Everything in his worst nightmare scenario and it was driving to the base, and he didn't have a damned idea how it was going to play out.

Anticipate the target?

One of the first things he'd learned under Jason Constance. Anticipate where your target will be. Well, he wasn't trying to take Ace and Cramer out, but he *was* trying to acquire them. If Lacey didn't kill them right off, where would he put them?

The obvious answer was the brig.

Burton had been trying to bug Lacey's office again—it had been locked during his absence, and picking the series of three locks, two of them electronic, had been taking a maddening amount of time. But he'd come prepared every day.

Before he went back to the com room, he ran to the back of the nearly deserted administration building and hid the bug in the brig, up over the doorframe. Not the best hiding place in ordinary circumstances, no, but the whole place was about to go up like a wasp's nest, and Burton figured it would be overlooked. He made it back to his com station and slid into his seat like his world wasn't about to crash to the ground.

"Where the hell you been?" Manetti hissed. "Gleeson, Adkins, and Leavins are about to get here with Rivers and Cramer. Lacey's gonna be pissed you didn't tell him they were coming down here."

Burton worked hard at being innocent. "I didn't know—it's not my fault they found the damned bugs!"

It hadn't been, either. In fact, it had been *Lacey's* fault for trying to take Rivers out while he was running the investigation—but that wasn't the important thing.

"How in the hell did they get Rivers and Cramer anyway?" Burton asked, masking his stab of relief. Rivers and Cramer. Lacey didn't know Ace wasn't Rivers. Oh, thank God for bad intel.

Manetti grunted. "Cramer activated his phone this morning. Lacey must have called in a favor with someone who's got big bucks—they managed to track it even after he turned it off. I'm thinking it was a satellite or something."

Burton looked at his display and saw the same dead space he'd been seeing since they'd gone dark. "How do you know he activated it this morning?" Burton said, staring at him. "I didn't even see that."

Manetti rolled his eyes. "Showed up before you reported in. It was just sort of blinking there—I alerted Lacey since he's the one so all-fired excited about these guys."

Burton grunted. "How long have you worked for Hamblin?" he asked, wondering if he even owed Manetti the time of day at this point.

"About three years, why?"

"Would you say you're loyal to him?"

Manetti shrugged. "Like any other job, I guess. I'm gonna trade up."

"Great. A word of advice, though, from me to you. You can't trade up to a sinking ship. Lacey's people are cray-cray or incompetent, and Lacey's a raving lunatic. You take that any way you want to and go ahead and tell anyone you feel like that I said that. But if you can, maybe avoid hitching your wagon to that particular star, you hear me?"

Manetti gaped at him. "Wow. That's… wow. Don't burn any bridges or anything on your way out of here."

"Man, if bridges are gonna blow, I'm not the one who's torching them. Shit."

At that moment there was the ring of boots on the tile. Nobody walked in front of the coms room, but Burton's entire body was tingling—it was all hitting the fan. Manetti went to his own coms, and Burton pulled out his Jason phone.

Shit's going down. Have men and medivac on standby. They've got Cramer.

Rivers?

Cramer and a civilian they think is Rivers. Cramer'll keep up the charade.

Roger that.

Burton expected Jason to ask him why later, but he was going to have a hard time answering how he knew that was the way it would go down.

It's just that he'd spent months monitoring these guys, and he felt like he knew them. If Lacey found out Ace was a bystander, he'd have him taken out. Cramer would cover for Ace because that would be the decent thing to do.

God help them all when Ace's life depended on the word of a decent man.

Pain of the Shattered Bowl

RIVERS'S PAIN was going to unmake Ernie one silent howl at a time.

He'd been almost excited when the car had pulled up the drive, right after Alba's left—he really *did* want to meet the guys he and Burton had been watching for the past few months.

But then Rivers had stepped foot over the threshold, and Ernie had almost doubled over.

Sonny Daye was in a lot of pain—but he hid that pain down the well with the hurt child he had been.

Rivers's pain was entirely adult, entirely self-aware, and entirely running near the surface of his skin. They'd shaken hands, and Rivers had locked eyes with him and damned near disappeared.

He was apparently stronger than Ernie, because he'd managed to surface when Ernie would just as soon he go under into a healing coma and let Ernie sing his psyche to sleep until it stopped screaming.

But part of Jackson's pain was fear over Ellery Cramer, and Ernie's plan wasn't going to work.

Which sucked. Something needed to work.

Especially because the plan they came up with to get the guys out was both dangerous and simple.

And thanks to Jai, who Ernie had texted while he was waiting for Sonny, it involved the land mines around the military base and a shit-ton of C-4.

"Uhm, Jai?" Ernie hissed while Rivers was studying the schematic on the computer.

"What?"

"You *do* know how to handle munitions, right?"

Jai all but rolled his eyes. "I did many things for my former employer," he said with dignity.

"Don't you still officially work for that guy?" Ernie wanted to know. His understanding was that Jai was out on loan to Ace and Sonny, and he had no idea how that worked.

"He does not pay me unless I do jobs for him. I am usually busy with cars." Jai didn't need to shrug his massive shoulders, but Ernie got the picture.

"Does he know you have his C-4?" Because God help them all if a Nevada-based Russian mob boss decided to come looking for it.

"It's not his," Jai said, sounding defensive. "I have many things left over from those days. It's not even all the C-4 I have. It doesn't take much, really, to create a smoking crater out of a Toyota."

Ernie tried hard not to panic and remembered that Burton had faith. Then he heard Sonny on the phone to Alba, telling her to check in on Duke in case she didn't hear from any of them, and realized Sonny assumed Ernie was going with them.

Burton had told Ernie to stay put.

Ernie was unprepared for the flare of anger in his chest. God*dammit*. He cared about these people, and they were driving onto a fully loaded military base full of mercenaries with no better plan than to blow up the Toyota and grab their guys while the rest of the world went apeshit?

And Burton? Where the hell was Burton anyway? Burton was sitting in the middle of the mercenaries, and he was going to fix this clusterfuck single-handedly? Bullshit! Just pure fucking bullshit.

Rivers—dirty-blond hair sticking straight up, pretty green eyes bloodshot from worry—was trying not to implode at their kitchen table, and the only thing keeping Sonny from being equally as fucked up was the damned dog he wouldn't let go of.

They needed Ernie. If Burton thought of Ernie as a goddamned inconvenience, these guys needed him. Of course he was fucking going.

The drive to the abandoned air base was as tense a thing as Ernie ever hoped to live through. He had to touch-calm Sonny down in the first ten minutes because Rivers was gonna pop, and every conversation he had with Rivers to calm him down, maybe just take some of his pain so he could freakin' function, came to a dead end.

They rolled up to the military base, taking a dirt frontage track to the main road before they were close enough to be spotted. Ernie could feel palpable waves of fear roll off the man—not for himself, but for everybody in the car, including Ernie.

"You know what you're doing?" Rivers asked one last time.

"I'm taking the SUV and following Jai in the Toyota. When we get to the land mines, we're rigging the Toyota with a brick and a bungee cord, and it's going to drive over one of the mines so it can explode." The land mines were an unpleasant surprise—and one of the things Burton had clued them in

153

on that had probably saved all their lives. It was good to have the intel, and Rivers had spotted them off the dirt track as they'd ridden, but it had been even better that they could use the explosive devices for their own needs.

The hope was when the Toyota went *kaboom*, all the people in the base would run toward it. Sonny would stay at the airstrip to serve as cover fire if they needed it, and Rivers would be free to run inside the camp itself and pull Ace and Cramer out.

Simple and hopefully effective—Jai had confessed quietly to Ernie that he wasn't sure if the land mines would actually set the C-4 *off*, but Ernie had hope they'd find *something* that could set it off by the time things got dire.

Except here they were at the base, and so far all Ernie knew was that Jackson Rivers was so tightly wound, his entire intestinal system was probably coiled like a spring.

He didn't show it, though. He and Sonny got out of Rivers's SUV, and after some discussion with Jai, they took off for the back of the hangar, Sonny trotting almost cheerfully next to Rivers's fluid run. Ernie had to leave them to themselves and hope, while he and Jai made their way down the pitted jeep track toward the west side of the base.

Ernie had all his senses on high alert or he would have plowed into the back of Jai's Toyota when it came to an abrupt halt just as they cleared the last building of the base.

He sat for a moment, heart hammering in his ears, and Jai got out of the Toyota, leaving it to idle while he came to talk to Ernie.

"What?" Ernie asked as the window was still rolling down.

"I'm pretty sure there is a land mine in my way," Jai said casually. "I'd like a second opinion before I decide to drive the car over it."

Ernie gaped at him and backed the Infiniti up damned quick. When he had about twenty yards between him and the Toyo, he put the car in Park and trotted back to look.

The lump of ground looked like the land mines they'd seen coming in—like a hump of land, newly unearthed, that had been left undisturbed for the green of January to cover it. Ernie stared at it in confusion.

"But why would you put a land mine right here?" he asked. "It's right in the middle of the path—how would you transport back here?"

"Maybe there is something they don't want people to see on this section of land?" Jai suggested tentatively. It was not like the big guy to show curiosity—this really must be an anomaly.

"You know"—and he hated to do this—"I'm going to have to ask Burton."

"Yes. Why haven't you done so already?"

"Because he doesn't know I'm here?"

Jai's rolled eyes were a thing of beauty. "Children. He tells you to stay safe so he doesn't need to worry, and you get upset because you think you are a burden. He is a very smart man and so are you, but together you are tremendously stupid. By all means, have a text war about how much you don't love and need each other. We only have, what? How much time did Rivers give us?"

Ernie looked at his phone. "Thirty minutes?"

Jai let out a sigh. "There needs to be a way. Here—I've got something in my car that might work."

Ernie looked at his phone again and took the coward's way out.

Jai found a land mine on the service road, south side of the base heading west. He wants to know if it's the only one and why it's there.

He waited a moment, watching as Jai rummaged through the trunk of his car, which proved surprisingly full of camping gear.

"You go camping?"

"Da."

"Where?"

"Tehachapi Mountains, by the lake. It's not a forest, but it's not a garage in the fucking desert either."

For a moment the time crunch they were in was completely forgotten. "But… but… *when*? And you don't say anything to Ace or Sonny!"

"On my days off, once a month or so. And I say nothing because then there's confusion. Do I want them to go, do I want company—they don't want to come camping with me, any more than I want to go to Disneyland."

Ernie almost bought it—stoic Russian bastard. But there was a faint whine in his voice, a disclaimer. "Do you get laid in the Tehachapi Mountains?" he hazarded.

Jai grunted. "Often and well. But he is married and I don't really like him. What can I say—a man has needs. Yes! I knew it was here!"

He held a small electronic device aloft in triumph, and Ernie blinked. "What the hell is that?"

"I used to work construction. It's a stud finder. Let us see what it finds, yes?"

Ernie couldn't help it. "You point your penis at it and see if it lights up."

A terrible sound came out of Jai's mouth, a cross between an elephant choking and a donkey dying of asthma. Ernie gaped at him for a moment, unsure if he needed to run for his life or start the Heimlich maneuver, and then he realized what that sound was.

Jai was laughing.

"Oh my God! You are very funny!"

Ernie felt a weak smile at the corner of his mouth. "I do my best. Do you want me to—"

"Stay there and talk to Burton," Jai ordered summarily. "It's not that I don't trust you not to walk on a land mine because you suddenly see a bird, but I don't trust you not to walk on a land mine because you suddenly see anything *not* a land mine."

Ernie grimaced. "Very on point," he admitted. "Just don't blow yourself up or anything."

"You want to help?" Jai asked, as though considering something.

"No, Jai, I just defied my sort-of boyfriend and risked my life to drive out to a military base and watch you blow shit up."

Jai held out his hands in placation. "Yes, yes, you're very fierce. Hiss, kitten, hiss. And when you are done ruffling your fur, look through the car you are driving. I need a detonator."

"I don't think that's standard issue in a lawyer's briefcase, Jai—besides, I don't know what one looks like."

"One looks like a battery or an electronic doodad of some sort. The irritating one who got kidnapped probably has three laptops all on his own. Even the cop—"

"Ex-cop—"

"He stinks like bacon. He probably has one because he is not stupid. Look for those—now shut up and let me point my penis at the hole." He snickered then and started to aim the laser pointer, first at the mound of dirt and then away from it, paying close attention to the LED readout on the screen. Ernie left him to his stud finding and started his search, feeling a little sad as he pawed through Rivers's and Cramer's belongings.

Cramer had what Ernie had expected—garment bags, a neatly packed suitcase with a few adult goodies, and a briefcase with an easily pickable lock. Yup—there you go—the laptop! Ernie set it aside and prepared himself to dive through Rivers's stuff.

Unlike Cramer's things, there was a fine residue of the pain Rivers carried. Ernie wasn't usually touch sensitive—he couldn't read objects with just a brush of the fingers. But because he'd met Jackson—and because the man's psyche was so strong and so wounded at the same time—he could definitely feel it now.

It made his hands ache, like arthritis, and he really hated that, once again, these two men were being invaded for their usefulness, their privacy and dignity sacrificed with barely a thought. And that's when he found them. Rolled up in a pair of tattered underwear sat a couple of child's action figures from a show Ernie didn't recognize. The figures themselves were plastic, cheaply made, and most of the paint had been rubbed off from hard use.

The love, the simple joy these two toys carried with them soothed some of Ernie's anguish for not being able to help Jackson.

Jackson had joy in him. He'd find it. Ernie had to have faith.

And, hey, while tucking the action figures back in their place, Ernie also found Jackson's *Doctor Who* computer case and the laptop inside it.

Faith he had indeed!

While he was pulling Jackson's laptop out and setting it on top of Cramer's, his phone buzzed against his hip.

There are several active land mines on the path. Tell Jai to avoid at all costs—they apparently put the big meat-grinder ones there—not a lot of noise, but a lot of shrapnel.

Ernie stared at the text and grimaced. Oh dear. *Will do*, he texted. *Glad you're safe.*

Oh. Oh—there was guilt. Burton just hit him with a giant guilt burger, and Ernie wasn't sure how to bite.

Do the ones on the outer perimeter make more noise? He was mostly asking to diffuse curiosity—but he had an idea too.

I have no idea—but they're a different make.

Ernie gnawed on his lower lip. *Will tell Jai.* Then, on a burst of indignation, *And you stay safe too! How's Ace?*

He and Cramer are fine. Bored and pissed and worried, but fine.

Good.

I'm so glad you're not with them.

Guilt, guilt, guilt, guilt… oh fuck it—he couldn't even answer that.

He tucked the phone back in his pocket and waited until Jai returned from stud-finding the next three mounds on the track.

"All land mines?" he asked, guessing from Jai's expression.

"Fuckers."

"Well, we're going to have to set them off here, right?"

Jai scowled. "We have no choice. The other site was better—there was a building to hide behind. This is harder. The Toyota only goes straight for so long—we need to be hauling ass the other direction."

Ernie grunted. "Well, I found your laptops—you set up the C-4, I'll turn the SUV around—"

"Open the back," Jai said judiciously. "I'll jump in as you're driving away."

Ernie blinked. "That's a little dramatic, isn't it?"

"So is having your entrails found in a nearby tree."

"Uh, yeah. Take the computers. Maybe, you know, think happy thoughts, right?"

Jai drilled holes into him from two obsidian eyes. "Yes. That will make us live. Happy thoughts." He contorted his lips back to reveal white, even, ginormous teeth. "Everybody is fine."

Oh yeah. Ernie was peachy-fucking-keen.

It took him a full five minutes to turn the damned Infiniti around because at this point he was so freaked out by the giant land mine *on* the track that he was terrified of every hillock and hump of grass *off* the track. The result was a six-billion-point turn that was probably the origin of the Spirograph and a cold sweat that soaked his underarms.

He finished and checked his rearview mirror to see Jai still sitting in his driver's seat, tinkering with the laptops, and then, because he knew Rivers was probably losing his mind, he texted *Wait for it*, just to let him know they were working on the situation.

He was about to ask if Jai needed help when his phone went off, Kaleo's "No Good" playing for Burton, although Burton had never called—until now.

"You're *here*?" Burton hissed. "Here! What in the actual fuck are you doing *here*?"

"Hi, Lee!" Ernie said cheerfully. "Good to hear from you! Sort of busy!" In his rearview mirror, Jai was rigging the Toyota's steering wheel with a bungee cord, and Ernie had a sudden thought. "Jai!" he hollered out the window. "Not *over* the mine, *on* the mine!"

Jai stared at him for a moment like he was trying to parse what Ernie was saying, and then his eyes got really big. "Mother*fucker*!" And he got back in the car to mess with the steering some more.

"Oh dear God, it's like Abbot and fucking Costello!"

"Well, it's not Burt and Ernie!" Ernie snapped into the phone. "Because if it was Burt and Ernie, *you'd be here* and I'd be with *you*!"

"You think maybe we could have worked this issue out some other time?" Burton asked, and to his credit he sounded legitimately worried.

"I'm *sorry*!" Ernie dropped his voice, because the hell of it was, he really *was* sorry. "They needed me, Burton. I don't know what to tell you. Rivers showed up and he was in pain, and Sonny was there and he just assumed, you know? I was part of the team? And I wanted to be part of the team. I mean, you left me with a *family*, and we worried over Rivers and Cramer like our children—and they were all in danger. And I wanted to help!"

He heard Burton's deep breath dragging at his lungs. "But, baby," he said, voice cracking, "you're... you're the one person I count on being safe."

Ernie gnawed on his lower lip and started to twitch. They were running about two minutes off the schedule Jackson had given him, and he knew their timing had to be close. "I'm a burden," he said, hating himself for saying it right now, but apparently the last thing he might say to Burton had to be the truth. "You can't make yourself break up with me, but you don't want to keep me—"

"*That's not true!*" Burton was whispering, his voice echoing in what sounded like a bathroom. Suddenly Ernie remembered that Burton texted him from the bathroom in an enemy camp and felt a little queasy. Their every interaction had put his life at risk, and Ernie hadn't appreciated that until right now. "I needed time someplace not *here*. But I think about you every fucking minute of every fucking day, do you hear me? As soon as this shit's done with, we can—"

"Burton? Who in the fuck are you talking to?"

"My person," Burton said vaguely, and as much as Ernie didn't want to be a dirty secret, he certainly didn't want Burton to come out about them *now*. "H—it's important."

"Were you going to say he? Get out of the fuckin' bathroom and tell me you weren't gonna say he!"

"Dammit, Manetti, what's it to you?"

"I'll see you later," Ernie muttered, heart in his mouth. Oh God. No wonder Burton thought he was a burden.

"No, dammit—"

"Ernie!" Jai called. "Ernie, step on the gas! Go, dammit, go!"

Ernie looked in the rearview and saw Jai running hell-for-leather toward the back of the SUV while the Toyota took off at alarming speed.

"Oh shit, that's going fast!" He stomped on the gas and the back wheels dug in, spraying Jai with mud just as he leaped into the back of the car. Jai's weight, combined with the traction, dug them in deeper, and Ernie swore.

"Goddammit!"

"Foot off gas!" Jai hollered, and Ernie felt the vehicle rock, *hard*, as Jai pushed it forward, then let it go back, then forward, then back, then forward. *"Now!"*

On the phone Burton was saying, "Manetti, why in the fuck do you give a shit who I'm on the phone with!" and then there was a sharp pop like a fist hitting a metal partition.

"Burton!" Ernie screamed, and Jai yelled, *"Go go go go go!"* as the Infiniti scrabbled for purchase and lurched out of the trench and onto the track, fishtailing as it went. Ernie dropped the phone by necessity and got hold of the wheel as Jai scrambled inside. Jai was reaching for the hatch, hauling it down to close the door, when the Toyota hit the land mine and the whole world went boom.

Boom Fish!

SHIT SHIT shit shit shit.

Burton knew better—he *knew* better than to contact anybody by phone. It was, like, black ops 101, right after Don't Shoot Your Dick Off and Wear Dark Clothing During Night Work—Don't Call Your Motherfucking Boyfriend from the Bathroom When You're Undercover.

But he had to.

First he'd seen Cramer and Ace, and Ace had read him the riot act about how, maybe, if he'd been able to calm Ernie down, Ernie would have been able to calm Sonny down, and, well, this entire shitstorm might not be about to come down on his head.

Great. Ace Atchison, a guy who had retired at master sergeant and who knew shit about black ops, could apparently manage Burton's love life better than Burton.

It stung because it was true.

And Rivers... oh God. Fucking Rivers.

Cramer had been everything Burton was expecting. Slim, disdainful, dry. Cool under fire. But Rivers... the man had been all business, focused entirely on getting Ellery and Ace out alive. But he'd also been sharp, cocky, and smart as fuck.

And boiling sex on two legs.

Burton had been acutely uncomfortable at the same time he'd been scared to fucking death.

"Eight minutes?" Burton asked soberly, keeping his voice too low to echo. "That's not a lot of time."

"Less than you think. Did you know they were gassing a plane for wherever in South America? We've got to get them out of here."

Burton scowled. "Oh, for fuck's sake. There's people at the hangar?"

Rivers shrugged, and in spite of the fact that his whole life was on the line, he made it look like this was easy. "Sonny's got a surprise going. I got no idea when it's going to pop, but we've got—" He checked his phone again. "—six minutes until chaos ensues."

161

"Sonny? Where's Ernie?"

Jackson grimaced. "Dumping a Toyota full of C-4 in a minefield?"

Oh no. Oh hell *no. Everything in Burton's chest, his bowels, his lungs, all of it, froze. "I'm doing you a solid and this is how you repay me?"*

"Hey—you let that kid know he's got you when he's got you and I don't think he'll be so eager to prove himself. But Jai's with him—I think that guy would rather blow himself up than let Ernie get hurt, so he's safe."

Burton scrubbed at his eyes with one hand while he pounded a tattoo on the sink with his other palm. Ernie. Jesus Christ. Ernie was here. *"Goddammit— you couldn't have stayed in Sacramento for a couple more days?"*

"While these assholes listened to us have sex? God no—"

"I listened to you having sex, and I've got one word for you. Soundproofing."

Burton barely managed to let Rivers go without throwing himself on the guy's mercy and begging him to call it off. He couldn't—he knew he couldn't. Rivers had said Hamblin's men were gassing the plane—Ace's and Ellery's lives really *did* depend on getting them out *now*. And even if their lives weren't on the line, Lacey was trying to get away. All the fucking illegal shit he'd been doing, and he was going to be felled by a traffic accident. If a woman hadn't died, it would almost be funny, but Burton wasn't laughing. Lacey was going down, and Burton had to get out of here with the jackets of the other nightmares Karl Lacey and his "training techniques" had loosed upon the world.

Which meant that he had to trust Ernie and Jai and the car full of C-4. Right?

He managed to make it to coms, sweep a look inside, and then wheel around. He was back in the bathroom, in the stall, before he even knew what he was doing. Ernie's voice over the phone was both the best and worst thing he'd ever heard in his life—right up until the part where Ernie started shouting about going *on* the mine and not *over* the mine.

God help him, that was the man he *loved* out there with a load of C-4 in a minefield, and Burton hadn't once told Ernie Caulfield how he felt.

And then Patrick Manetti barged in and Burton didn't have a chance.

Manetti swung at him and missed, hitting the stall door and yelping, until Burton caught his other fist in his hand and bent his arm around his back before shoving Manetti's face up against the wall.

"What's it to you?" Burton hissed. "Who I'm seeing? You don't even know for sure, do you?"

"Lacey hates you," Manetti told him. "He wants you dead so bad he's been offering guys cash out of pocket to take you on. I wasn't gonna, but knowing you're a faggot just makes it—"

The blast hit, throwing Burton against Manetti's back, his arm bent at that impossible angle. The concussion of the blast and Burton's grip forced Manetti's shoulder out of its socket, and he howled, his bladder voiding before the room stopped shaking.

Burton let go of his wrist, and Manetti fell to the ground, moaning—so Burton kicked him in the ribs. "Call me names one more time, asshole," he snarled. "See where it fucking gets you."

"What in the hell was that?" Manetti whined. "We're under attack!"

"God, I hope so." Burton kicked him again. "You got a brain in your fucking head and you will stay there, you hear me?"

"I need a medic!" Manetti wept, and Burton took off from the bathroom at a run.

First he hit the coms room, not surprised in the least to see Hamblin's entire assembly fleeing, whatever equipment they could carry in their arms. Hamblin had run drills on this sort of thing—and the coms had been his people. Burton went to his unit in the corner, hissing when he realized someone else had grabbed the main drive. Well, shit. The good news was, he'd sent a backup of all his research to Jason's and his own account, both of them on encrypted servers. Good luck to anyone trying to figure out who Calvin Oscar really was, but still.

Burton would have wanted his goddamned unit back just on general principle. Since it wasn't going to happen, he pulled his weapon out and held it at ready, taking off at a trot toward Lacey's office.

He was halfway there when Hamblin stopped him, hand to shoulder.

"Everyone's meeting out front," he said. "The explosion came from the west corner—it looks like someone was trying to sneak around the back and got caught up in the minefield. Their vehicle was completely destroyed. Coms is evacuating, and my people are going down to South America—there's room on the plane if you want to come with me."

Ernie.

But Burton had to go on faith, right? Ernie had faith in Burton; it was time for Burton to hope a little.

Otherwise he might as well go out hard, gun in Hamblin's mouth first, Lacey's mouth second, his own mouth third.

Only faith stilled his hand.

Burton swallowed, trying to decide if now was a good time to expose his cover or not. "Won't Lacey want in?" he asked, unfeigned disdain dripping from each syllable.

Hamblin's nose wrinkled in disgust. "Lacey? Lacey sent his pets up north to find Rivers's family—Manetti's surveillance said he stashed a witness of some sort with his brother near Nevada."

Burton gaped. "Now? We're under attack and he sends out a hunting party *now*?"

Hamblin shrugged. "He was a bad bet, Oscar. The worst of my career. But I still have enough to start again. Will you start with me?"

God. He could. Right here and now he could make the call to go undercover with Hamblin. To find more bad guys. To keep the chain going.

To be away from Ernie for another year or more. *Please let him be alive.*

To not know if his boy would be there waiting when he got back. *I'll do anything if he's still breathing.*

"I'll think about it," Burton lied. He didn't want to quit his job, not yet. But a year undercover was someone else's gig. "If you and Lacey are making the split, I want Lacey out—now."

Hamblin shrugged. "It would be... of benefit," he admitted, "to not have that man dogging my shadow."

Burton saw that for what it was—an offer to let Burton take out the guy who'd orchestrated this madness, put the hit out on Ernie, sent psychopaths out into the world under the guise of training.

Do the job the US military was going to ask him to do for free.

"What'll it get me?" he asked, playing for time.

"Anything you want," Hamblin said, meeting his gaze. "For one thing, I won't have my men take you out for being black ops."

Burton gasped. "I am no—"

Hamblin held out a hand. "Don't bother lying. You're too good for Lacey and too good for me. You're well trained, smart, and you obviously have your own agenda. I need Lacey dead. Your government will want the same. Tell me what you need."

Burton's finger trembled on the trigger, but dammit. This guy knew too much they needed. "I need *complete* jackets on the pet snakes Lacey turned loose," he said. He had research—but Hamblin would have it all. "And I need that fucking flag off of US fucking soil." The tattered scrap of corduroy that Lacey had flown since Burton arrived there. The thought of it flying where good troops had once served made Burton's fingers slippery with rage.

Hamblin grimaced. "Done." He paused. "But Lacey needs to be dead by the end of the op. And I can't control his men."

From outside came the sounds of battlefield chaos—men shouting, shots fired, and a really fucking big piece of machinery *kathunk*ing against the ground. Hamblin's look of confusion was a genuine treat.

"I can't control my men either," Burton said, grim humor dripping from his voice. "That explosion was *not* my idea!"

Hamblin's mouth twisted, and for a moment they were sane allies in a sea of crazy. Burton wasn't sure whether to hate himself for that moment or not—it took him years to decide.

But by then he'd blinked first.

"Stay alive," Hamblin warned darkly. "Kill that asshole. Me and my men will be out of your hair and off your territory for a good long time. You've got other things to do."

A particularly loud *thunk* from whatever machinery was going haywire made them both grimace, and Burton lowered his gun. He'd been heading for the back way out, which was where he'd directed Rivers to take Ace and Cramer, and Hamblin had obviously been heading toward the front.

With short, sharp nods, they both took off in their intended directions at a run.

Lacey's men were milling about without direction—Burton heard a lot of shouted questions and no single answer, and not one of them thought to maybe go investigate the explosion on the west end of the base.

As Burton passed between the admin building and a barracks, he could see Hamblin's men gathering in a well-ordered group and Hamblin addressing them. Hamblin's voice rang out and groups of men would break off, heading for the parking lot for probably their personal vehicles and a regroup wherever the plane in the hangar landed.

There were two hangars—a big one, where Hamblin's Cessna sat, along with a Jayhawk and a crippled Black Hawk parked out front, and a long, low one where smaller planes used to be stashed for personal use but now was used to house a few Jeeps and a lot of munitions. Burton entered through the open front of the long garage-style hangar and then moved, staying along the back wall, hiding behind the crates and land vehicles that were stored in the place now. He was nearing the far corner when a short burst of shots rang out.

The place he was using for cover was old and in disrepair, and he found a spot where the aluminum had separated from the four-by-four that held it up. He peered through the space in the building just in time to see Ellery Cramer, weapon pointed at the thin aluminum of the big hangar, staring at a cluster of holes he'd just shot through the siding while Jackson tried to get him to move.

Before he could call to get down, three shots rang out from the hangar itself, and Cramer flew back, gun falling from his fingers, and Rivers fell on top of him, a second too late in trying to save Cramer from his inexperience—and himself.

Oh God. Burton stared, stunned, unsure of himself for the first time he could remember since boot camp. Since high school.

If it had been Ernie, his heart would have stopped.

If he'd just rolled off Ernie's bloodied body, had just checked Ernie for a pulse and come back with bloody hands, he would have died. *Ernie's still out there. Oh God, Ernie's still out there.* And then, while Burton swallowed his heart and tried to form a plan, Jackson Rivers did what Burton wasn't sure he'd have been able to.

He rolled over to his back and fired his clip into the hangar, opening up a grapefruit-sized hole where individual bullet puncture wounds had peeked.

He called out for Lacey once, twice, and then ran to the hangar and checked.

Burton was waiting for the short, quick nod, the one that indicated his work was done, and then Jackson Rivers went back to the only thing that mattered.

The man bleeding on the ground in front of him.

Burton forced the aluminum out farther and pointed his gun, searching the area for enemies, covering Jackson while he and Ellery were helpless, much like he'd spent the past few months covering them by taking their surveillance.

He heard the mechanical *thunk* again, and looked toward the open area in front of the hangars, his eyebrows going up when he saw the Black Hawk performing a deadly dance as it spun around, hindered by the broken propeller Lacey had been bitching about for weeks.

Someone had rigged the thing to go, and just when Burton was admiring the initiative, he realized that Ace was *in* that helicopter, gun pointed out the side bay, as Sonny worked the controls on the inside.

Oh wow.

Go, Sonny Daye—Burton was reluctantly impressed. He was just about to drop his gun and go to help Jackson when he saw a wiry thin figure, snazzily dressed in a pinstripe suit and shiny black shoes, heading out from the other side of the hangar Lacey had just died in.

Burton stayed out of sight, gun trained on Hamblin as he spoke to Jackson.

Hamblin—right there in his sights.

Lacey was dead, as offered, and Hamblin was *right there*, and there were no rules in the combat handbook about letting a mercenary king live.

"My plane is intact," Hamblin told Rivers, "and I'd like you to let me and my men leave."

Even from his position, Burton could see Rivers's confusion. "My gun is empty. What in the fuck—"

"Your friends—they will back off?" Ace and Sonny shouted from the Black Hawk, and Hamblin rolled his eyes. "They can fix the rogue helicopter—as entertaining as it's been. You order them down, and I'll take the Cessna and my six decent men and leave."

"Why should I do that?" Burton could hear Jackson's desperation, and his heart ached. But.... But *Hamblin*.

"Because if you know someone who can fly, I can let you have the Jayhawk," Hamblin said, unmoved by the man bleeding at Rivers's back. "Provided your men haven't sabotaged it, of course. And I've already promised to send files of Lacey's... assets."

Rivers caught his breath and then showed Burton what a true soldier is made of. "The psychopaths—"

"Yes—and their intended targets. This is your call, Mr. Rivers. Lacey was not a good soldier—he was easy to kill and foolish to shoot blind. I *am* a good soldier—and my men *are* well trained."

"They are," Jackson said, making Burton wonder who he'd faced. "Give me the keys. I'll call to my men."

Hamblin half laughed and Burton wanted to cry. "Oh dear God. Who *are* you?"

"I'm nobody. What's your fucking problem?"

"Helicopters don't have keys. All you need is a pilot—and *not* to get shot when you're trying to get in it. Now what's it going to be, young man?"

"Sonny!" Jackson screamed at the top of his lungs. "Ace! Stand down!"

Hamblin held a walkie-talkie to his mouth. *"Corduroy!"* he barked. "Stand down!"

Abruptly the shots, the shouting, the chaos that had filled the air around them ceased, and Burton heard the resignation in Jackson's voice. But still, he had to ask.

"Rivers? Status!"

"Ellery's down!" Rivers shouted back. "He's injured but still breathing. Lacey's dead. I've got an offer of a helicopter and jackets on Lacey's trained killers if we just let Hamblin the fuck out of here. I'm taking it!"

"Fucking Jesus," Burton swore. "Hamblin, I could kill you from here!"

"Oscar, is that you?" There was a certain disappointment in Hamblin's voice. "Oh dear. I find myself owing this young man instead of you."

"Turns out he and I want the same things. I'd say choose your men better," Burton snapped, "but—"

"But you're the best of them. And now I know why. Your friend here is right. Standing down is your best option. I like you, Oscar, but I won't hesitate to kill him as he sits. You know that."

"Fuck."

And then Rivers gave Burton a reason to let him go. "Sonny's friend is here!" he called. "He's safe now!"

Oh God. Sonny's friend. *Ernie.* "But not for long. I hear you. Go, Hamblin—but don't count on the US military to just let this go. This is a mercenary flag on American soil. It might not be me, but—"

"But we will all live to fight another day!" Hamblin called back. "I understand. I was offered assets—that was all. The rest of this—the flag, the base, all of it—delusions, you understand? A dead man who wanted to make the world in his image. All petty demagogues are like that." He gave a razor-thin smile. "I should know. I've killed plenty. Good luck with your man there, Nobody. You should be proud. You toppled a minor king."

He didn't even know who Jackson Rivers was. For some reason that seemed to Burton to be the gravest injustice, but Burton wasn't going to do anything about it now.

Hamblin turned then and walked unhurriedly toward the front of the hangar, and Burton rushed to Rivers's side.

"Ellery?" Jackson said quietly, turning to see him. "Ellery, you with us?"

"Fucking. Ouch," Cramer mumbled, lips thick with blood. "What in the hell?"

From the corner of his eye, Burton could see Ace advancing, and he ran to intercept. "Is the Black Hawk controlled?" he asked tersely.

"Yessir—want me to get a backboard?"

"And any supplies you can find."

Ace nodded and jerked his chin to the road behind the hangar Burton had just run from. "Jai and Ernie are right there, in case you were interested."

Burton felt like he was moving in slow motion as he turned his head. Sure enough, Ernie and Jai sat in a... well, a semitorched SUV, Lacey's gangly, hapless medic getting in the back seat as Burton watched. Ernie's hair looked... crisp, and even from this distance, he could see scorch marks on Jai's clothes. Oh God. They were singed, but... oh hell.

Alive.

"What the hell is Saunders doing over there?" Burton asked, his voice cracking. That's not what he wanted to know at all.

"I think Rivers saved him," Ace said, a tinge of admiration in his voice. "Everything I can see, the boy's a hero."

"Well, let's save his man," Burton told him and then rushed back to Rivers's side. "Rivers!" Burton snapped, his voice like a slap to the face. "Move! Ace and I got a backboard—we're gonna get him to the Jayhawk, you understand?"

Rivers nodded dumbly, and Burton and Ace secured Cramer. When Rivers *did* speak, it was pure practicality. "Is that the Jayhawk warming up?" he asked.

"I can fly it," Burton said, kneeling by Cramer's head while he belted Cramer to the board. "Just pull your shit together and follow us." Ten minutes. The copter would get them to help in ten minutes, when the SUV would take them an hour. Half an hour if Ace drove. Judging by Cramer's ragged breaths and the extent of his bleeding, Jackson had just negotiated to save his lover's life.

And Hamblin had let him.

Burton couldn't hate the guy—neither of them.

"Saunders is a medic," Rivers mumbled, and Burton didn't have the heart to tell him that he wasn't much of one.

"So I fly, you and Saunders come with, everyone else meets us there. Let's hurry—your guy's breathing, but he's gonna need a little help. Rivers, you and Ace get the board to the copter—it'll be a squeeze, but you can make it fit. I'll go get the medic. We got shit to do."

Burton trotted across the field, hoping Ace and Rivers could get Cramer secure—Jayhawks weren't known to be roomy. Part of him figured

Sonny would help them, and Sonny could jury-rig anything that didn't work on its own—but most of him was focused on the SUV.

"Saunders!" he called, getting the guy's attention through the open window. "Go help the guy in the copter."

Saunders looked at him in confusion. "But.... Oscar? Don't you work for Lacey?"

"No," Burton said, holding on to his patience. "I work for the actual fucking military. Now go help the guy bleeding, and I'll see what I can do about getting you out of a court martial."

"I didn't *do* anything!" Saunders wailed—but he was getting out of the vehicle and heading toward the copters, so Burton let it slide.

Ernie was staring at him through the open window with ginormous limpid eyes, and Burton.... God, for this one moment he wasn't a soldier or an operative or an assassin.

He was a guy damned glad to see his lover alive.

"Burton?" Ernie said softly. "Lee?"

"Get out of the car for a minute," Burton said, voice shaking. "I gotta hold you. Just for a minute, okay?"

"Yeah, sure." Ernie messed with the latch and the door swung out, the rattle of broken glass echoing from inside the panel. Oh. That explained why the windows were all open. Jesus God.

Burton stared at him for a moment, swallowing hard before raising his hand to Ernie's crispy, wild hair.

"There was a big ball of flame," Ernie said apologetically. "I was driving as fast as I could, but Jai didn't get the back hatch closed and some of it got inside. I think Jai needs bandages on his hands, but he said he's got stuff at home—"

"Shut up," Burton whispered, cupping both his boy's cheeks. "God, Ernie. Please. Don't... don't ever scare me like that again. My heart stopped. My fucking heart stopped, do you know that? The explosion happened, and... and I thought you were dead and I wanted to go with you. I almost... I almost killed all the fuckin' things, do you get that? 'Cause if you weren't there on the planet, there wasn't any reason to hold back."

Ernie gazed at him, mouth slightly open, black smudges on his cheeks and nose. "Have faith, Cruller," he said, voice low and sweet. "I've loved you when all I knew about you was thunder on the horizon. Now that I know you, I love you even more."

Burton nodded, closing his eyes against the worry, the fear, and he groaned, pulling Ernie tight into his arms.

"Burton!" Ace called, trotting back from the copters. "You gotta get a move on—he's not doing so hot!"

Burton pulled away reluctantly and placed a gentle kiss on Ernie's forehead. "See you at home," he said.

"We're going to the hospital to be with Rivers," Ace told him as he headed for the driver's seat. "He needs someone—Cramer goes south and he's gonna fuckin' lose his shit."

"See you at the hospital," he said softly.

Ernie grinned. "You can tell me more about how I keep you from killing all the fuckin' things," he said happily. "That's pretty damned romantic, don't you think, Ace?"

"It's damned near flowers and chocolate," Ace said, and Burton didn't hear the rest because he was heading for the Jayhawk, pulling his phone out to talk to Jason as he went.

Places You Can't Go

ERNIE STARED at Jackson Rivers in dismay as he crouched on the floor of the bathroom, bleeding from a really nasty series of cuts on his hand.

They'd gone back to Walmart so Jai could drive Ace's SHO back to the garage and Ace and Sonny could pick up some food and clothes for Rivers. By the time they'd gotten to the hospital, Cramer was in surgery and Rivers was....

Well, Rivers was losing his shit. As he told them, his voice wrecked, that hospitals were a weight pushing on his chest, stopping his breath, Ernie had a sudden real and terrible fear.

Rivers couldn't be fixed.

Ernie had always thought he had his gift for a reason. His gift had given him Rivers and Cramer, but Cramer was in surgery and Rivers was...

Broken.

He wished suddenly, fiercely, for Burton, but apparently Burton had to take the medic guy back to his superior and wrap up all the loose ends in the world, and the one thing—the *one* thing—Ernie thought he could do, well, Rivers wasn't letting him do.

"I've got it," Rivers mumbled, standing up and cleaning his hand. Ace and Sonny and Ernie dogged his heels as he stumbled into the waiting room, and Ernie heard the nurse there tell him where the chapel was—and threaten to put him in the psych ward, and promise to call up a stitching station so she could tend his hand.

Ace, Sonny, and Ernie were left staring at each other and guarding the big bag of takeout Ace had bought on the way there.

The oppression in Ernie's head wouldn't go away. He was a heartbeat away from curling up and sobbing, his head hurt so bad, when suddenly there was a *pop!* Like when people went up too high on a mountain or an airplane.

It was like pressure being released, and Ernie almost cried again—but this time from relief.

"What?" Ace asked him, watching his expression change with perception.

"He's… crying. Praying. Something. I thought his head was going to pop open, but he's… I don't know. Trusted something."

"I'm sorry," said a female voice from the door. "I'm looking for Jackson Rivers—he's here for my son, Ellery Cramer?"

Ernie looked up and saw... well, a goddess, really. Brown eyes crackling with intelligence and a long face with a bold nose and chin, this woman had the bearing of a queen and an expression of high expectation.

Ace stood up to go greet her, and Sonny hid behind Ace's shoulder.

"Mrs. Cramer?" Ace asked, surprising Ernie.

"Yes, sir? You know me?"

"I... I know your son. He's still in surgery, ma'am, I'm sorry. We don't have any news."

Mrs. Cramer nodded regally. Her hair was scraped back into a severe ponytail, and only the gray roots at the base told Ernie she was older than thirty-five. "And Mr. Rivers? My son's associate?"

"Jackson's in the chapel," Ernie said, drawn to this woman forcefully. It wasn't just that her presence was magnetic—he missed his own parents so badly sometimes. This woman had an air about her—sort of like she could be everybody's mother if only the world would move to her bidding.

"The chapel?" And the surprise in her voice indicated she really *did* know Jackson Rivers.

"Yeah—the pressure released, so he must have figured out what to do there."

Mrs. Cramer nodded, looking relieved, and followed the nurse's directions down the corridor. Ernie, Ace, and Sonny were left feeling superfluous again until, after about half an hour, Ernie heard a booted tread in the corridor.

And felt the wall of safety that was Lee Burton.

He darted for the hallway and launched himself into Burton's arms.

For once he wasn't disappointed. For once Burton didn't hold back. There was no sex in Burton's touch—although that simmered between them always—there was only tenderness and joy.

"Hey, kid," Burton whispered against his ear. "You doing okay?"

"We're waiting for news," Ernie told him, needing to be in his arms more than nearly anything else in the world. "Lee, I'm so sorry—I didn't mean to put you in danger or distract you or—"

Burton stepped back from him for a moment and smiled, his eyes tired and at peace at the same time. "Baby, you *are* a distraction. But you're a distraction I can't live without. If you can live with me going on missions, you can distract me all you want."

Ernie gasped, almost too afraid to hope. "Really?" he asked. "Can we—"

"Hey, guys!" Ace called, looking up from where Sonny was digging into their takeout. "You hungry? I mean, you're not going to solve all your problems *here*, are you?"

Lee laughed a little—but he still looked tired. So tired.

"So," Ace said as he passed out cheeseburgers. "You staying around for a while?"

Burton shook his head. "As soon as we hear how Cramer is doing, I need to take off again."

"Oh." Ernie's disappointment was acute. After the things Burton had just promised him, Ernie had been hoping... oh God. Just some time alone. Like Christmas but longer. Some time where they could cement this thing they meant to each other.

"Some of Lacey's men left before shit went down," Burton told them, and Ernie was forcibly reminded that his man worked for a higher cause. "And they're headed overland toward Rivers's family. My boss says I got the Jayhawk and some backup troops to stop them—my bet is they've all gone dark until their job is done, because that's just how Lacey did his thing. But I need to talk to Rivers—"

"He's barely functional," Ace warned. "I'm not sure what magic Cramer's mother can work—"

"He'll be okay," Ernie told them, that remarkable lightening of the air still ringing in his ears. "He'll make it through. As long as Ellery lives, he's going to be fine."

Burton regarded him soberly. "Any ideas on that one way or the other?" he queried with delicacy.

Ernie grimaced. "Sorry—no. Jackson's internal screaming has pretty much spun my gears all day."

Burton's hand, soft in the small of his back, told Ernie all the things they hadn't had time to say about how things had changed between them. "Been a rough day on your noggin, hasn't it, kid."

Oh. Kindness. Sympathy. Ernie leaned his head against Burton's shoulder. "Yeah, Cruller," he said, melting a little, letting some of the trauma of the day ease up off his shoulders. "I'm glad you're here, if only for an hour."

Burton kissed his temple, and at that moment, Rivers and Mrs. Cramer entered.

Meetings and Partings

BURTON SAT next to Jackson Rivers as he was getting his hand stitched and wondered at human endurance. The nurse stabbed his hand with a needle and he barely flinched, but his voice as he talked about his fear of hospitals was the sound of a man in pain.

And Burton had to add to it by telling the man that there were people after his family. In the back of his head, he could hear the clock, plan the op, have people gathering around Rivers's people in Truckee and in Sacramento, but he couldn't seem to force Rivers to choose: stay here in the hospital with Ellery Cramer or leave and join Burton on the op to protect his family. With an ordinary civilian, Burton wouldn't have even offered—but Jackson wasn't ordinary. Burton had seen him be a soldier and a protector with a single-minded ferocity and a stunning competence. Jackson Rivers was a man to be reckoned with, and Burton wouldn't mind him on Burton's team.

He put off the decision until after they heard news. They could wait another half hour, right? And in the meantime, Rivers called up his brother and handed Burton the phone.

"Is Jackson okay?" Kaden Cameron sounded… well, street. Much like Rivers himself did, to be honest, but with a deeper voice.

"The vote's still out," Burton said lowly, not wanting Rivers to hear him. "We're waiting on news of Cramer—"

"Is Jackson bleeding," Kaden demanded, voice hard.

"Yes, but he's getting stitched."

"Goddammit. Ask him about his head—he just healed from a concussion!"

Burton peered into Jackson's eyes and saw that they were shadowed and bloodshot—but not blown. "He might live," he muttered. "But I'm worried about your family now, so focus." While he was talking, Jackson pulled up a picture of Kaden, his wife, Rhonda, and their two children, River and Diamond, on another phone and showed it to him. They were playing with a little boy about twelve who Burton knew as Anthony, who Adkins had been dumb enough to pay to do his dirty work for him. Anthony was probably the reason Gleeson and Adkins had left on their little adventure, but that wouldn't save the rest of the family, or the young man in his early twenties with them, who was a family friend.

Burton stared for a moment and then shot a quick glance at Jackson. The Camerons were black.

Burton had never gotten a picture of them—neither Kaden nor Jade Cameron, who he gathered to be twins, nor the rest of Kaden's family.

Jackson, eating his heart out about whether he should stay with his boyfriend or go help the op that would protect his family—these were step- or foster siblings, and Rivers would die for them.

And the little boy in the picture was as pale as Cramer had been—*after* he'd been shot. And the twentysomething kid was a bronze tone between them.

It was a stupid detail, really. Something Burton had never realized he'd believed, the idea that families would look the same.

His family had looked the same, but he'd decided a long time ago that *his* family, the one he'd grown up with, wouldn't be the kind of family Lee Burton could sustain.

But this was a family. He could easily see Jackson Rivers in these pictures, could see Cramer there too, helping to build a snowman, drinking hot cocoa, being real people here.

Burton and Ernie and Ace and Sonny and even, God help him, Jai and Alba, could be a family.

It wouldn't be anything like this one, with kids and uncles and aunts and days playing in the snow. Burton would come and go, but when he was there, he could help Ace and Sonny in the garage and take Ernie on vacations and cook dinner for them all so Ernie didn't have to.

And when he was gone….

Ernie was already a part of their family. He'd told Burton that himself. It was why he'd had to get into the car.

This had happened without Burton's conscious decision. He'd been telling himself for three months that he "had to decide" what to do with Ernie, but the truth was, Ernie had already achieved complete and total Ernie-dom with or without him.

Of course they were going to buy a house and live together. Of course they were going to stay in Victoriana and be part of Ace and Sonny's life. Ernie was the distraction he couldn't live without? That was weak shit, right there. Ace and Sonny were his family—but Ernie? Ernie was his *church*.

Burton finished up talking to Kaden Cameron and explaining that a group of soldiers would arrive by helicopter, probably landing in the nearby school parking lot, and then looked up to see the focus of the waiting room had changed to the man wearing bloody scrubs who had just come through the door to the OR.

He held his breath until the doctor made his pronouncement and had to breathe through spots when he was finished.

"Burton!" Cameron barked. "Burton, are you there?"

"Cramer's out of surgery," he said hoarsely. "It's looking good."

"Oh." He could actually hear Cameron swallow. "Thank God. Jackson… Jackson wouldn't make it without him."

No. And now Burton knew what that felt like.

Burton signed off with Kaden and watched, heart aching, as Ellery Cramer's mother, who had seemed a pillar of granite, melted like sugar in the rain. And Rivers—who had seemed irreparably broken—shored her up and held her, looking surprised the entire time.

Burton could relate.

At a quiet moment, he pulled Ernie aside and out of the waiting room and tried to make "You're my church" make sense with "I don't know when I'll be back."

"I want a house," he said without preamble, not making any sense and not caring. "I want to live by Sonny and Ace and have cats. And I won't be there every day and I might not be able to call, but I will always come back to you. Can you do that, kid? Can you be my haven, my church, and my lover, and know that, if there's breath in my body, I'll come back to you? It's a lot to ask—it's weak sauce to even offer it to you, but…. God, kid. I can't—whatever lies in store for me, I'm just like Rivers in there. I can't deal with it if you're not there. Can we do that? Can we—"

Ernie kissed him. Fully, joyously, without inhibition.

Burton groaned and kissed him back, devouring him, his last meal, his last sip of wine, before he went back into battle.

IN THE end, Rivers chose not to come with them.

Cramer's mother had said it best—Burton was a soldier, and a soldier's job now was to protect. Jackson's job was to be there for the other chamber of his heart.

A year ago Burton would have seen it as cowardice, but then, a year ago he hadn't met Ernie—and hadn't been an unwilling fly on the wall between a shark and a shattered fish.

Now, creeping through the snowy woods in the Tahoe National Forest, he could recognize Rivers's sacrifice for what it was: making the best of a brutal choice and learning to trust a heretofore indifferent universe.

He could also be damned glad for the heavy Marine-issue sweater Jason had scared up for him before they'd taken off from the now secured abandoned base outside of Barstow. The unit had arrived ready for winter ops at night, but Burton was wearing cargo pants and a hoodie, which was standard gear for a mercenary apparently, and not damned warm enough.

"Bravo, this is Alpha," Jason said in his ear. "Do you see anything?"

"Negative, Alpha," Burton responded, searching the darkness of the thick woods intently. "Charlie? Delta? Do you see them?"

Caspar Klein and Donnie Yamane were the other two members of the impromptu team Jason had thrown together, and they both gave negatives over the headsets.

"I'm going in," Burton told them. "I have contact with the civilians. They know my voice."

He neatly holstered his service weapon, grateful to have his Marine-issue Glock by his side again. Calvin Oscar had been an Army man and had carried a Sig Sauer, which had been entirely too small for his hands. Burton was really glad to be himself again.

Stealthily, he walked from the woods to the clearing where the Camerons' house stood, two stories of kid-riddled domesticity, and looked around.

And tried to figure out what was wrong.

"Alpha, Charlie, Delta—it's too quiet. It's not ten o'clock yet, and the house is completely dark—"

"Maybe they're early risers," Jason said, but he sounded nervous too.

"Not when they've been told there's a threat coming," Burton said decisively. "Psst." He melted back into the forest, taking station behind a hefty-sized pine tree and trying not to stand close enough to get any sap on himself.

"What do you see?" Donnie asked in his ear. Burton scanned the woods to his right and barely made out the slight, deadly form of Donnie Yamane in the dark of the woods.

"There's someone standing in the living room, back toward the window," Burton murmured. "He's got his gun out in front of him, and he's heading up the stairs."

"I see him. Do you see the night goggles?"

"Yeah."

"Flash-bangs?"

"No! Silent running!" Burton looked around one last time and sprinted across the yard to the front door. With a twist of his wrist, he found it was unlocked. "The house has been breached," he hissed. "Charlie, Delta, swing up to the kids' rooms. Jason, you and me take the ground floor. Go! Go! Go!"

Burton and his team converged on the little house, and he had no doubt that Jason was breaking in through the back door if it hadn't been breached already, while Donnie and Caspar were swinging up to the top. Burton burst through the door just in time to hear a high-pitched child's scream from the upstairs bedroom. The intruder on the stairs swung around, gun out, to take down anybody behind him.

"Gleeson!" Burton barked. "Weapon down!"

"Oscar?" Gleeson sounded legitimately puzzled—right before he adjusted his shoulder just enough for Burton to know he was going to fire.

"Got him!" Jason called, and Burton rolled to the right as Gleeson fired at the space he'd just vacated.

And Jason fired three shots into him.

But Burton didn't hang around to see the face of his former antagonist. Instead he ran up the stairs, vaulting the body as it bled, faceup, on the landing. By the time he got to the upstairs bedrooms, things had gotten damned bad.

"Anthony!" A giant of a man wearing Star Wars pajamas stood outside what looked like a guest bedroom. "Anthony, calm down!"

"Kaden! Kaden, he's got me! The bad man got me!"

"The bad man wants something!" Kaden Cameron roared. His family pressed up behind him, and he waved his arm at them in a fruitless attempt to make them get back. "I'm sure the bad man can negotiate, right, asshole?"

"I want safe passage the hell out of here!" Adkins demanded. "That's all I want. But I got two assholes at the window with guns and you fuckers in front of me—just move and I'll take the kid with me!"

The child in the room broke into tears, and another voice, adult, male, soothing, spoke up. "Let him go. Take me. He's, like, a baby—I'm grown. I can deal."

"You're not nearly as fuckin' cute," Adkins snarled. "Now get out of my way!"

Burton took advantage of the chaos to whisper into his com. "Delta, Charlie, his name is Alan Adkins—ask him how many of his friends are out there. There should be three of them, and we've only accounted for two."

"Roger that," Donnie said softly, and Caspar echoed him. "Hey, Alan—we'll give you safe passage, but we need to know how many of your people are here. You know, so we don't walk around a corner and get our heads blown off!"

"Just two," Adkins said, desperation clear in his voice. "There were gonna be five, but two of us went after Rivers's sister, and Leavins said he had another job to do."

While they were talking, Burton tapped the shoulder of the little girl in front of him. She turned, startled, and he held his fingers to his lips and pointed to the far end of the hallway. She nodded, obviously scared but also damned brave, and tapped on her brother's shoulder. Both of them eyeballed Burton suspiciously, and he leaned forward to whisper "Jackson sent me" under the sounds of Adkins and Team Delta Charlie as they negotiated.

Both of them pulled away, eyes big, and the girl grabbed her mother's hand and tugged. The mother—a gorgeous woman in her early thirties—looked at Burton, startled, but kept quiet as Burton held his finger to his lips and pointed. All three of them retreated silently across the carpet to the end of the hallway by the bathroom. Burton made a little fluttery motion with his hands, and they all went inside, hopefully to hide in the bathtub in case bullets started flying.

But Burton didn't think they would.

Silently he dropped to a crouch behind Kaden Cameron's big, solid dad-body and pulled his pistol from his holster, peering up from the gap between Kaden's leg and the doorframe.

He could see Adkins in there to his left, holding his arm around Anthony's throat and a gun to his head while Donnie and Caspar peered in through the window. Across the room a slight young man—AJ—stood, hands out, looking at Anthony in anguish.

Adkins had a big head—so big it was catching light from the moon through the window—and it made an amazing target.

Burton took a deep breath, aimed, and squeezed the trigger.

Adkins went over backward and the world erupted into chaos, and all Burton could think was that things weren't over by a long shot.

CASPAR AND Donnie took cleanup, asking Rhonda Cameron nicely for some spare sheets and some bleach, both of them promising they'd have new furniture sent and a new coat of paint on the walls within the week. In the meantime the family gathered around the two frightened boys who had been in the bedroom and... and hugged them. Both. As often and as warmly as possible. Burton pulled Kaden aside as the family huddled in the kitchen and told him that was the best medicine he could offer the kids.

Kaden nodded once, a hard gesture that made Burton think maybe Jackson called this man brother because they'd grown up in the same hard place.

"You asked if there are others—what does that mean?"

Burton grimaced. "It means I've got my commander calling the unit we assigned to your sister to make sure they got everybody."

"What about Jackson and Ellery. Do *they* get a unit?"

Burton stared at him. "Why would they need—"

"Why wouldn't they?" Kaden asked bitterly. "I love my brother, man, but if a chunk of ice falls off an airplane wing and falls through a building to hit somebody on the head, you can *bet* that someone is Jackson Leroy Rivers."

"I'll call him and warn him," Burton said, a hard knot of anxiety congealing in his stomach.

"Now." Kaden pointed to the phone in his hand, and Burton nodded, pulling off to the corner of the living room.

As he was pulling up Jackson's number, Jason spoke in his ear. "Jade Cameron and her boyfriend are fine. Well armed and apparently scary as fuck, but fine."

"Were there any shots fired?" Burton asked nervously. Adkins had his arm around that kid's throat, a gun to his head. How had they let that happen?

"Yeah, by the civilians." Jason gave a bitter laugh. "I am going to have to cash in my retirement, Burton, because apparently I can't train my guys to protect a doghouse, much less civilians. No—two guys tried to crawl in over the fence. The dog barked, the residents opened fire, and now we've got two mercenaries in the hospital whining about dog bites with a bullet chaser."

"I'm going to check on Rivers and Cramer, sir." Burton sighed. "One of Lacey's scumbags is MIA, and he claimed he had a special mission."

"Shit. I'll call the hospital—"

"I'll call Rivers."

Rivers picked up on the first ring—but he sounded fucking unhinged.

"Rivers? How you doing?"

"Fucking peachy. How's my family?"

Burton met Kaden Cameron's grim gaze. "They're rattled but okay. We've got most of the mercenaries sent to mop up accounted for, but we're missing one operative. A snake-mean fucker named Pruitt Leavins."

"Missing one?" he said, sounding damned near insane.

"Yes, sir. We've got the others, including Adkins and Gleeson—"

"You got Adkins and Gleeson, but you're missing one."

"Yeah, Rivers—"

"You're *missing* a bad guy. Missing. Heh-heh. Missing one. Uh-huh. Like a shoe. Sorry, y'all, got all the bad guys, but we're missing a homicidal shoe." Uh-oh. This did not bode well for Jackson's night. "Why, yes," he continued. "Yes, we found your homicidal shoe. Why the fuck do you ask?"

"Can I talk to him?" Burton asked—but he didn't hold out a lot of hope.

"Can you talk to him?" Jackson gave a hard bark of laughter. "No, Burton, you can't talk to him. Because he's dead. Yes, that's what I said. Dead. Your missing shoe is *bleeding out* on the hospital floor. Yup. You heard me. Bleeding out. No—everybody's fine."

The phone was grabbed, apparently by Cramer's mother.

"Jackson's being admitted momentarily. You can debrief him when you return. I take it the Cameron families are both in good shape?"

"They are, ma'am," Burton said, struggling not to stammer like a kid. "Yes? Good."

"Could you make sure Rivers knows?"

"Yes, I will. I'll tell him that just as soon as he *goes to the ER!*" Her voice rose shrilly on that last note, and Burton grimaced, holding the phone away from his ear while he struggled to find words.

He didn't have to, because she hung up. Burton let out a grunt and scrubbed his face with his palm and met Kaden's sardonic gaze.

"So?"

"The good news is he's still alive," Burton said, feeling ill. Bungled. This whole thing was bungled so badly.

"And Cramer?"

"Jackson said everybody was fine."

"Was Jackson injured?"

Burton cringed. "Uh, Mrs. Cramer said something about him needing medical attention, yes."

"God*dammit!*"

"I'm so sorry." Burton was starting to wonder if he was in the wrong line of work.

"Don't worry about it," Kaden Cameron said, surprising him. "I know, I know—you feel like you fucked up. And you sort of did—but everybody *I* care about is still breathing, so I'm gonna say job well done."

Burton's head ached fiercely, and he wanted Ernie's unconditional acceptance in a way he'd never wanted anything in his life.

"I thought he'd be safe, at least, with Cramer," he confessed, feeling as foolish as a child.

Cameron shrugged. "Jackson's never safe. It's why my sister and I worry so much about him being right with God."

Burton gaped at him. "That's a terrible thing to—"

"We don't want him to *die*," Cameron told him, obviously annoyed. "But dammit. He's come close so many times. It's just… if the moment comes, we want him to be at peace. To have known happiness. To know he's loved."

Burton looked around the nice two-story house that Jackson's family had turned into a cozy, tastefully decorated home. Everything was stain-resistant and brown-and-plum-colored—probably to hide any stains if they couldn't be resisted—but it was cozy.

"He's loved," Burton said softly. *And so am I.*

He still had a long stretch ahead of him.

He and Jason needed to account for every mercenary who'd been at the base when things went south and every mercenary who'd been sent off the base with a mission. They needed to take a look at the jackets Hamblin had sent Jackson and cross-reference them with crimes that had been committed since November.

And they had to send out members of Jason's unit to either bring the mercenaries in or take them down.

The task was monumental. Herculean.

Bigger than a day, or a week, or a year.

Neither of them was getting fired, and neither of them was resigning—but something had to change.

In the end Jason simply commandeered Lacey's old base, since it had a functioning administration building and barracks and all. He pulled the entirety of his unit in on the operation, and they held meetings every morning, after they'd caught a few scant hours of shut-eye after working sixteen-hour days.

Burton would hit the hard wood of his barracks dreaming of mad-eyed men, blood dripping from their fingers, as they tore through Ace's little house and murdered its inhabitants and ate his dog.

One night, about two weeks after he'd taken out Adkins in the Camerons' home, he sat up in bed screaming, only to see his CO sitting quietly at his feet.

"What?" Burton muttered. The base was big enough that they got the CO's barracks—the privacy was great, not that they used it much.

"You were calling out for someone named Ernie," Jason said, a quiet smile on his face. "I figured you wouldn't want the rest of the unit to hear you."

Burton groaned and scrubbed at his face with his hand. "I, uh…."

Jason waved his protests away. "The people in your life are yours, Lee. I know what we tell you—no connections. But I'm not training automatons. I'm training soldiers—and real soldiers are human." He grimaced and looked around the plain barracks room. "If nothing else, Karl Lacey's little experiment should have taught us that the people who defend our country need to be allowed to be human."

Burton nodded, his heart suddenly so sore from missing Ernie, he wasn't sure it could beat.

"Lee?" Jason said, kindness unexpected in the corners of his eyes.

"Yessir?"

"We're going to be at this for years. We need to make this a nine-to-five job, something with hours and downtime and weekends, or my people are going to burn out, and I *like* my team. Do you understand me?"

Burton's eyes started to burn. "Sir?"

"You have a week off. Come back here in a week with a place to go every night from here that's *not* in this compound, do you hear?"

Oh God. He took a shattered breath. "*Sir?*"

"Find a home, Lee. And go there. See you in a week, when we'll start working shifts for the duration. You may still get assignments, but for right now the Lacey Project will be our priority, and my team will work hours that won't make their eyeballs bleed. Go home, Lee. Find Ernie or whoever you're calling for, and go home."

...And Cats

ERNIE FELT him coming in the middle of the night. He hadn't texted, he hadn't called—but Ernie knew.

He got home and put Duke in his crate, nodding at Ace and Sonny as they sat on the couch and argued over TV.

"You're back early," Ace said midkvetch, and Sonny looked up and nodded.

"Burton's coming," he said shortly. "Getting ready." He didn't explain that this time would be different than the other times—he'd told Ace about the promises that had been made, about his belief that they'd be kept. The energy he felt from Burton was fully focused and completely on him.

And needy. So damned needy.

Ernie wanted to be ready.

He hopped in the shower, and when he got out, he grabbed water bottles and snacks for the room.

He wasn't planning on coming out for a while.

Lee's knock on the front door was weaker than Ernie had expected. A timid request for sanctuary, as opposed to the confident demand for it he'd employed when he'd first brought Ernie there. Ernie let him say hi to Sonny and Ace for a moment before opening the door and ushering him inside his room, dressed only in a towel.

Burton took two steps in, closed the door behind him, and wrapped his arms around Ernie like he was drowning and Ernie was his last best hope of safety and air.

Ernie hugged him back just as fiercely, raising his mouth for a slow, greedy, painful kiss.

Slow. This was seduction, slow and simple. His mouth on Ernie's begged—when Burton should never have to beg.

Ernie gave, everything, without reservation. What would he hold back? He'd been in love with this man from the very first, and giving him sex had been incidental.

But giving him trust and faith, stability, a home—those were things he'd had to learn, lesson by painful lesson, until this moment right here, when he could offer every one of them with each and every careful touch.

Burton's hands turned the last of the moisture on his skin to steam, and he moaned softly, sliding his own hands up under Burton's regulation OD-green shirt.

Words later.

They needed to communicate skin to skin.

Ernie let the towel drop and yanked at Burton's shirt until he shed it voluntarily and then pulled at his belt to remove his pants.

"Let me get my boots," Burton rumbled—the first words he'd said.

Ernie moved so he could sit down on the bed but tormented him with openmouthed kisses on the back of his neck, his ears, the back of his shoulders.

He sucked on Burton's earlobe, pleased when he let out a frustrated whine while he was working a stubborn bootlace.

"Kid," he begged breathlessly. "Please. Just... gimme a minute. You're so naked, and it's not fair."

Ernie let out a strained chuckle. "We're not gonna talk about what's fair, Cruller. Get rid of the goddamned boots. We've got shit to sort."

The boot went flying across the room with a *thump*, and the other one followed in short order, along with socks, pants, and shorts.

Burton stood by the bed, naked and beautiful, and Ernie crouched on hands and knees to wrap his mouth around Burton's cock.

He was starving for the taste of it.

But Burton stopped him, catching his chin under two fingers and tilting his head up. "I haven't showered," he said gruffly. "I'm not... you're so clean and soft...." He trailed a finger down the side of Ernie's neck, and Ernie closed his eyes. It wasn't the sweat of an honest day that was bothering him— Ernie could tell. It was the film of deeds he couldn't wash away.

"All of you, Cruller," Ernie said softly. "That's who I love." And with that he took Burton into his mouth entirely, to the back of his throat, swallowing as he went to put pressure where it would feel best.

Burton moaned, fingers massaging Ernie's scalp through his overlong hair, and Ernie kept sucking, kept stroking with his fist, kept *pleasuring*, using every trick he'd ever learned in a random hookup to make Burton forget any reservation he had about being right here, right now, in Ernie's arms, in his bed, in his *mouth*.

Ernie tugged gently on Burton's testicles, fondling, and Burton jerked his hips. "Kid... I'm gonna...."

Good.

Let him climax.

Let him flood Ernie's mouth, lose his mind, come undone.

He was lost—Ernie could see it, could feel it. Burton's need was like a tattoo needle on Ernie's skin, etching his pain with every touch.

Let him fuck Ernie's mouth until his pain exploded. Ernie pulled him deeper, slid his fingers more daringly behind Burton's balls, teased more tauntingly between his cleft, and just when he found Burton's pucker, Burton gave a strained shout and orgasmed, coming until Ernie couldn't swallow any more and it ran out the corners of his mouth and down his chin.

Ernie looked up at him in the dim light of the bedside lamp and let Burton see him, his mouth shiny and dripping with come, his lips swollen, his eyes fierce.

"Get down here and love me," he ordered, and Burton fell upon him like a lion with a lamb.

He pressed Ernie back against the pillows, licking at his mouth, the last traces of his own spend, and then pushing back for more. Ernie spread his legs, letting Burton rut against him, sloppy and hardening and not taking a break, even a little, from the kiss.

And his hands moved possessively, restlessly, like he could gather Ernie in fistfuls and keep him near. Ernie wrapped his legs around Burton's hips and pressed them even closer, whimpering when Burton's hardness jammed in the space between his thighs.

He fumbled under the pillow for lube and handed it to Burton demandingly. Burton managed enough self-possession to rock back on his knees and drip some on his fingers.

"Thinking of me?" he teased, closing the bottle with a little *snick*.

"Yes," Ernie told him unapologetically. "I'd think of you and touch myself and stroke myself, and sometimes I'd use two fingers and... ah! Ah! God yes!"

Burton thrust two slick fingers into him, and Ernie splayed his knees, opening himself up, begging for full possession. The stretch, the burn, the ache—these were things he needed, and he needed them bigger, with all of Burton inside him.

It was the only place Ernie could keep him safe, inside his body, in the haven of his heart.

Burton put himself in position and thrust in, glorious and huge, and Ernie raised his hips to meet him, swallow him down to the hilt, and again and again and again.

"Gonna be quick," Burton apologized. "Need...."

"So bad," Ernie agreed. "So bad. God, Lee, fuck me harder."

The tenderness was overwhelming, and Burton must have felt it too. His hips picked up speed, harder, faster, brutal, claiming possession, and Ernie gasped breathlessly, needing, oh God... just a little pressure on his aching untouched cock to... please just... oh please....

Burton bit his shoulder hard, roaring into the hollow of his neck as he came again, and Ernie gasped "*No!*" because he wasn't there yet, needed just... just a little touch.

But Burton wouldn't leave him hanging. Not now. Still thrusting slowly, still not soft, he kept fucking, powerfully, while he grabbed Ernie's cock and squeezed.

Fireworks, bright and beautiful, exploded behind Ernie's eyes, and he came in Burton's hand like Burton possessed all of him, his ass, his cock, his come.

Burton *did* possess all of him, and not just the sex parts, tingling with hard use and climax.

He fell against Ernie, covering his body protectively, murmuring nonsense in his ear, and Ernie wrapped his limbs around Burton's body to keep him safe.

All of him. Burton owned all of him. Cock, ass, mouth, come.

Heart, soul, body, love.

All.

HE HAD to roll off sometime, but Ernie didn't want to let him go. "Stay," he murmured. "Stay inside me."

"Am I in your heart?" Burton asked quietly, his voice rumbling.

Ernie caught his gaze then, unflinching. "Always, Lee Burton. Always."

Burton swallowed and nodded, his eyes squeezing shut. "I don't deserve that."

"Are you going to stay? I mean, not *stay*, but stay?"

Burton really did roll off, stretching his arm over his head and facing Ernie on the pillows. "Yes," he said. Then he reached down and grabbed the comforter to pull it up over them. February was still chilly, even in the desert. "I have a week to get a home. A place not work. Then I go back to work like a nine-to-five for a while. An hour commute, but there's worse things."

Ernie gaped. "Like… like an everyday job?"

Burton's mouth grew grim. "We had to set up a database and trackers. My commander's entire unit is dedicated to getting the guys Lacey turned loose. We don't even have time to go after Corduroy—too many of these guys are showing markers, coming up on DNA matches. Everything from serial rapists to quickie-mart robberies—it's insane."

Ernie nodded. "So… so your job changed."

Burton's mouth lost its tightness. "My life changed," he corrected, reaching out to trace Ernie's mouth with his fingertips. "My heart changed."

"So, your home…?" Oh God. Ernie's heart was hammering so hard in his chest he was surprised it didn't explode outward.

"You are my home. I'll have you buy a house and set it up. Not too far from here—"

"There's a little stretch of property a half mile away," Ernie said promptly. "I looked. It's isolated, but it's got a giant kitchen and a big bedroom and a porch and even sod—Ace is so jealous. And it's got a hot tub—I mean a *hot tub*, and I can walk here every night and cook dinner for Ace and Sonny, and we can eat together when you get home and then we can go home, to our own house, and—"

Burton's finger over his lips was the only thing that would have stopped him from spilling out his hope, his silly pipe dream, the thing he'd longed for with the fierceness of pain since Burton had left him last time, promising him everything right before he left.

"Cats," Burton said softly. "You can feed every cat in Southern California. It's okay, Ernie. You get the whole dream. You're my heart. It's the least I can do."

Ernie started to laugh then, and cry at the same time, finally sobbing on Burton's shoulder while Burton rocked him and crooned in his ear.

They'd talk about all of it later.

The fallout between Rivers and Cramer, who were going back to Sacramento in a couple of days after being released from the hospital finally. Lee's agony over almost letting Rivers's family down.

189

The way he'd thought about Ernie every minute of every day, until he knew he'd have no peace unless they were together, settled, a home in each other's hearts even if he couldn't be home every day.

That last part was the important part.

It was all Ernie had ever dreamed about, all he'd ever wanted in his life, all he believed could be true between two people, even people as unlikely as he and Burton were.

As long as Burton was in his arms, or dreaming about his arms, or needing him in any capacity that would eventually lead him back to Ernie, holding him fiercely, loving him always, Ernie knew he had a home.

Choose your Lane to love!

Orange

Amy's
Dark Contemporary Romance

AMY LANE lives in a crumbling crapmansion with a couple of growing children, a passel of furbabies, and a bemused spouse. She's been nominated for a RITA, has won honorable mention for an Indiefab, and has a couple of Rainbow Awards to her name. She also has too damned much yarn, a penchant for action-adventure movies, and a need to know that somewhere in all the pain is a story of Wuv, Twu Wuv, which she continues to believe in to this day! She writes fantasy, urban fantasy, and gay romance—and if you accidentally make eye contact, she'll bore you to tears with why those three genres go together. She'll also tell you that sacrifices, large and small, are worth the urge to write.

Website: www.greenshill.com
Blog: www.writerslane.blogspot.com
Email: amylane@greenshill.com
Facebook: www.facebook.com/amy.lane.167
Twitter: @amymaclane

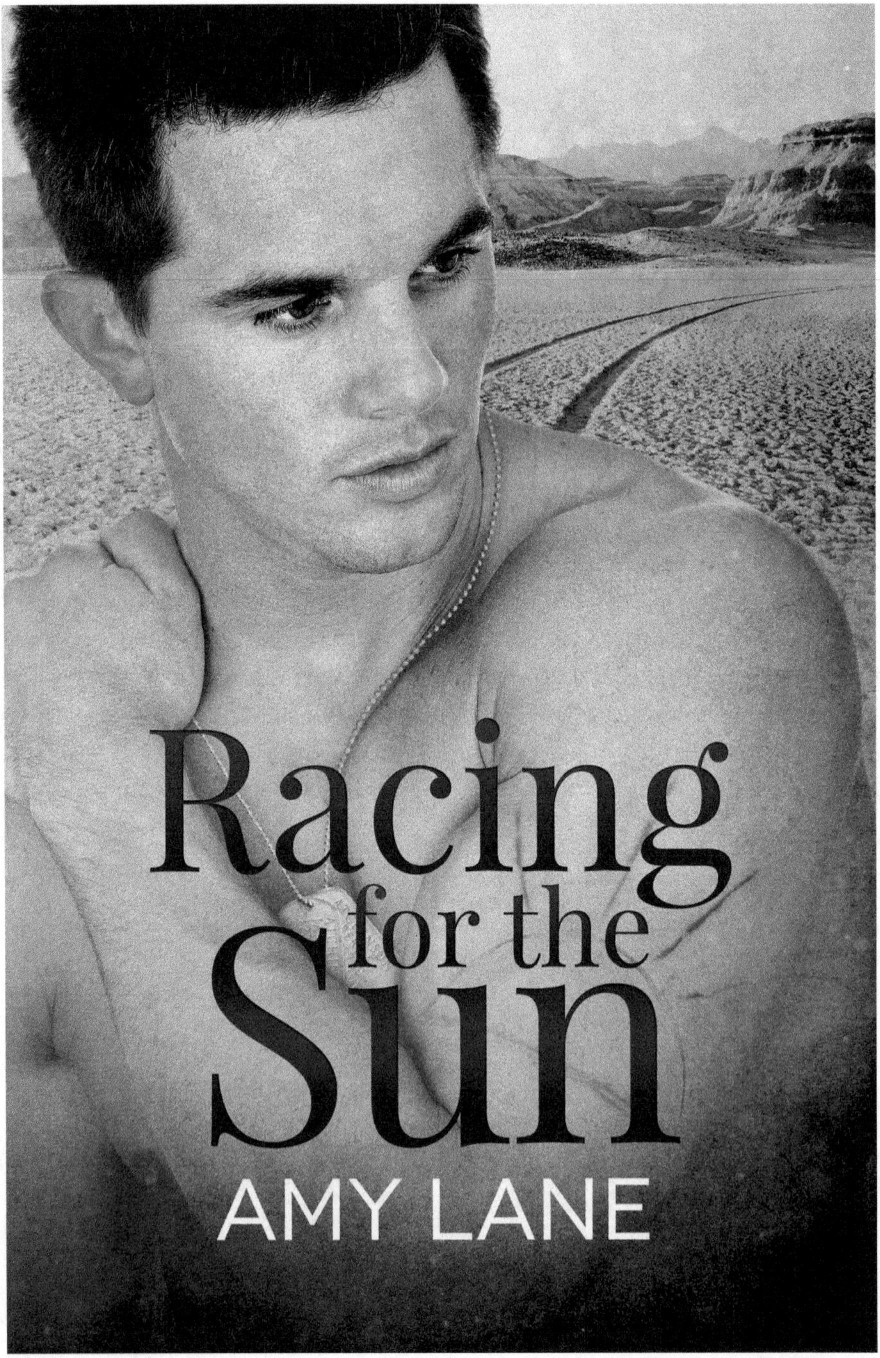

Racing
for the
Sun
AMY LANE

"I'll do anything."

Staff Sergeant Jasper "Ace" Atchison takes one look at Private Sonny Daye and knows that every word on paper about him is pure, unadulterated bullshit. But Sonny is desperate, and although Ace isn't going to take him up on his offer of "anything," that doesn't mean he isn't tempted.

Instead, Ace takes Sonny under his wing, protecting him when they're in the service and making plans with him when they get out. Together, they're going to own a garage and build race cars and make their fortune hurtling faster than light across the desert. Together, they're going to rewrite the past, make Sonny Daye a whole and happy person, and put the ghosts in Ace's heart to rest.

But not even Sonny can build a car fast enough to escape the ghosts of the past. When Sonny's ghosts drive them down and run their plans off the road, Ace finds out exactly what he's made of. Maybe Sonny was the one to promise Ace anything, but there is nothing under the sun Ace won't do to keep Sonny safe from harm.

www.dreamspinnerpress.com

Guess who's swimming in the same pond...

FISH
OUT OF
WATER

Amy Lane

Fish Out of Water: Book One

PI Jackson Rivers grew up on the mean streets of Del Paso Heights—and he doesn't trust cops, even though he was one. When the man he thinks of as his brother is accused of killing a police officer in an obviously doctored crime, Jackson will move heaven and earth to keep Kaden and his family safe.

Defense attorney Ellery Cramer grew up with the proverbial silver spoon in his mouth, but that hasn't stopped him from crushing on street-smart, swaggering Jackson Rivers for the past six years. But when Jackson asks for his help defending Kaden Cameron, Ellery is out of his depth—and not just with guarded, prickly Jackson. Kaden wasn't just framed, he was framed by crooked cops, and the conspiracy goes higher than Ellery dares reach—and deep into Jackson's troubled past.

Both men are soon enmeshed in the mystery of who killed the cop in the minimart, and engaged in a race against time to clear Kaden's name. But when the mystery is solved and the bullets stop flying, they'll have to deal with their personal complications… and an attraction that's spiraled out of control.

www.dreamspinnerpress.com

There's blood in the water and
death in the air...

RED FISH,
DEAD
FISH

Amy Lane

"Deliciously tense . . .
a satisfying mix of sweet
angst and steamy suspense."
KAREN ROSE,
NYT Bestselling Author

Fish Out of Water: Book Two

They must work together to stop a psychopath—and save each other.

Two months ago Jackson Rivers got shot while trying to save Ellery Cramer's life. Not only is Jackson still suffering from his wounds, the triggerman remains at large—and the body count is mounting.

Jackson and Ellery have been trying to track down Tim Owens since Jackson got out of the hospital, but Owens's time as a member of the department makes the DA reluctant to turn over any stones. When Owens starts going after people Jackson knows, Ellery's instincts hit red alert. Hurt in a scuffle with drug-dealing squatters and trying damned hard not to grieve for a childhood spent in hell, Jackson is weak and vulnerable when Owens strikes.

Jackson gets away, but the fallout from the encounter might kill him. It's not doing Ellery any favors either. When a police detective is abducted—and Jackson and Ellery hold the key to finding her—Ellery finds out exactly what he's made of. He's not the corporate shark who believes in winning at all costs; he's the frightened lover trying to keep the man he cares for from self-destructing in his own valor.

www.dreamspinnerpress.com

Getting out alive is going
to take help from...

A FEW
GOOD
FISH

Amy Lane

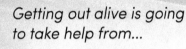

Fish Out of Water: Book Three

A tomcat, a psychopath, and a psychic walk into the desert to rescue the men they love…. Can everybody make it out with their skin intact?

PI Jackson Rivers and Defense Attorney Ellery Cramer have barely recovered from last November, when stopping a serial killer nearly destroyed Jackson in both body and spirit.

But their previous investigation poked a new danger with a stick, forcing Jackson and Ellery to leave town so they can meet the snake in its den.

Jackson Rivers grew up with the mean streets as a classroom and he learned a long time ago not to give a damn about his own life. But he gets a whole new education when the enemy takes Ellery. The man who pulled his shattered pieces from darkness and stitched them back together again is in trouble, and Jackson's only chance to save him rests in the hands of fragile allies he barely knows.

It's going to take a little bit of luck to get these Few Good Fish out alive!

www.dreamspinnerpress.com